I COULD GIVE YOU THE MOON

Also by Ann Liang

If You Could See the Sun
This Time It's Real
I Hope This Doesn't Find You
A Song to Drown Rivers
I Am Not Jessica Chen
Never Thought I'd End Up Here

I COULD GIVE YOU THE MOON

ANN LIANG

HARPER

An Imprint of HarperCollinsPublishers

HarperCollins Children's Books, a division of HarperCollins Publishers, 195 Broadway, New York, NY 10007

HarperCollins Publishers, Macken House, 39/40 Mayor Street Upper, Dublin 1, D01 C9W8, Ireland

I Could Give You the Moon

harpercollins.com

Library of Congress Control Number: 2025946547
ISBN 978-1-335-01411-5 — ISBN 978-1-335-00240-2 (int.)

Typography by Alice Wang
26 27 28 29 30 LBC 5 4 3 2 1
First Edition

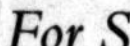

For S

1

CHANEL

The best thing about heartbreak is how spectacularly predictable it is.

I've watched it play out enough times to know exactly what to expect, how to react. First, there's flat-out denial. *He won't hurt me, I swear. He isn't like that. He was just getting lunch with her, and he said himself she was only sitting on his lap because there weren't enough seats in the cafeteria. He never lies about anything, so why would he be lying to me now?*

If well-meaning friends remind you about the twenty-five instances where he was, in fact, lying, you pretend not to hear them. You're too busy clinging to whatever's left of your time together, holding out hope that you can find a cure, even if the relationship is gray in the lips. . . .

Until at some point, the denial collapses under the weight of suspicion, and that's when the anxiety kicks in—the second stage. Casual messages from months ago turn into vital evidence, every punctuation mark analyzed for proof of how he texted when he loved you, if he ever loved you, and when he stopped. In a selfie, the blurry reflection of a girl standing beside him in a coffee-shop window becomes a killing blow. The rage hasn't arrived, not yet. But it will, during that third stage, in a violent spiral of midnight venting sessions and deleted conversations and tossed pillows.

My friend Haili is clearly still stuck in the second stage of heartbreak—by far the least fun of them all.

"Maybe this is a bad idea," she mutters to me, the worried line between her brows illuminated by the warm hotel lobby lights. She's fiddling with the diamond charms on her wrist, a nervous gesture I've seen her perform like a ritual a hundred times in the decade I've known her. "Maybe I should just ask him. . . ."

I shake my head. "You're never going to get an actual answer if you just ask about these things. Like, okay, what could he possibly say? 'Yeah, you're right, I snuck out to get dinner with another girl even though we've been a thing for two months already'?"

"But . . . what if he gets mad at me for following him here?" she whispers. "What if he never wants to talk to me again?"

Even though this is yet another expected symptom of second-stage heartbreak, it's still mind-boggling how the sufferers tend to focus on how the *other* person feels.

A memory sneaks up on me: my own mom, sobbing to her friend on the phone when she thought I was out of the house, a silk bathrobe draped around her shaking shoulders, the crack in her voice as she spoke. *He doesn't love me anymore. Why doesn't he love me anymore?*

I shove it away. Lock it up before bile can rise to my throat.

"The question isn't whether he wants to talk to you," I tell Haili firmly, loudly enough to drown out the rattling in the back of my brain, and give her slender arm a squeeze. "You should start thinking about whether or not you'll ever talk to him again."

"I . . . okay." Even through the dark tint of my sunglasses, I can see her complexion turn pale. "Okay, let's go find him."

I make a beeline for the front desk, through the bamboo groves designed to look like they've sprung right out of the black marble floors, and around the indoor pond that's been trending as *the* new aesthetic photo spot on Xiaohongshu. Everything here is sleek wood, subdued colors, sophisticated in a way that isn't too try-hard. Perfect influencer bait.

Two businessmen stop and stare at me as I brush past them, but I don't slow my steps. The trick to fitting in anywhere is to act like you already belong there. Walk with purpose, shoulders straight, eyes ahead.

"Hello." I greet the receptionist in my brightest voice. "Can you please point us in the direction of the Sky Restaurant?"

The receptionist glances up from her laptop and offers a smile almost as fake and wide as mine. "Yes, sure." Then her attention slides past me, to Haili, and I follow her gaze with a wince. Haili looks like she's on the verge of having a breakdown right in the middle of the perfect lobby. "Is your friend . . . okay?"

"She's fine," I say. "She's just really hungry. We haven't eaten since breakfast."

"Right," Haili squeaks out unconvincingly. At least she's stopped gnawing on her lower lip. "I'm really, *really* hungry. Super hungry."

But the receptionist studies us with growing suspicion. "Sorry, before I let you through—could I actually have your room number first?"

I feel Haili stiffen beside me.

"Um," Haili says. "We don't . . . we aren't staying here—"

"I see." The receptionist's smile slips all the way off her face. "Well, I'm sorry, then. The restaurant is only open to our guests and VIP members."

"That's okay," Haili begins to say, but I make a quick motion behind my back for her to leave it to me.

"I'm one of your VIP members," I say smoothly, though I'm unsure if that's true. Of course, this in itself wouldn't have been an issue a few months ago. My father's a titanium member at practically every major hotel and airline in the world; if I ever needed to pop into the lounge or visit a restaurant like this one, all it'd take was a quick phone call from him for the staff to let me through. But that might prove a little harder now, seeing as I've blocked his number and cut off every channel of communication between us.

"Do you have your membership card with you?" the receptionist presses. "Or your membership number?"

No, and no. But a quicker solution springs to mind—just a considerably more obnoxious one. "You can search for my name," I tell her.

"Pardon?" The receptionist blinks at me.

"I'm sure I'm in your system," I say. "It's Chanel Cao."

I wait as she types, her long nails clicking against the keyboard. "Chanel Cao," she murmurs to herself. A pause as she frowns at the screen, then a slow shake of her head. "No, I'm sorry. Your name's not coming up."

Okay, fine. Another way then. I scan the lobby and spot two girls around my age posing by the bamboo. One of them has paired a cropped Louis Vuitton shirt with simple sweatpants, the ultimate fashion statement to let you know she's rich but totally casual about it. The other is in a full floor-length gown, her makeup so heavy that her eyeliner is visible from here, like Sharpie on a white wall. They rotate between taking photos using their phones with the flash on, then the flash off, then the digital camera that every influencer has been recommending lately, then their phones again but video this time. Definitely my target demographic.

I wait until they've finished assessing their newest photos before lowering my sunglasses a few deliberate inches, right as they glance up.

They both do a double take.

Then Louis Vuitton Girl elbows Ballgown Girl, and they exchange a look, curiosity and confirmation at once. *Oh my god, could it really be her? Are you seeing this too? Yes, yes, I think so, let's find out.* And they unanimously make the decision to approach me.

"Excuse me," Louis Vuitton Girl says in a breathless voice. "*So* sorry to bother you, but are you . . . are you Chanel Cao?"

I grin at them like I'm surprised to be recognized, a little shy, even. "Yeah, I am, hi."

They exchange another look, that shared language between best friends, a silent scream of excitement and *I can't believe this is happening*, and they both start gushing.

"Oh my god, you're even prettier in real life—I didn't think that was possible—"

"We're huge fans. We *worship* your Instagram, you have no idea—"

"I've been following you for years—"

"You're literally so pretty, like, for real—"

"I *love* your leather jacket," Ballgown Girl coos, and makes a motion as if to stroke the material, then thinks better of it, though her fingers still twitch in my direction. "It's the limited edition one, right? I heard they only sell it at their flagship store in Venice and it's, like, fifty thousand dollars."

"Yeah, I don't think they make these anymore," I agree, though I can't remember the price. I'm not even the biggest fan of this jacket—I'd bought it on a whim during my last trip to Venice because it was getting chilly and I happened to be walking past the store. "I have another really similar jacket at home, to be honest—do you want this one?"

Ballgown Girl's eyes widen. "What? Are you being serious?"

"Yeah, if you don't mind that it's secondhand," I say, shrugging off my jacket and holding it out to her.

"I . . . Would I *mind*?" Ballgown Girl makes a choked sound as she takes the jacket from me. "I can't even . . . there's no way—"

"That's so sweet of you, what the hell," Louis Vuitton girl says.

Without turning around, I can sense the receptionist watching the exchange from behind us, the scales of her risk assessment tipping heavily in my favor.

"Do you have an event at this hotel or something?" Ballgown Girl asks.

"We actually had plans to go to the restaurant, but I forgot my ID," I tell them, glancing over at the receptionist. "So it's just taking a while to get my identity verified. . . ."

Ballgown Girl makes an indignant sound on my behalf. "Oh my god, since when did *Chanel Cao* need verification?" She whirls toward the receptionist. "She's literally famous. Just look her up right now."

Before the receptionist has even turned back to her laptop, I know what will show up. The professional photos and viral selfies and family portraits, everything from my reported height (a few inches above my actual height) to my reported weight (a few pounds below). All the suggested search results:

> *is Chanel Cao related to model Coco Cao?*
> *Chanel Cao net worth*
> *Chanel Cao boyfriend*
> *what high school does Chanel Cao go to*
> *Chanel Cao interview*
> *what is Chanel Cao famous for*
> *Chanel Cao Instagram*

"*Chanel Cao* . . ." the receptionist says again, this time with recognition, her eyes widening. "Oh!" Her smile springs back into place with such speed even my actress friends would be impressed. "Please do forgive me for the inconvenience here, Ms. Chanel Cao. Hotel policy, you understand. The restaurant is on the seventy-third floor. Turn around the corner and take the lift on the farthest left to go straight up. Would you like me to show you there myself? I'll ask them to prepare some drinks for you—a mocktail, perhaps? Or something warmer, like our brown sugar and ginger tea?"

"That's fine, we can head over ourselves," I say graciously, then turn to the two girls. "Thank you so much—"

"No, no, it's our pleasure," Ballgown Girl says. "I'm just so glad we got to meet you in person—"

"I'm glad I got to meet you guys too," I say, and this goes on for about as long as I would expect from past experience, more compliments passed back and forth, three different attempts to say "We'll let you go, we know you're busy," a quick selfie of us together after finding the best lighting, a promise to tag me once they post it. It's all very flattering, no matter how many times it happens.

Then I wave goodbye to them and grab Haili's wrist, pulling her along with me inside the lift, which is better equipped than most actual hotel rooms are. There's a plush velvet sofa sitting in the corner, a wooden stand offering scented tissues and alcohol wipes and cotton swabs, and a bamboo basket of complimentary tea bags to take to your room. There's even a gold-framed vanity mirror I'd put to good use under happier circumstances.

"Welcome to QiXing Luxury Hotels," a lilting, questionably seductive female voice plays overhead as the lift ascends. "We hope you enjoy your stay."

"Oh god. I was so scared we were going to get kicked out of the hotel," Haili says.

"The only person who might get kicked out today is Yaozu," I assure Haili. "Though for your sake, I hope it doesn't come to that."

She swallows. "You think there is still hope? That it might all be okay? That maybe I'm just overthinking it?"

I don't want to lie to her, so instead I hold out my hand. "Show me the last thing you sent him?"

She fishes out her phone and passes it carefully over to me like it's a DNA sample from a crime scene. Her WeChat is already open to her old conversations with him. I've seen most of the messages before, sent in screenshots from her over the past few weeks, alongside key details about their relationship.

It's a familiar tragedy. In the beginning, *he's* the one who's more interested. He adds her on WeChat, asks for her alias, shamelessly comments on how nice her figure looks in her latest posts, invites her out to parties. She humors him with one-word responses, or sometimes straight up ignores him, but that doesn't stop him from texting again an hour later, with an entirely new conversation starter.

There's a brief moment in time where they're both equally into each other, affection almost dripping off the screen, "I like you" exchanged as easily and naturally as breathing.

But of course it doesn't last, because he senses it. The instant she's hooked, he starts to pull back. The exclamation marks disappear, and the "good morning" texts taper off, and there's a vague note of annoyance to his responses when they do eventually come in, eighteen hours later.

And then I land on her most recent messages. They're hard to miss, because the text basically takes up the entire screen.

can u please call me when u get the chance??

i really want to talk to u

idk if it's just me and i'm overthinking like i usually do but it feels like you've been kinda distant these days? again idk i could be over-thinking. it's just unfair bc you're on my mind 24/7 and u make me so sad and angry and confused sometimes and i've put in all this effort to keep u and open up to u in a way i haven't with anyone else before but you never let me in. and then you'll say something that makes me think u actually like me. but do u actually like me? i don't even know where this is going or why i'm this upset and i'm sorry if i'm being super annoying rn but i need u to tell me what you're thinking bc it's literally driving me insane. . . .

"I know I sound pathetic," Haili mumbles. "I tried to control myself, but I couldn't."

"You're not pathetic. You're just . . . in love," I tell her, suppressing a shudder at the very thought of it. *Love.* By far the worst idea humans have ever come up with, even worse than mesh ballet flats. "Happens to everyone."

"It doesn't happen to you, though," she says quietly.

And thank god for that, I think to myself. Watching yet another one of my beautiful, smart, talented friends fall apart because of some random douchebag just reaffirms my personal motto: You can cry over a stained dress, but you should never cry over a boy. "I just don't think romance is really my thing," I tell Haili as the lift doors part with a soft *ding.*

The Sky Restaurant has been effectively designed to feel like you're really dining in the sky. You can see the entirety of the hotel sprawled out below in all its gorgeous, glistening luxury: the traditional gardens and pagodas, the canopied sunbeds, the curved man-made lake that transitions seamlessly into a swimming pool. Lanterns float over the dark waters, their yellow flames clarifying the shapes of canoes strung to the decks and the lily pads dotting the edges. The rest of the city waits just behind it, the Beijing skyline glowing against the night.

It doesn't rank anywhere near the top ten restaurants I've been to—maybe not even the top fifty—but I suppose it does make for a pretty nice venue. Before our school wisely opened up its wallet to hold our annual prom at Rivera Restaurant, making it *the* most extravagant, buzzed-about international school event of the season, they used to rent out this place.

It's also the perfect spot for a romantic dinner—peaceful, scenic, and most important of all, private. Rather than having the tables spread out across the floor, there's a single narrow corridor that forks off into individual sets of steps, leading down into what are essentially glamorous pits, encircled by ferns and white marble. Each table occupies its own corner, with a sectional sofa and a balcony to lean over; spacious enough to move around and take pretty photos before the appetizers come in, but cozy enough to make out against the satin cushions after dessert.

Most of the diners here are couples, their heads close together in the intimate candlelight, but as I search the area, my eyes land on a tall figure standing alone by the railings. He's holding an empty glass, his expression alert, as if he's waiting for something to happen.

I blink in surprise.

Ares Yin.

The new boy at Airington International Boarding School.

Dropped like a bomb into our classes at the start of this semester, no warnings given, no further information provided.

From the second he walked in, his shirt collar rumpled, his blazer conspicuously missing and his black hair left to grow out to a length the teachers would deem "distracting" or "unruly," he'd become the Number One Trending Topic on campus. Most of my classmates are as scared of him as they are fascinated by him.

Even now, standing in the restaurant, he appears not just intimidating, but actually dangerous—something about the severe cut of his jaw, the hollowed-out look to his cheekbones, the dark brows angled over his pitch-black eyes. In the weeks since school started, I haven't seen him smile once, not even when people are speaking to him. Everything about him is sharp and unyielding, like he's prepared to enter a knife fight.

For a moment, his gaze swings to me.

I deliberately hold it and lift my hand in a casual wave, waiting for him to acknowledge me. It's not as if we've ever really spoken to each other before, but it's what any guy from school would do: wave back, grin, invite me over. They'd be eager to make our acquaintance known, to come closer. And honestly, I wouldn't mind coming closer to Ares. He's more than attractive enough, even by my standards, and I still haven't finalized my prom date. Based on all the buzz around him, he could be a *very* valuable asset in my campaign—I simply need him to make a move.

But Ares stays right where he is, expression unchanged, and turns his head away, as if my presence is of zero importance to him.

I blink again, this time in disbelief, heat rushing to my cheeks. There's no way he just chose to *ignore* me—

"He's over there," Haili says on a shaky breath, yanking my attention to the table at the back.

I force myself to focus, forget Ares, and crane my neck for a better view. I only know her guy through photos, all preselected by Haili and shown to me while she explained sheepishly and insistently that he looked *way* better in person.

As expected, he does not look better in person.

He looks like the kind of guy I'd go out of my way to avoid at a club. The overwaxed hair—so shiny I can see it glinting like a beetle shell even before I start marching my way over—isn't helping, but it could be forgiven, if he didn't have his arm around the girl beside him. They're laughing together, practically falling into each other's laps, and just when I didn't think the evidence could be any more damning, he plucks the cherry off one of the mini cupcakes on his plate and feeds it to her.

Bile threatens to creep its way back up my throat. This feels far too familiar.

"Okay, I'm going to kill him," I decide, my stomach twisting with outrage on my friend's behalf. "That *asshole*."

"I . . . can't believe it," Haili whispers. "I—I can't believe he's actually . . ."

"Unfortunately, I very much can believe it," I say darkly. "Look, you stay here—I'll handle it for you."

"Can you?" She grips my arm tight, like she might lose her balance otherwise. "Are you . . . are you going to splash water on him or something?"

"No. Water dries. Humiliation lasts much longer."

And with that, I march straight over to their table, my hands curled into fists.

Yaozu jerks his head up, his fingers still stained red with cherry juice, and scowls at me, like I must have accidentally lost my way around the restaurant, before he focuses on my face. His mouth goes slack, a familiar, mesmerized look that would be satisfying if it weren't coming from a piece of total trash. "Have I met you somewhere before?" he asks, his attention shifting away completely from the girl sitting right next to him.

"Are you fucking *serious*, Yaozu?" I hiss, letting all my disgust and rage spill into my performance. "Where's the ball?"

His features freeze into an expression of comical confusion. "Huh?"

"I said, where's the fucking *basketball*? You told me you were playing *basketball* with your *bros* tonight." I jab my thumb toward the girl. "How long have you been sneaking around with her behind my back?"

The girl pushes away from him. "Who is she?" she asks sharply. "You already have a girlfriend?"

"I—I don't know," he splutters.

She glares at him. "You don't know if you have a girlfriend or not?"

"No, that's not what I—I don't know who she is—"

"Oh, right, sure you don't," I scoff. "I actually should've figured you were an asshole ages ago. I mean, I rented out your favorite restaurant and invited all your friends just to surprise you for your birthday, and you couldn't be bothered to see me in person on my birthday because you just *had* to see some emerging indie artist called Pipplo perform live in Shanghai, and you know what? I saw his sets after, and he couldn't even keep up with his own backing track." The words flow easily from me, unscripted and unrehearsed. Maybe a little too easily. Because even as I'm speaking, it's my mom's voice I hear ringing inside my head, bitter and betrayed and broken, every argument she and my father waged against each other after the truth came out.

"What are you *talking* about?" Yaozu demands, his brows scrunching up in bewilderment. He whips around to face the girl, hands half raised above his head like her gaze is a gun, pointed right at him. "I—I don't listen to anyone named Pipplo, I swear! I've never heard that name before!"

"You said you'd pick me up from the restaurant, but then you got sidetracked playing video games," I talk over him, really on a roll now. "You said you'd introduce me to all your friends from your old school, but every time I ask about it, it's like they vanish into thin air. You said you wanted to travel to Italy with me, but suddenly you can't afford plane tickets or your schedule's too full or you're concerned the weather won't be warm enough or you need more time to buy a bigger suitcase. You said you *wanted* me."

"I have no idea who you are," Yaozu insists, red in the face, and turns again to the girl, repeats with urgency, "I literally have no idea who she is."

"Yeah, sure." The girl grabs her black leather clutch and lurches onto her feet, her lower lip curling. "Feel free to delete me on WeChat."

"Wait. *Wait!*" he calls, scrambling after her.

She's already gone.

I breathe out, letting my scowl loosen, but my fists won't unfurl. The anger is still there, the acid searing my stomach, burning me from the inside out. I don't know if it'll ever go away. I used to think it would at some point, maybe after the divorce was finalized and everything went back to normal, but these days I'm starting to worry that there *is* no going back to normal after what my father did. This is just how I am now.

As I walk back over to Haili, I can sense someone staring. Instinctively, I glance back and spot him right away. Ares. It's clear from the way his dark brows are furrowed, his mouth pressed into a thin line, that he overheard everything. But there's no trace of sympathy anywhere on his face.

My fingers tingle with a strange, unfamiliar, out-of-control feeling, my insides clenching. I've always prided myself on being able to detect exactly what someone's thinking about me, but between him ignoring me earlier, and how he's looking at me now, I have no idea what he's thinking.

Part of me is tempted to march right over and find out for myself. Does he have a problem with me? Did I accidentally smudge my makeup on his favorite shirt or something? Or, the most mortifying possibility of all: Does he just *not like me*?

But then I notice Haili, who's been hiding behind one of the pillars, her cheeks streaked with tears, and I push my questions away. I can deal with Ares Yin later. Right now, my friend needs me.

"Are you okay?" I ask Haili.

"No, but . . . I watched the whole thing," she says, and manages a weak smile. "Thanks for doing that. I wouldn't have had the guts to even confront him."

"I held back, honestly. If you *really* want to make him miserable, I have plenty of other ideas," I say. I reach into my purse, rifling through several tubes of lip gloss and a tin of strawberry mints and a new bottle of Chanel No. 5 perfume, before I find the packet of tissues I'm searching for. I hold it out to her.

"I don't think he could ever be as miserable as I am right now," she mumbles, scrunching the tissue up into a ball and dabbing at the mascara flecks under her eyes. "He doesn't care the way I do."

"Remind me again," I say gently, "why you like him."

"I don't know. . . ." She pauses and thinks for so long that I start wondering if she's planning on skipping over my question entirely. "He's . . . I guess he's nice to me?"

"He's nice to you," I repeat, less gently, unable to keep the skepticism out of my tone.

"He gives me all these little compliments—like, he'll say that I'm cute or that he thinks my necklace is pretty or he can't stop thinking about my body," she elaborates in a hurry. "He carries my bags, and he holds the door open for me, and sometimes he helps me stab the straw into my bubble tea, and . . . and there was this one time where I spilled water on my shirt and he got me a napkin. . . ."

I take a deep breath and silently lament the fact that the bar is so low these days you'd have to dig through hell's basement to find it.

"Also," Haili goes on, to her own detriment, "once I was running seven minutes late to go meet him, and he didn't even get mad."

"Okay, no. I'm sorry, but literally any human with basic decency would do those things. An old woman held the door open for us on our way into the hotel just now. And I've seen actual *pigs* who are trained to carry bags," I add, which makes her snort a little, even as more tears slip down her cheeks. "It's truly not that difficult, and more importantly, it's not that rare. Like, give me half an hour, and I could find you another boy with his exact same haircut and nose ring and love of clubbing and Jack Daniel's off a random street in Beijing."

"I just wanted it to be him," she whispers. "I so badly wanted it to be him."

"I know," I say, my voice softening again, and consider how I should phrase my next words to get the point across without rubbing the salt deeper into her wounds. "But you said that he's had plenty of girlfriends before, right? What was it, six? Seven?"

She nods slowly. "Yeah. Seven. And a half, if you count that summer fling."

"Okay, so, the way that he was behaving around you—that's like, muscle memory for him. He knows what he's doing. He's got all his tricks tried and tested. It only seemed special because it was your first time experiencing it with him—and *you* are special. You're gorgeous and way too good for him. And you can cry about it, or get angry, and you can call me whenever you need to vent, but on days when you miss him, and you're fighting the urge to text him, you have to remind yourself that what you miss is the experience. The *feeling*. Not him, the person."

She nods again, faster, though I'm not sure how much of it is sinking in. "God, I'm so done." She sniffs, leaning back against the gray stone. "I'm going to become a nun. No more feelings for me; I'm never liking anyone ever again."

But I know she will, and soon. Haili is one of those people who's simply in love with the idea of love. She'll lock eyes with a stranger in the grocery store or see someone helping an old lady across an ice-slicked road, and that's it for her. She's already gone, heart on her sleeve, twenty thousand feet in free fall, with no thought for self-preservation at all.

I genuinely can't fathom how she does it—how anyone does it. How she can bear to put herself through the pain of wanting someone, only to lose them again and again. It sounds like signing yourself up for torture.

"Do you want my driver to give you a ride home?" I offer. "I can also hang out here with you."

"It's okay, it's getting late. I think . . . I just need some time alone right now," she says with a wobbly smile, and I wish I could magically make everything better, spare her from the last two stages of heartbreak: the rage, followed by the grief. But this is where love always leads. "Thank you, though, for coming with me tonight. I seriously have no idea what I would've done if you weren't there. . . . Just so you know, I'm definitely voting for you."

It takes me a moment to realize she's talking about the election for prom queen. "You don't have to thank me—I'm always here for you," I tell her. It's the diplomatic thing to say, but I really mean it. "Just text me when you get home safe, yeah?"

"You too."

I glance back at her a couple times on my way to the lift. She remains standing in the same spot, arms wrapped around herself, her hurt palpable, everything about the wounded, betrayed look in her eyes so reminiscent of my mom's that I consider running back to hug her—or running after Yaozu to punch him.

But I know it wouldn't help, not really, no more than I was able to help my mom. The only way to prevent heartbreak like that, from what I've seen, is to avoid the ordeal of falling in love altogether. Save yourself before you're in too deep. What's romance really good for, anyway? I can buy myself nicer gifts than any guy could afford, I already enjoy the full princess treatment everywhere I dine and shop, and I regularly receive messages from followers that are sweeter and more sincere than any kind of love letter.

The doors to the lift slide open. A couple in their twenties walks out first, the woman gazing dreamily at her boyfriend like he's the moon in the sky while he's busy checking a stock-trading app on his phone.

I step inside, more grateful than ever to be alone.

2

CHANEL

I've always liked Beijing better at night.

There's something thrilling about the cloak of darkness, the same reason why parties only *really* start to get exciting as the hours tick by and drinks are poured and layers are stripped off. Mornings are for the self-disciplined, the ambitious, the hard workers with Big Plans in life, people like my best friend, Alice Sun. Nights are for secrecy and spontaneity, for cocktail dresses and covering up messes, for all the people who don't have their shit figured out but are desperate to put it off until dawn.

The air is cool against my cheeks as I wait on the sidewalk, the stars above half concealed behind a thin veil of smog and clouds and distant city lights.

Cars and mopeds whir past me, their shiny metal edges glinting under the neon signs of surrounding shops: rice noodle stores and grilled squid stands and karaoke bars, all in full swing. Even though it's almost one in the morning, this city is used to staying up late, just like its overworked twenty- and thirtysomethings.

I check my phone again. My driver's been stuck in traffic for the past ten minutes, and I'm debating whether to just cancel and call a DiDi instead when I spot Ares leaving the hotel.

He doesn't see me. He's too busy surveying the street, and as a bus rounds the corner, its headlights throw the hostile edges of his profile into clarity. There's an odd sense of urgency to his movements as he checks the time on his phone. Glances up at the sky, his eyes sharp and focused, as if there's a secret message written in the clouds. Then he checks his phone again.

I frown, my mind whirring faster and faster with suspicion. Why had he even been at the Sky Restaurant anyway? He wasn't eating, and he wasn't with anyone. *How* was he at the Sky, when they'd almost denied me entry? And what is he planning on doing tonight?

Something shady, for sure. I swear I have a sixth sense for this kind of thing, or maybe that's just what happens when your dad's been hiding something awful from you half your life. You know how it looks when someone doesn't want to be caught.

Whatever he's up to, Ares definitely doesn't want to be caught right now. And I need something to soothe my pride after he ignored me, something to hold over his head and make me feel in control again. It's not just because I've never met someone like Ares before, someone so wholly immune to my glamour; it's the fact that he's a wild card, the only contender for prom royalty who I know next to nothing about, and with only weeks left until the most important night of my high school career, I don't want any disruptions to the social order. If he can't be an *asset* in my prom campaign, I sure as hell won't let him become a threat.

So when Ares starts walking down the street, his steps quick and purposeful, I follow him.

Every muscle from my stomach down to my calves is tensed, as if my body is convinced that something terrible will happen.

Ares walks a few yards up ahead, his silhouette sharp against the darkness, his back turned toward me. He makes his way down the block with the purpose and certainty of someone who's navigated this route a thousand times before.

I move faster, as if propelled by some invisible force, a single thread drawing me closer and closer to him, until there are only five feet of distance between us.

Then, to my utter confusion, he turns the corner and heads into a park.

"What the hell?" I mutter to myself as I follow him in. The single lane is basically empty save for a few late-night joggers, the upbeat music from their earphones fading in and out as they pass me, heaving and puffing. Soon the stone pavement dips down into a short flight of stairs, and a lake opens up in full. Lights dance off the black-glass surface, outlining the slick stone banks on either side.

This is where Ares stops.

He stands on the water's edge, almost frozen to the spot, staring intently down at the lake. A minute passes. Two. Enough time for my confusion to nosedive into complete bewilderment. Nothing about any of his actions tonight make sense, but this might be the strangest of them all. If he were someone else— say, the poetic, super-in-touch-with-his-feelings type—I might think he was simply marveling at nature and ruminating about life. Yet there's an unnerving intensity to the way he's watching the water now, as if he's reading a grim report.

A chill stirs my spine. I hesitate, then tiptoe up to him from behind, hoping to catch a glimpse of whatever it is he's focused on—

He whips around so fast I register only a dark flash. A blur, as if the shadows themselves have peeled from the willow trees to attack.

Cool hands close around my wrists, tight enough to restrict movement, but not tight enough to hurt. Then his face looms over mine, even more dangerous and deadly from this angle. His lips part.

"Chanel," he says, both a question and an accusation. It's the first time he's addressed me by name—the first time he's addressed me at all—but he makes it sound like a curse. "What are you doing here?"

My head spins as I try to invent a believable excuse. "What do you mean? This is my favorite park," I say. I've never set foot in this park before. "I always like to go for a quick jog at night."

"Really." His gaze drops from my face down to my outfit, slowly taking in my thigh-high boots, my leather corset top, the impractical length of my miniskirt, before finding its way back to my eyes. "Nice jogging clothes."

I've learned from businessmen and politicians that the best way to pull off a lie is to bite down on it, no matter how outrageous it is. Even if people don't *believe* it, they'll eventually get tired of trying to confront you about it. So I smile at him like he's just paid me a genuine compliment. "Thanks," I tell him. "They're from Versace's new activewear line."

He doesn't return my smile. Doesn't even accept it. "Are you done with your jog now?" Despite the flatness of his tone, there's an urgency bubbling beneath the surface. He clearly wants me to leave as soon as possible, which only confirms my suspicions: He's hiding something.

"Almost," I hedge. "You'd probably need to let go of me first, though."

His hands fall away from my wrists, but he doesn't step back. This is the closest we've ever been, I realize unhelpfully. Maybe the closest anyone has dared to stand near him in a while. At school, everyone steers clear of him by at least a few feet, as if there's an invisible barrier erected around his body.

Up close, his eyes are such a deep, bottomless black that instead of reflecting the light from the park's lamps, all the light seems to die in them. A single freckle is dotted on the sweep of his cheekbone like an isolated star. Proximity is meant to breed warmth, if not familiarity, but his face remains cold and hard.

"In the future, I'd recommend a different jogging route," he says, barely looking at me now. He keeps glancing up at the moon like it's a clock. "This one can get . . . crowded."

An obvious lie, as outrageous as mine. I grit my teeth. Even though I'd been lying too, there's nothing that enrages me more than the lies of men. "It's a public park," I point out, cutting straight through his bullshit. "I can jog anywhere I want."

"And yet you chose this specific spot," he says. "Interesting."

"If you think coincidences are interesting, sure."

The clouds part overhead, revealing a moon as perfectly round as the Sanya-imported pearls dangling from my ears. A stream of silver light falls over the lake, in the same direction

Ares was facing before, and something ripples across the surface right as the moon reaches the highest point in the sky.

Ares whirls back toward the lake as if someone's just called his name, and I follow his gaze, frowning. It should just be a trick of the moonlight, but the dark shapes in the water seem to bend and shift, like ink swirled by a brush. . . .

And then I notice it. Only a hazy impression in the beginning, but it grows clearer by the second, like a Polaroid picture developing, the details solidifying, and my blood roars in my ears as the impossible unfolds, every rational thought I've ever had fleeing my body, leaving behind only: *What the actual fuck is happening?*

Because I can see myself in the lake.

Not my reflection, not a memory, either, but some other version of me, playing like a film reel over the water—

I'm at school, about to leave the math classroom, when Ms. Hoang beckons me over to her desk. She's pointing to a test paper and saying something, but I can't make out the words, can only watch her mouth opening and closing, her expression grave. From the doorway, my friend Rainie shoots me a concerned glance, but I just smile like I'm not fussed and motion for her to leave without me. Then Ms. Hoang waves Ares forward, which he does, reluctantly, his hands stuffed deep in his pockets, his gaze pinned on me. . . .

The scene changes. The classroom fades away, and everything darkens. It's nighttime, I'm standing in an alley I don't recognize, have never set foot in before, and my face is pale, my hair falling wild and messy over my cheeks. Fresh purplish bruises cover my wrists, stark as ink, and there's something dark splashed across my dress—*blood*, I realize with a sickening lurch. And in the strange reflection of the water, Ares is yelling at me, his eyes pitch-black, blazing with such fury that my breath constricts. The version of me in the lake flinches back, and he seizes my arm, danger rippling through his movements—

Then a house, burning down.

My stomach heaves. I recognize that house.

I recognize the apricot tree in the front yard moments before it catches flame; it's the one my father bought as a replacement after he accidentally killed our old one by feeding it an alarming amount of fertilizer, the one that bore so much fruit every summer we always ended up collecting them in baskets and sharing them with my father's clients. I recognize the traditional low table set out on the porch, where my parents would drink Tieguanyin tea and read through contracts and crack open sunflower seeds between their teeth; the table I know was made from the wood of old shipwrecks, an overpriced metaphor about how anything can be salvaged from the ruins. I recognize the swing set we painted over because it wasn't blue enough, then repainted because it was *too* blue, and my followers would recognize it as well, after it featured in one of my most liked posts. And I recognize those French country curtains, which my mom thought were *classy* and my father thought made the house look older than it was, but didn't care enough about interior design to argue over it.

I had left that house only a few hours ago, when Haili called me in distress. I'm meant to return to that house tonight. It's my childhood home.

And in the lake, it's on fire.

Everything in the vision is engulfed in flames, and there's someone trapped in the house. A woman. Through the smoke, I can only see the slim silhouette, the sharp profile, the pointed chin, but that's enough for me to recognize who it is. It's like watching a horror film unfold—I can't do anything but stare, helpless, as my own mother bangs on the doors, screaming for help, while a window shatters to her right, revealing the crimson glow of a blood moon.

Ares is there too, outside my house, watching everything burn down. His features are half blurred, but it's most certainly him; he's even wearing the Airington school uniform, his hair long and dark and rumpled, his sleeves rolled back and collar unbuttoned in his usual fashion. A lighter in his hand.

My heart is pounding so fast that I feel lightheaded from it. I think I might double over and vomit into the water.

"Do you see something too?" Ares asks, the sharpness in his voice startling me. I tear my gaze from the lake back to him, and my blood runs cold. His expression isn't filled with the terror beating through my veins. He looks . . . *hopeful.* Not like he's watching my greatest nightmare unfold, but like he's just been granted a miracle, a dream about his ideal future. There's a glint in his eyes, the lines of his face blazing with intensity.

I lurch back from him. "What the actual fuck?" is all I can choke out. "What did you just do?"

"So you see it too," Ares says on a drawn breath. He sounds almost awed. "It's not just me. It's never been that clear before—"

"*Before?*" I repeat, my knees trembling. *Wake up,* I command myself. *Wake up from whatever simulation this is.* "What do you mean, *before*? This . . . this has happened more than once?" I jab a finger at the lake, but the vision is gone. There's only water now, the reflection of the willows and my own face, drawn tight with horror, rippling across the surface.

"You won't be able to see it anymore," Ares tells me. "The moon is starting to go down—you have to wait until it's at its highest point every night, and the moonlight has to actually be visible over the water. That's as much as I've figured out by myself, anyway—"

"No. Stop. No, this isn't . . . this isn't possible," I say, shaking my head fast. "That was—"

"What did you see in the future?" Ares presses. "Was there also a fire in your vision?"

I feel like I've run headfirst into an invisible wall, my skull reverberating from the impact. "What are you talking about? It can't be the future."

"Well, it's not in the past, and it's obviously not happening right now," Ares says with a conviction bordering on desperation, and again I can't fight the feeling that he wants the fire to happen. But *why*? What did I ever do to him?

"It can't be," I repeat, louder. Even though the lake looks normal now, the images won't stop flickering through my head: me, standing in that alley, bloodied and bruised, my mother caught in the fire, screaming. And Ares, the culprit at the center of it all.

The trembling has spread from my knees to my fingertips.

I'd figured that Ares Yin wasn't my biggest fan, that I

couldn't trust him, but if what I saw in the lake is any indication of the future, this changes everything. He doesn't simply dislike me—he's out to ruin my life, to hurt me and the people I love.

I stare at him, at those wild, dark eyes, the fine-angled face that holds no room for remorse, and I wonder if this is how prey animals feel, looking into the mouth of a beast right before they're eaten.

"Chanel—" he starts to say.

I twist around, away from him, and I run.

3

CHANEL

As the car swerves onto my street, I brace myself for sirens.

An ambulance, firefighters, the flames already spreading through the walls, eating away the fences and incinerating the rosebushes. The destruction promised by the vision. But as my house comes into view, lit up by the orange porch lights, it looks perfectly normal. It stands as extravagant and beautiful between the rows of villas as it always does, with its marble pillars and massive garden and five-story modern wood exterior, the glass lift gleaming from the ground level up to the turret roof. Easily the best villa in the area—my father had made sure of it when he bought the house as a first-anniversary gift for my mom.

My ears are still ringing when the driver parks outside the front gates and opens the car door for me with one white-gloved hand, reaching for my purse with the other. "Welcome home, Cao Nüshi," he says.

"Thank you, Hong Shushu," I tell him, my voice smooth and warm despite the quiver in my chest. Even when my boots land on firm concrete, I feel like I'm suspended in another reality. I should be relieved everything is the same as it was, but the clamp around my heart only loosens slightly.

The fire hasn't happened. But that could just mean it hasn't happened *yet*.

I pause at the front door, taking care to smooth the fear out of my expression before stepping in.

My mom is upside down.

"... and hold for one ... two ... three ... four ... five ... *feel* the burn. Engage your core ... ," a smiling, serene-looking woman instructs from our TV screen. "Now, very slowly, lower yourself back down. ..."

My mom eases her famously long, toned legs off the wall, one at a time. Once she's the right way up again, she dabs the sweat on her forehead and moves into squatting position. She looks like she could walk into the TV and take over the fitness instructor's job at any second, with her perfect posture and purple activewear set.

"You're home late," she says. Totally oblivious to the fact that I'd seen this room on fire less than an hour ago, the white-oak cabinets behind her collapsing, the high ceilings black with ash, and her pounding on the doors, trying to escape. I swallow the lump in my throat and fight the urge to rush up and hug her and make her promise me she'll stay safe, now and always.

It takes me a moment to even remember how to talk.

"I ... was just out with a friend," I say, unzipping my boots, my fingers quivering as I yank them off. "I'm going to go shower—"

The fitness instructor speaks over me. "We're almost there! Just three more to go. You *feel* that?"

I feel like I need to lie down and scream into a pillow.

"Three . . . two . . . one . . ."

My mom finishes her set, her face pink and dewy and somehow still photoshoot ready, then turns around. Looks at me properly for the first time since I entered the room. Frowns.

I'm wondering whether she's sensed that something's off when she steps closer. "When was the last time you got your hair done?"

I pat it self-consciously, try not to let my smile fall. "I don't know. Like, three weeks ago?"

"Well, it's looking *really* dry." She picks up a strand between two crimson-painted fingernails to inspect it more closely, like it's a frayed thread sticking out from her favorite blouse. A problem she needs to snip away. "Have you been swimming? You *know* how badly chlorine damages hair—it's already going yellow at the ends."

"No, Mom. I haven't been swimming. And I've been doing that treatment you recommended." Honestly, I'd wanted to stop the treatment three days after I started it. It requires an hour to complete, from washing your hair to slathering it in products to combing it all the way through—*gently*, so the product has time to be absorbed—before washing it again. I'd rather go to bed an hour earlier, but my mom's always said that beauty requires sacrifice.

"The treatment isn't enough. You should still book an appointment to get it checked out," she tells me, in the same somber tone you'd tell someone to schedule a doctor's appointment for a suspicious lump.

Ringing up the hairdresser isn't exactly a top priority for me right now, but I nod to placate her. "Okay, I'll call Tony."

"Not the Tony who cut off two whole inches when I asked for only one and a half—I wouldn't trust him with my hair again even if every last salon on earth went into bankruptcy."

"No, not him," I agree quickly. "The other Tony."

"The one in Sanlitun?"

"The other *other* Tony."

She nods, the little crinkle between her brows lightening, and I release a small inward sigh of relief. It's all I can do these days—not make her happy, because nothing seems to make her happy anymore, but find and eliminate everything that might upset her further. Like purchasing business-class tickets for a long-haul flight; you can't avoid the turbulence, or the jet lag, or the fact that you're stuck in a metal tube, but you can at least make the ride a little more bearable.

I'm about to retreat to my bedroom, where I can freak out over the vision in private, when her gaze snaps from my hair to my waist. And just like that, her frown is back, her mouth puckering as if she's taken a sip of expired mung bean milk. "Have you been eating?" With her, this question is never the conversation starter you so often hear over the phone in Beijing, the friendly equivalent of "How are you?" It's an accusation.

My stomach twists. "Not much. I mean . . . I had some California rolls for lunch, but I only had like, two of them." I speak faster, feeling like I'm pleading guilty in court. "And the serving was small to begin with."

She repeats the same movement she used with my apparently damaged hair, except this time, it's the flesh above my waistband that she pinches between two nails. It hurts a little, but I resist the urge to flinch away. Or shove her hand away. *She's going through an extremely difficult time,* I remind myself. *She's grieving a marriage. She means well. She's your mom.*

She's your only parent left.

But even though I've vowed to erase my father from the family portrait, and I absolutely should not be missing that lying, cheating asshole, I feel a twinge deep inside my chest. Before, whenever my mom slipped into a lecture about cutting out rice or trying some new, model-approved trick to suppress your body's natural hunger cues, my father would jump in to defend me faster than my mom could push my food out of reach. "Aiya, just let our daughter eat what she wants," he'd said one night, sliding a plate of pork potstickers across the table to me with a wink. I'd been eyeing them all dinner, my mouth watering through bites of cold cucumber. "She's still growing."

"If she eats whatever she wants, she's not going to be able to take any photos," my mom had protested.

"Now, Coco, my dear, that's literally untrue. There's no prerequisite to getting photos taken," my dad had said. "Do you think cameras ask you to enter your body mass index before you're allowed to use them?"

My mom had rolled her eyes. "You know what I mean. I want her to eat well, but if she doesn't look her very best, those netizens will tear her to pieces. I'd rather that I be the one to warn her beforehand than for her to have to suffer the consequences after."

"Those netizens are bored, lonely strangers making meaningless comments about other strangers' bodies on the internet. They won't care if your daughter's starving, but you should," my dad had pointed out, with the air of authority he often employed to wrap up his big annual meetings. "Chanel," he'd said, turning to me, his expression warm. "Eat."

". . . eat less," my mom is saying.

I nod again. I can feel all the remaining energy in my body leaking out.

Finally, my mom releases me, and I make my escape down the hall, into the bathroom, where I splash ice-cold water on my face, as if I can simply wash the events of tonight away. But even with my eyes closed, the water running down my cheeks, I can still see the vision. . . .

This house going up in flames, and everything I've ever known burning down with it.

There's a brief, blissful lag in my memory when I wake the next morning: those colorless moments between sleep where all I know is the stiffness in my neck muscles and the soft, lavender-scented fabric of the blankets cocooned around my body.

Then I remember everything.

The lake and the fire and Ares Yin.

It doesn't feel real, not when the moon is gone from the horizon and the buttery daylight is spilling over one side of my bedroom. Maybe it *wasn't* real, I think hopefully, pushing the blankets off and stretching, my toes finding the fluffy pink slippers laid out on the floor. Maybe I imagined it.

I try to tell myself this on the ride to school, until I'm almost convinced. As I head off to math for first period, my panic from yesterday starts to feel like a silly overreaction. It had *felt* like the world was ending in the darkness, with the eeriness of the park after midnight, the surreal quality of the moonlight falling over the waters. But it could all be smoke and mirrors, like the atmosphere of a haunted house on Halloween. Terrifying when you're in it, yet so clearly fake when you're out of it.

I breathe a little easier and lift my chin, remembering to smile at everyone who greets me in the corridors:

"Hi, Chanel!"

"Hey, girl."

"Chanel, holy crap, your dress in your last post? *So* gorgeous—"

"Did you hear about the party Jake Nguyen's throwing at his place?"

"What outfit are you wearing to—"

"Morning, Chanel!"

"I *love* your lipstick shade—where did you get it?"

"Chanel, are you free next weekend for—"

"Oh my god, did you see?" Rainie Lam asks excitedly, dropping into the seat beside me. She runs a hand through her long hair, which she's recently dyed a honey brown that looks almost blond beneath the classroom lights, and opens up her laptop to a school email.

"See what?" I ask, squinting to read the text loaded on her screen.

We would like to congratulate our prom king and queen candidates. . . .

My pulse skips. I'd been so caught up in last night's events that I'd managed to completely forget about prom nominations. I don't have to scroll very far to see the results; my photo is listed first. Copied straight from my Instagram. I'm sitting in my favorite French restaurant in Shanghai, the one that looks out at the Bund, my hair curled, my crimson dress fitted snugly around my bare shoulders.

I smile wider than I have all morning. Yes, I'd expected to be nominated, but it's nice to have the confirmation. It means I'm on track to being crowned prom queen, the one thing I've dreamed of for years. It would be the perfect finale, but more than that—it would be the ultimate confirmation of my status, tangible proof of how much everyone loves me. I have a whole vision board ready—spiritually, and literally, smack in the middle of my bedroom wall.

"Congratulations," Rainie squeals over my shoulder as I keep scrolling.

There are four other candidates for prom queen. Rainie is one of them, thanks to the star power of her mother, the famous Hong Kong singer Krystal Lam. But all the girls are gorgeous and influential and lovable in their own way: There's an actress who's been popular at school ever since she filmed a variety show with the C-drama star Caz Song, an actual royal who spends her summers riding Friesians around her castle in Europe, and a transfer student with goddess proportions who's repeatedly gone viral for lip-syncing. The competition will be tight.

"Congratulations to you too," I tell Rainie sincerely. Even if she's competition, we've been friends since we were kids, and I know she cares about prom almost as much as I do. "You're going to look *so* good."

Then I pause over the prom king candidates. Henry Li is, unsurprisingly, the first to appear. But right next to him, just as I feared, is Ares Yin.

"I heard he received one of the highest number of nominations for prom king. Like, *ever*," Rainie whispers, following my gaze. "Do you think he even owns a suit?" she asks with a giggle, as if she's already picturing him wearing one.

I can only picture him setting my house on fire. I suppress a shudder and busy myself with reading.

We're delighted to share that the theme will be Total Eclipse of the Heart. As you might have heard, this year's prom is very special, as it will coincide with the lunar eclipse! If the weather conditions allow, you'll even be able to see the blood moon.

Voting opens at 3 p.m. today and will close on prom night. You can vote again a second time at the entrance of Rivera Restaurant. Your prom king and queen will officially be announced at the event.

Get your dresses ready and your suits ironed—just three weeks to go!

The blood moon. I stare at the words, my throat tightening as the vision resurfaces in my mind. The glass shattering, the red moon hanging high in the sky.

Is the fire destined to happen on prom night?

No.

No, the fire isn't destined because the vision isn't *real.* It can't be real.

". . . thinking about getting this ballgown from VCL," Rainie is saying. "You should know it. It's like the one your mom wore for their spring campaign? I *loved* that photo shoot, by the way—the fact that they got your dad to shoot it with her? It's *so* cute. Truly, such a power couple."

There's enough noise rattling around my brain without this unwelcome mention of my father, so I just make a soft sound like *hmm,* hoping she'll move on. It's been getting harder to maintain the facade of the perfect family when my parents haven't even stood in the same room together in months. But if anyone found out, it would ruin everything, taint my image irreparably—and with it, my chances of becoming prom queen.

"Your parents should do more photo shoots together," Rainie continues. "Oh, speaking of—my mom's been meaning to ask them over for a little get-together. She says it's been ages since she last saw them. What do you think? Are they free next week?"

"That would be *amazing,* but I'll have to double-check with them," I say. "Their schedules have just been so hectic lately, and my dad's reserved a cottage in the countryside for the two of them on Thursday or something." It's scary how smoothly the lies slip out, how intuitive it feels to just say whatever sounds good.

"Wait, that's so sweet of him," Rainie gushes. "I don't think my dad's taken my mom out on a proper date since . . ."

But I barely hear the rest of her sentence, because Ares Yin walks through the classroom door. His gaze locks on mine right away, like he's been searching for me, and my chest constricts. Just one look from him is enough to undo all my wishful thinking this morning. Confirmation that what we experienced last night *was* real.

My eyes follow Ares as he takes his usual seat in the back corner. Alone.

I don't get any work done in math.

This isn't exactly a new problem. For the past few months, I've been finding it difficult to concentrate at school—it's like everything has been reduced to white noise. But even by my own standards, I'm hopelessly unproductive for the entire fifty-five minutes. My notebook lies forgotten on my desk as I glance over at Ares again and again, remembering how he'd looked last night by the lake. Dark-eyed, dangerous, like the fifth horseman of the apocalypse. When the bell rings and everyone scrambles out of their seats, he takes his time standing up, pausing before he reaches for his bag.

"Chanel, can you stay behind for a second?" Ms. Hoang calls, beckoning me over to her desk. She flips open a binder and points to what I recognize as my math test. Or a mutilated form of my math test, because more than half the page is marked with red. "I wanted to talk to you about your . . . somewhat concerning math results."

I freeze, struck by a horrible sense of déjà vu.

Rainie shoots me a concerned glance, and I force myself to smile like I'm not fussed and motion for her to leave without me, but the déjà vu only grows. This shouldn't be possible. I'd seen this exact scene playing out in the vision last night, and it's happening now, beat for beat.

"I'll find you later," I tell Rainie, my voice holding strong, even though breathing feels difficult. "Won't be long."

While everyone starts shuffling out of the classroom, Ms. Hoang glances up and says, "Ares. Can you stay behind too?"

He lets his bag fall back to the ground. Nods, only once, and makes his way forward, stopping beside me. Just like in the vision. I feel physically ill, lightheaded. I try to breathe in, but all I inhale is his scent—it's like the aftermath of a fire, the burnt, barely sweet notes of smoke.

"Thank you," Ms. Hoang tells Ares, then fixes me with one of her classic stern, over-the-spectacles looks, the one that tends to precede a lecture or detention. "Look, Chanel," she says, drawing in a deep breath. "I didn't want it to have to come to this. But I am extremely concerned about your math grades. You barely touched the last page in this test—and no, drawing a sad face and writing 'Sorry!' in the working-out space will not help you earn any pity marks."

I clear my throat, my cheeks burning. I'm carrying so much dread inside my body that I didn't think there'd be any room for embarrassment, but it's still humiliating to have my failures aired like this for Ares to witness. I already know that I'm not smart, but does *he* have to know as well?

Ms. Hoang tuts softly, shakes her head, seems unsatisfied by her previous tutting and tuts some more. "Do you know what your current average is?"

Something awful. Something that would probably send Alice into a state of shock if it were to appear on any of her tests.

"It's fifty-two percent," Ms. Hoang says, her voice grave. "And that's me being *very,* very generous already, Chanel." She sits down on her leather armchair and heaves a heavy sigh, like this conversation is sapping her strength. "I don't want to fail you. I think you're a bright young woman with lots of potential, and I understand you have far more social demands than I ever did when I was your age. But you seriously need to get your grades up. You may have heard about our school's robust peer tutoring program. The program will officially commence next week, and luckily for you, Ares here will be available to help you—"

"What?" I actually step back in alarm. "What do you mean—"

"Getting mentored in math by a fellow classmate will be highly beneficial for you, Chanel," Ms. Hoang says, like this is the most reasonable suggestion in the world. Like she's not making me learn algebra with an arsonist. "Although Ares hasn't been with us for long, his math grades are perfect."

Even through my panic, this registers with some surprise. I've never even seen Ares answer a question in class, and the only time I've glimpsed one of his scores was the forty percent he got for his English essay. I'd figured he was flunking all his subjects, just like I am.

Out of the corner of my eye, I check Ares's face for his reaction, but other than the faintest crinkling of his brow, he gives nothing away.

"Is there a problem, Chanel?" Ms. Hoang asks, her mouth thinning into a hard line.

Yes, many problems, I think. *He hates me. He'll hurt me. He wants my house to burn.*

"Can't I just . . . study by myself?" I ask desperately.

"You need the help," Ms. Hoang says. "If you can score higher than ninety percent on your next test, then I might reconsider the arrangement. But for now, I'm going to ask you to please cooperate. This isn't optional, Chanel."

"But—"

"I don't think you're grasping the severity of the issue," Ms. Hoang speaks over me, her patience visibly wearing thin. "If you fail this class, you won't be able to graduate. Maybe you're under the impression that your parents' wealth will insulate you from failure your whole life, Chanel, but this isn't something that money can fix. You have to fix it yourself."

Her words land like a punch. I swallow, my face prickling, my protests drying in my throat. Is that what she thinks of me? Just another spoiled girl who relies on her parents for everything?

I dart another look at Ares, who shifts for the first time, betraying the slightest reaction, but I can't tell if it's because he agrees with the teacher. If that's what he thinks of me too.

"Thanks again for all your help, Ares," Ms. Hoang says in a much friendlier tone. "If you have any questions, feel free to shoot me an email."

Ares shrugs and makes a noncommittal sound.

And with that, the teacher gathers her papers and heads out of the classroom, leaving me alone with the very last person I want to be near.

"Since when were you involved in *peer mentoring*?" I can't help asking. Can't help hoping that this might be a gross misunderstanding I can wriggle my way out of.

Ares turns slowly to face me. "Since I had five unexplained absences in a row, the school threatened to kick me out if I didn't make some kind of contribution." He cocks his head. "What, you don't want me to tutor you?"

"I . . . it's not that," I lie. "I just—"

"Then why are you so jumpy?" he asks, his brows furrowed as he studies me, like he's trying to understand a book written in his third language. "Is it because of last night? Are you scared or something?"

Yes. I'm scared of you. More terrified than I've ever been of anyone. But I can't let him know that, so I dodge his question with one of my own. Media Training 101. "How long has the lake been . . . doing that?" I ask.

"Not sure," he says. "I first saw the vision three months ago. A coincidence—I was just walking around the lake at night when I noticed something in the water. I assumed I was hallucinating. Especially because it disappeared after just a minute, and when I returned to the lake the next morning, it was gone. Must've visited the lake twenty, thirty times before I figured out there was a pattern to it."

"The moon," I murmur, remembering.

He nods. "Once the moon reaches its highest point, the

vision starts—and it always ends on the same scene. The same house burning down."

My heart skips with a new realization: He doesn't know the house is mine, or else he wouldn't be talking about it like this. And if he has no idea *where* the house is, he can't set it ablaze just yet—that gives me an advantage. Or at least more time.

"The thing is, other people have passed by that lake, but nobody else has reacted. I thought I was the only one who could see the vision . . . until you," he says, his gaze fixed on me with the pressure and precision of a knife. He's staring at me like I have all his prized possessions locked in my basement and the key dangling from my pinkie finger, and he's calculating when to lunge for it.

"And what does that mean?" I ask. My voice sounds breathless to my own ears.

"You tell me," he says, his eyes narrowing as if I'd implanted myself in the vision on purpose. "For some reason . . . for better or worse, you're part of my future, Chanel."

A violent shiver courses through my body. He's leaning in close, too close, the darkness of his gaze inescapable, and I'm scared that if he were to touch me, he'd feel just how hard I'm trembling, how fast my heart is beating. I can't remember the last time someone had such an overpowering effect on me. I'm transfixed. Too terrified to stay, too terrified to move.

Even his beauty is terrifying.

Then the classroom door creaks open somewhere behind us, and I startle, lurching away from him like I've been shoved. Two girls from the lower-year level are standing in the entrance, openly ogling us, their expressions scandalized. I can feel the flush in my cheeks, and I can only imagine what it seems like we were doing alone in here.

"Um, we're so sorry to interrupt," one of the girls says with a giggle.

"It's fine. I was just leaving," I tell her, smoothing my hair with a quick smile, careful not to look over at Ares again.

"Remember our session," Ares says from behind me, which sets off another round of giggling. No doubt our uninvited viewers are thinking *hook-up session* rather than *math tutoring*.

"Yeah, got it," I say briskly, and hurry out of the classroom— but not before I overhear the girls whispering to each other.

"Oh my god, do you think they're running for prom queen and king together?"

"I feel like they'd definitely win."

"No, don't sound so sure. There's also Henry Li."

Henry. Of course. I make up my mind on the spot and change course midstep, turning down the corridor. He's exactly who I need to find right now. He should know what to do.

After all, who better to turn to for advice about the supernatural than the creators of Beijing Ghost?

4

CHANEL

"Henry. Henry Li. *King Henry.*"

Airington's unanimously recognized royalty slows his foot-steps, but just slightly, letting me catch up to him outside the humanities building. The group of wide-eyed girls who've been tailing him from his last class step aside when they see that it's me.

I make eye contact with each one of them as I stride forward, and they take it upon themselves to quickly disperse. Everyone knows by now that Henry Li is extremely, happily taken by my best friend, Alice, but that still hasn't stopped some of the newer students from trying their luck. They've probably watched too many movies and have deluded themselves into thinking that if they can drop a pen near Henry at just the right moment, he'll notice them and fall head over heels.

As if he's capable of seeing anyone except Alice Sun.

"Chanel," Henry greets in his typical posh, reserved manner, like he's reading my name out of an old British newspaper. He looks like he could be on the front page of a newspaper too,

"You could assume that, yeah."

He clears his throat. "And are they of a . . . positive nature, or—"

Despite myself, I have to laugh. "Are you fishing for compliments? Why not just ask her yourself if you're so keen to hear her praise you?"

"It would be rather undignified," he says, adjusting his tie. "But yes, she should be free after five."

"Amazing. And . . ." I hesitate. It feels strange to ask for help, even from Henry and Alice. Under normal circumstances, I'd iron out my problems by myself, all while smiling like I'm having the time of my life, so nobody else could guess that I'm struggling. Because It Girls don't struggle. Future prom queens don't struggle. They just do everything effortlessly. But these aren't normal circumstances, and so I force the words out of my lips. "I kind of need your help with something. Can the three of us meet in private? Somewhere nobody can overhear us, I mean."

His brows knit together. "Is everything all right?"

"Yes. Well, no." Ares's face flashes through my mind again, and I suppress a shudder. "I'll tell you and Alice later."

"We can meet at my house, then," Henry says, already unlocking his phone to add the details to his calendar. "My father's away at a conference and my mother's at her flower arranging class until after dinner. Would you like me to prepare anything? A whiteboard? Pens?"

In Henry Li's world, over ninety percent of problems could be solved with a whiteboard and pens. "Maybe some alcohol," I say, only half joking.

★ ★ ★

The first time I visited Henry's house, I'd assumed it was fake.

One of those places you rented out for a photo shoot or a promotional video with *Vogue*. Everything looked a little *too* perfect—the traditional Chinese furniture, the crystal fruit bowls filled with fresh mandarins and dragon fruit, even the engineering magazines spread out on the coffee table, which I refused to believe anyone would actually flip open until Alice confirmed that it was Henry's idea of leisure reading.

The only evidence that he really does live here can be found in the photos lined up along the bookshelf. Multiple high-resolution shots of him receiving flowers and certificates, standing tall and posh like a Burberry model while someone drapes a medal around his neck, lifting up trophies with his name immortalized in gold italics. Lower-quality photos of him and Alice holding hands on the table at a Peking duck restaurant, her face self-conscious and half shy, probably taken when they first started dating. Another photo of them at the park on a perfect sunny day, lounging around on a picnic rug, wildflowers springing out of the grass, and a strawberry vanilla cake misspelled to say, "Happy birthday, Henny."

There are more photos of his father, the founder of SYS: a dark-browed, bright-eyed man, handsome for his age, with a face recognizable from all the business magazines and interviews he's done in the past. In one of them, he's cutting the crimson knot stretched across a sparkling new office building, the air thick with firecracker smoke; in another, he's smiling and shaking hands with some old, stern-looking gentleman.

"Henry told me we're having an emergency meeting," Alice says, reaching for the slippers Henry's already laid out for her by the entrance. Her high ponytail swishes back and forth as she shrugs off her blazer. It still feels strange seeing her in a different uniform—red and yellow instead of the Airington colors, the iconic tiger crest swapped out for a swan on her front pocket.

Alice Sun isn't like any of my fuerdai friends. We didn't meet through our parents, or mutuals on social media, or at a promotional event. If it weren't for the fact that we were randomly assigned to the same dorm room at Airington—back before I moved home to be there for my mom—our lives might never have overlapped. On her first day at Airington, before she'd even finished unpacking her clothes, she'd stuck a giant poster with only the word *valedictorian* next to the window. Then, catching me staring, her expression had melted from fierce determination to something softer and sweet. "Sorry," she'd said. "Is this blocking your view? I can move it."

"No, no, you're good," I'd told her, grinning. I had a feeling then—or maybe it was a hope—that we would become best friends, and though it took a few years for it to happen, I was right.

And as much as I miss catching up with her in class, the change has clearly worked in her favor. These days she stands taller, straighter, like she's finally settled into her own skin, and the tired circles that used to appear permanently stamped around her eyes have disappeared.

"What's going on?" she asks me.

"It's going to take a while to get through," I say, making

myself at home on Henry's couch. When we first launched the Beijing Ghost tutoring app, we used to gather here for semi-official business meetings, brainstorming new ways to get the word out and refine the app's features. But now that the app has gained traction, we mostly just come here to take advantage of Henry's home theater and swimming pool.

"We have time," Alice assures me, sitting cross-legged on the other end of the couch like a student in a discussion circle.

"Well, to be precise, we have approximately three hours and fifty-three minutes until my mother comes home." Henry's voice floats over from the kitchen.

Alice rolls her eyes good-naturedly. "Ignore him. Go on."

"Before I do—you know who Ares is, right? Ares Yin?"

"Oh yeah, Henry mentioned something about the new guy," Alice says. "Apparently he's super scary?"

"I did *not* say he was scary," Henry corrects, returning from the kitchen with our usual drinks: an iced water for himself, a warm lemon tea for Alice, and a Diet Pepsi for me. He hands the tea carefully over to Alice before sitting down with his own glass. "I merely observed that many people find him intimidating. I, for one, am not intimidated by him. I would just be wary of someone like that."

"For good reason," I say grimly. "Because something really, really weird happened with him the other night, and I thought you might have a better idea of what to do after your little . . . situation."

This is how the three of us have been referring to the fact that Alice suddenly started turning invisible last year—like literally, actually invisible, something I refused to believe until I watched her vanish right in front of me. We talk about her *situation* as if it was a random, mildly embarrassing early-teen phase, the same way some people might go through a pony phase or a boy-band phase.

"Don't tell me Ares can turn invisible too," Alice says, her eyes widening.

"No. That's the thing—I don't think it's *him*. Like, it's not something within his control. But there was this vision. . . ." I go over everything from last night in as much detail as possible, from him sneaking onto a rooftop where he definitely didn't belong, to me following him into the park, to the vision and his reaction afterward.

When I'm finished, both of them are silent for a long time.

"So do you think it's real?" I prompt. "What I saw in the lake?"

They exchange a glance.

"Ares said he saw a burning house too, right?" Henry asks slowly.

"Yeah, and I didn't even describe the vision to him. So it couldn't just be a coincidence."

"And you're sure you saw a lighter in his hand," Henry confirms. "You think he's the one who set your house on fire."

I nod. "I definitely saw a lighter. And the house was definitely my house. He seemed eager for it to happen too. Like, really, disturbingly eager."

Alice's face tightens with worry. "What's his deal? Why would he want to burn your house down? Should we—I don't know, should we tell the teachers? The police? If this guy's out to get you . . ."

"But that's the thing," I say. "I have no idea why he's out to get me."

"And unfortunately, they can't arrest Ares for something he's yet to do," Henry says with a grimace. "We don't have any proof he'll harm Chanel or her mother, aside from the vision—which, if what Ares was saying is true, nobody else except the two of them can see."

"So . . . what do I do?" I ask. But despite the churn of dread in my stomach, I also feel steadier than I have since yesterday, with Alice and Henry next to me.

"Let's go over the facts first," Alice says, standing up and pacing in circles around the couch, the way she always does when she's stressed or thinking hard about something, as if her body needs to be moving in sync with her mind. "We know the vision involves Ares, it's at your house, and—do we know when the fire will happen?"

"Prom night," I say. Just one day ago, nothing excited me more than the idea of prom. Now there's nothing I dread more. "The night of the lunar eclipse. In my vision . . . I saw the blood moon."

"So that's three weeks away," Henry says.

I take a sip of my Diet Pepsi, but the sweet fizz of the drink burns like acid down my throat. *Just three weeks.* In three weeks, my childhood home might be turned to rubble, with my mom inside it—

"I suppose murder isn't an option," Alice says in a contemplative voice.

Henry and I stare at her.

"What? I said it *isn't* an option," she says, throwing her hands up. "Not the easiest one, anyway," she adds.

"Alice, you know I would break you out of prison in a heartbeat," Henry says very gently. "But I would most prefer not to."

Alice shoves his shoulder. "I'm only saying, we don't have to just let the future play out—we can take matters into our own hands."

"Right, yes, there are actually two main schools of thought regarding this," Henry says, shifting forward in his seat, his shoulders straight and eyes alert as if he's about to make an intelligent point in class. "To drastically simplify them both—this philosopher called William Livingston believes that the future is set in stone. Everything is predetermined, so no matter what you do between now and the night of the vision, you'll only be playing into fate's hands. His theory strips away any individual agency; we might as well all be hired actors, going through dialogue and stage directions and monologues that have been scripted out for us by a higher power."

My stomach sinks. "Wow, that's super comforting."

"But that's only what Livingston believes," Henry says. "This other philosopher, Ma Mengxu, argues the precise opposite. He considers the future to be fragile and malleable, and he interprets the butterfly effect to be proof of that."

"The butterfly effect?" I echo, my head spinning.

Henry nods, and recites, as if he has a textbook open right in front of him. "A seemingly trivial change in one part of a nonlinear system can trigger significant nonlinear effects elsewhere."

"That sentence means nothing to me," I tell him.

"It basically means that one event leads to another," Alice explains. "Even something small could set up a chain reaction down the line and act as the catalyst for a huge change in your life."

"For instance," Henry says, "a few months ago, I turned on my notifications for *National Geographic*."

I blink. "Congratulations?"

"Well, yes, thank you. But my point is, *because* I'd turned on my notifications, I received an alert about an exciting scientific discovery as I was leaving the auditorium from the Top Achievers' Assembly. I had originally been planning on heading down to my father's company, you see, but after I read the *National Geographic* update, I had a new train of thought for my science project, and so I decided to go straight to my dorm and make my edits. And because I was in my dorm room at that time, Alice was able to find me when she was panicking about suddenly turning invisible. If she hadn't sought me out, we might have never come up with the Beijing Ghost app, and you wouldn't have been our first client, and you wouldn't have found out about Alice's invisibility powers, and the three of us wouldn't be sitting together in this room right now," Henry says. "Now, Livingston would argue that us being here is inevitable, but Ma Mengxu would make the case that this current moment is comprised of all the little moments that preceded it, and there are hundreds and thousands of alternate timelines where things played out very differently."

"To sum it up," I say slowly, "Livingston thinks I'm fucked and I should just call it quits and let the fire happen, because it will, whether I like it or not, but my man Ma Mengxu thinks I've got a shot at changing the future."

"I wouldn't phrase it *quite* like that," Henry says, "but effectively, yes."

"For what it's worth, I'm like, a way bigger fan of Ma Mengxu's school of thought," Alice tells me, and I feel a deep rush of gratitude for her.

"I'm a big fan too," I say. "So—okay. Okay. If I'm going to change the future, then . . ."

"I believe Ares is key here," Henry says. "Your fates are intertwined, and judging from what you described in the vision, he's the one who's setting out to ruin your life. If you want to change the future, you'll have to stop him, somehow."

"But, like. How?" I ask.

The room lapses back into silence.

"Maybe we should revisit murder," Alice mutters after a beat.

"Alice."

"What? How else do we stop him from going after Chanel? Unless he has a sudden change of heart—"

"Wait," I say, springing up on my feet, my blood abuzz with adrenaline. "That's exactly what has to happen. If I can manipulate him into liking me, he won't want to hurt me, and he'll have no reason to set my house on fire."

Henry doesn't look super convinced. "Emotions aren't so easily manipulable or quantifiable, Chanel—"

"Emotions are *very* manipulable," I counter, tossing my hair over my shoulder.

"Even if that were true, how could you measure whether

he likes you enough? How would you know if your plan is working?"

"I just need him to ask me out to prom," I say, and as soon as the words leave my mouth, I can see it happening. The alternate timeline, a future where everything works out the way it's supposed to. My home will remain intact, and I'll be crowned prom queen. "Think about it," I urge them. "He's already been nominated as prom king . . . and the prom queen and king always stay back until midnight for photos and the special yearbook feature, right? So if he goes to prom as my date, spends the entire night with me, and we win, it's physically impossible for him to be setting my house on fire at the same time."

"It could work, in theory," Henry says slowly, exchanging another look with Alice. "And you know I'm fond of the theoretical. But in practice . . . how would you go about doing that?"

Ares's face flashes through my mind again, the memory that isn't a memory: those sharklike, remorseless eyes, the lighter gripped in his bruised hand, the glow of the flames against the hard lines of his profile. I try to imagine those features softening into a look of pure affection, his hands gentle around my waist, slow dancing under the chandeliers. It *does* seem difficult, almost impossible. But I'll do whatever it takes to prevent the vision from happening. I'll pry his ribs apart if it means forcing my way into his heart.

"Maybe we should break it down into steps," Alice suggests, turning to Henry. "Can you bring out your whiteboard?"

He perks up immediately. "Give me a moment," he says.

He returns with an entire set of markers in every color, and a whiteboard almost the same size as his plasma TV. At the top, he's already written the title: *How to Make Ares Fall for Chanel in Three Weeks*. Then he nods at me, expectant. "Well?"

I grab the hot pink marker, thinking back to every boy I've charmed and bent to my will, and start adding below:

Step one: Learn more about him (his family, interests, dreams).
Step two: Grab his attention.
Step three: Build a connection based on all the
      information gathered in step one.
Step four: Start dropping hints about prom and
      including him in prom plans.
Step five: Share photos of him on social media
      to build buzz for campaign.
Step six: Suddenly ice him out and show interest
      in another guy to make him jealous.
Step seven: Get invited to his house; hook up there.
Step eight: Give him a gentle push to ask about prom.

When I step back, satisfied with my work, Henry stares at the board for a long time. "Sorry," he says, shaking his head. "It's only . . . nobody has ever written the words *hook up* on my whiteboard before. Other than that, I don't see any glaring problems here. And at risk of sounding severely egotistical—"

"Trust me, it wouldn't be the first time you did," Alice puts in sweetly.

Henry offers her an affectionate eye roll. "I only intend to point out that I won't be competing for the title of prom king, so that is one less factor to worry about."

"You won't be?" I ask.

"No. I won't be in Beijing at all," he says. "My father wants me to attend this tech conference in London with him during prom week."

I hadn't realized how much I was counting on Henry's help until my stomach sinks. But I shouldn't be relying on anyone, even my closest friends. I'm meant to be stronger than that.

"That's all settled then," Alice decides. "Now, it just comes down to the execution—but, like, I have full faith in your charms, Chanel. If anyone can pull off this plan, it's you."

I have far less faith in my charms than I usually would, but I smile with practiced confidence and lift my glass from the table. It's left behind a ring of condensation on the red mahogany, like the outline of a target. I can almost picture Ares Yin's reflection inside it.

5

ARES

He's lost count of how many people he's asked tonight.

Always the same question. Always the same blank, unhelpful stares, the same crushing replies.

"Have you seen this boy?"

"No, sorry."

"Please . . . have you seen—"

"No."

Still, he braces himself to try again, taking in a deep breath as he approaches the vendor outside the subway station. The aroma of roasted sweet potatoes billows through the air toward him, and his stomach grumbles, despite himself. He hasn't had anything to eat since finishing school hours ago.

The vendor glances up from his makeshift furnace, where the sweet potatoes are squeezed around the fire in a circle, their undersides caramelizing to a deep brown, golden sap oozing out. "Want a sweet potato?" the vendor asks gruffly.

Ares shakes his head. "Have you seen this boy before?" He holds up the photo of his brother that he's been carrying around everywhere with him: a Polaroid taken on the first day of school, Luke's smile stiffer than it normally was, his curls brushed back and shirt collar buttoned too tight, something Luke had complained about before he left the house that morning.

For years now, he's presented it to strangers on the street like a salesman trying to hand out flyers, stopping by every spot he'd ever taken Luke: the arcade where he thrashed Luke in basketball, but Luke beat him repeatedly at Mario Kart; the swings where he'd taken Luke as a kid, pushing him high up into the air with one hand until Luke swore he could touch the sky; the aquarium where Luke would memorize the names of all the fish and point them out to him; the grocery store that always stocked Luke's favorite brand of orange soda and salt-and-vinegar crisps; the astronaut-themed restaurant where Luke had celebrated his tenth birthday.

"No." The vendor barely even glances at the photo. "Never seen him before."

"Take a closer look," he insists. "Please—"

"Do you want a sweet potato or not?" the vendor demands, swatting the photo aside. "If you're not here to buy something, then stop blocking the line."

Ares clenches his jaw and slides the photo back into his wallet, careful not to crease it. He can practically hear the policemen's voices echoing in his head, their pitying tone. *Give it up, kid. It's best you accept that he's gone.*

But there's the vision, he reminds himself. His last thread of hope. He had *seen* his brother in the lake. And the visions must mean something.

He joins the crowds swarming down the steps to the subway,

all of them in varying states of hunger and exhaustion. Follows them past the automatic glass gates and blinking lights signaling the next train. When the doors slide open, everyone pushes forward at once, sweaty bodies squishing against him, obnoxious elbows banging into his side. He manages to snag a seat in the corner, next to a middle-aged man in a wrinkly suit.

He's about to close his eyes for the rest of the ride when he sees the man's phone screen.

It's a photo of Chanel.

A recent post, the comment section already overflowing with praise and marriage proposals. She's somewhere sunny and beautiful, her arms stretched above her head like she's trying to reach the sky, her white lace top sliding up with the movement. She's smiling so wide you'd think she was getting paid for it—then again, she probably is.

He stares, somehow more jarred by her digital appearance on this man's phone than if she had popped up next to him in person. He shouldn't even be surprised that a stranger on the subway is following Chanel Cao; a good quarter of the national population follows her. She's the socialite of socialites, a fuerdai known for being more than a fuerdai, seemingly destined or designed from birth to become the icon she is today: gorgeous in an obvious, aspirational way, wealthy, young, popular, well connected, with a circle of equally fun, stylish, photogenic friends. Someone who very evidently had grown up adored, who was given everything she asked for. He can't imagine what that's like.

But for all her fame, he hadn't given much thought to her— not until she had seen the vision too.

And the visions had changed, once she appeared. The first few times he'd visited the lake, he'd seen himself standing alone at the Sky Restaurant, as if waiting for someone. And he'd seen the fire, the house burning down, and his little brother just across the street.

He suspects now that the person he was meant to be waiting for at the Sky Restaurant *was* Chanel. They were meant to cross paths, and she was meant to follow him to the lake, because once she did, new visions had surfaced.

Him shoving someone down in a boxing ring, the cavelike room dim and unfamiliar to him, his knuckles bloody.

A man with a crescent scar, slinking through the crowds at a nightclub. Club Sixty-Eight Hours, the name glowing neon pink above the bar counter. Posters advertising the club's special new blue lagoon cocktail, available on the eighth, which is just two weeks away.

He and Chanel together at a tattoo parlor, her sitting down right beside him like it was the natural thing to do, while the tattoo artist cleaned his needles.

He can't make sense of the visions, but the fact that they've grown clearer, more detailed, must mean that he's on the right track. That all his actions so far have led him closer and closer to being reunited with his brother at the fire. Like asking his father to transfer him to Airington International, after he'd seen himself wearing the Airington school uniform in the vision.

The train screeches against the tracks, pulling him back through time.

Beside him, the man is still staring at Chanel's photo. Then, slowly, he zooms all the way in to her chest, as if to try and see through the fabric.

Ares feels a sharp surge of revulsion, his mind flashing red. He almost can't believe it, even as he's witnessing it. That the man, *twice* Chanel's age, has the nerve to be doing this—and in *public*. Without shame.

When the train rattles again, Ares pretends to lose his balance and knocks the phone straight from the man's hand. It goes flying to the floor between them, where it lands with a *crack*.

"What the fuck?" The man scowls and picks up his phone. Ares is glad to see that the screen has shattered, a spiderweb of fissures expanding from the cracked corner. The photo is gone, the display showing nothing except tiny colored pixels.

Ares doesn't apologize.

The man swears under his breath, but the train has slowed at the next stop, and he only glowers at Ares before filing out the door, cradling his broken phone in his hands.

As soon as he's gone, another man takes his place in the seat next to Ares.

He's dressed in all black—black leather jacket, black gloves, black ripped jeans, though they've faded to the point that they could pass as gray—and there's a kind of restless energy to him, even as he slouches against the seat. They ride two more stops in silence when he stands up and suddenly swipes Ares's wallet from his pocket.

He's so fast that Ares barely sees him do it, just feels that his jacket is lighter. When he jerks his head up, the thief is already rushing out the doors right as they're closing.

"*Hey*," Ares yells, leaping to his feet. The doors slam against his shoulders, so hard that someone gasps. But he squeezes through them, tugging the end of his leather jacket free from where it had been jammed, and chases after the thief down the platform.

The thief glances back, eyes wide, and keeps running. Clearly he hadn't expected Ares to follow. This isn't even Ares's stop. And maybe Ares would've given up, simply let him take the wallet and go, except Luke's photo is in there.

They race through the subway station, past the throngs of commuters, then out into the night, down an empty alley that looks like the perfect home for serial killers and ghosts.

Ares ignores the needle-sharp stitch in his side and lengthens his strides until he's just a few inches away from the thief. He reaches out and seizes him by the collar. "Give it *back*," he gasps.

The thief jerks around. The next thing Ares sees is the flash of a black-gloved fist, but he doesn't feel it, because he has already ducked, his own hands flexing. Muscle memory. Years of boxing training kicking in. So it would come down to this. All right. He feels something spark to life inside him—not *excitement*, nothing that good, but anticipation. He wants to fight the whole world, but he'll settle for this one man.

When he swings his first punch, hears the *crack* of it against bone, his body aches with relief.

The thief staggers back but doesn't falter. He comes barreling at Ares, and now they're really fighting, knuckles against flesh, brute force and vicious determination. Even the bright, blunt pain of each collision is a release, so much better than the suffocating feeling Ares has been battling against alone.

"You're not bad at that," the thief says suddenly, appreciatively, stopping mid-fight like they're two friends catching up over coffee.

Ares doesn't lower his fists. For all he knows, this could be a trap. "Shut up."

"No, for real," the thief says. "Who taught you how to fight like that?"

Ares glowers at him. "What's it to you?"

"It could mean a lot." The thief nods once, as if having decided something important. "You've got a super solid foundation, good instincts. Not even Hongdan was this fast, and he almost made it to the finals. . . ."

"What?"

"I should've picked another target, that's my bad," the thief says. "But you know, I couldn't have robbed anyone else without breaking my rules."

"You have rules for . . . robbing people?"

"Course I have rules." He looks affronted by the question. "What do you think I am? Some kind of monster?"

Ares chooses not to reply to that.

"No, I don't attack pregnant women, kids under ten, or any old people over sixty. Or anyone with dogs," he adds. "Certainly not dogs. I could never do that, couldn't risk hurting an innocent puppy."

"What about cats?" Ares says dryly.

But the thief's expression is contemplative. "Depends on the cat. They can be pretty nasty sometimes."

Ares can feel his patience wearing thin. "Look, man, I don't give a shit about your rules or the wallet or whatever. Take the money if you want," he says. "But let me have the photo inside."

The thief raises his brows and flips open the wallet, extracting the Polaroid using two gloved fingers. Ares moves to snatch it back, but the thief is faster, holding it just out of reach and examining it in a pale stream of moonlight. "Wait. I know that boy."

Ares hears the words as if from somewhere deep underwater. He doesn't let himself believe it. It can't be. Too many times, he's dared to hope, only for nothing to materialize out of it. Still, his voice wobbles over the question. "You . . . know him?"

"Yeah, course." The thief rubs his jaw. "I've seen him around."

The world seems to slow. He can scarcely breathe. "You're sure it's him?"

"Well, he's a bit older now, isn't he? Fifteen or sixteen or something? Smart boy. Photographic memory, no wonder why Long Ge likes to keep him around." The thief squints off into the distance, as if trying to remember. "Started working for him, what, three years ago?"

Three years ago. That's around how long Luke has been missing. "Where is he now?" Ares demands. He isn't even sure if he's speaking properly anymore; his lips feel numb, and there's a high ringing in his ears. "Can you bring me to him?"

The thief merely extends a hand as if Ares hasn't spoken. "I'm Sangui."

Ares wants to slap it away. He doesn't care what the thief is called, doesn't care about anything except . . . "Where is he?" he repeats, keeping his own hands balled into fists at his sides. "Who is he with? Is he okay?"

"Now, now, don't be in such a rush." Sangui is studying him

with open interest. It's a measured, evaluative look, much like how wealthy men might study the racehorses in a stable before placing their bets. Ares can practically see Sangui gauging his stamina and endurance and market value in real time. "Here's the deal. I'd love to help you, really, nothing would make my little heart happier, but *I* don't have much of a say in the matter. It's all up to Long Ge. And if you want something from Long Ge—well, you'll have to fight for it." The sharp edge of a grin. "Literally."

"What do you mean? Who *is* Long Ge?" Ares asks, though it sounds more like a plea.

Sangui's eyes gleam. "There's this place—we call it the Cave. You ever been to a fight club before? Or seen one in a movie?"

But it's not the movies that Ares's mind jumps to. It's the vision. The one of him in the boxing ring, drawing blood. The dark room he's never entered before. *This must be it.*

"I know what a fight club is," he says. "When can I join?"

"Not so fast," Sangui says with a laugh. "We don't just let anyone in. You'll have to prove yourself first—"

"How?" Ares asks at once, his heart beating so fast it hurts. Whatever Sangui says next, it doesn't matter. He'll do anything.

Maybe Sangui can see the desperation in his face, because after a moment, he nods. "Meet me at seven on Sunday morning. The same stop where we got off earlier. Understood?"

This time, when Sangui holds out his hand, Ares takes it and shakes it firmly, even though it's splattered with his own blood.

CHANEL

Step one: Learn more about him (his family, interests, dreams).

I finish applying a fresh coat of lip gloss and scroll through the contacts on my phone.

Hundreds of names blur past. Assistants from past events and girls I've befriended inside nightclub bathrooms or danced with at parties and boys I've exchanged a few flirty messages with, then never spoke to again. Half the names I don't even remember anymore.

Finally I land on Jamie. The dial tone blends together with the incessant honking outside the tinted car window. Typical Beijing morning traffic.

"Qin, what's up?" Jamie's sweet, lightly Australian-accented voice comes over the speaker. Jamie likes to call everyone *qin*—a kind of alternative to *darling*—including her private chef and strangers in shopping malls.

"Are you busy?" I ask.

"Nope. Just heading out of dance practice." Some light

shuffling in the background, music fading with the click of a door. "And you know I'm never too busy for you."

I laugh. "Oh my god, stop it."

"You know it's true."

"Love you," I say. "Okay, there's someone I want you to help me search up. . . ."

"*Oh*," she says with instant interest. "Who is this? A new man in your life?"

"Something like that," I say vaguely, because it's easier to just go with that. It's not as if I could tell her the truth anyway. *No, he's my new enemy, and according to a bizarre vision in a lake, I have under three weeks to find out everything I possibly can about him to stop him before my house burns down.*

"What's his name?" she asks.

"Ares Yin," I say, and wait for her to work her magic.

Last summer, Jamie Lai joined an idol survival show and managed to sing and self-promote her way through to the end, where she was thrown into a girl group very misleadingly named The Eight. There were ten of them. ("A logistical nightmare," she complained to me. "At every event, we're always two seats short.")

They released a total of two singles, neither of which did well critically or commercially, and it seemed they were on the verge of disbanding when a clip of them from the show's earlier episodes went viral just this winter. No actual music was involved in the clip; they were heating a beef sandwich in the back of the dance studio using a regular clothing iron. This raised many questions—was it safe? Was it *hygienic*? Was it really kind of genius? Was it a sign of immense privilege, that they were willing to risk ruining both the beef and the iron just for one meal? Were they being denied proper food? Did beef sandwiches need to be heated? Were beef sandwiches even good?

The impassioned debates threw them into relevancy for long enough that all the members gained tens of thousands of followers. Then, quick to capitalize on the trend, the group rush-released a song with weirdly suggestive sandwich-themed lyrics, which was so horrible that people listened to it ironically, and soon the cafés in Beijing and Shanghai started playing it, and that was when The Eight *really* gained traction.

Now they're being invited to galas and award shows, and they even have a small but dedicated fan club.

But outside of being an idol, Jamie Lai is more commonly known in Beijing's young, elite circles for her impressive stalking skills. I've seen her locate a friend's ex using nothing but the sliver of his elbow in a blurry photo from ten years ago. There was a particularly desperate time when I'd considered asking her to find out if my father was cheating, but I couldn't bring myself to do it. And now I'm glad I didn't, because she would have had a front-row seat to my family's drama.

"Huh," Jamie says a few moments later. "He's not very active on social media, is he?"

"Yeah, I tried looking him up last night, and I couldn't find any accounts," I say.

"Don't worry, I'll find something," Jamie reassures me. "Give me maybe five business days to work on it. How urgent is this?"

Extremely. My-whole-life-is-kind-of-riding-on-this urgent. "Let's just say I'm . . . *very* interested in this boy," I say, hating myself, hating the world, hating Ares Yin for forcing these words to leave my lips.

"Damn, girl." I can almost hear her eyebrows rising. "I don't think I've ever heard you say that about a guy before. Just how hot is he?"

I pinch the bridge of my nose as delicately as I can without smudging my concealer. "He's . . . a special case."

"Two days then," she promises. "I have to pop into the studio tomorrow to record this new song—it's about cheeseburgers instead of sandwiches this time, and like, to be so real with you, I have super mixed feelings, but the team's confident it'll go viral—but after that, I'll get on to it."

"Okay, you're a lifesaver, oh my god. I'll treat you to malatang after." I lean against the back seat, watching the cars crawl along the highway, exhaust fumes spreading through the air like smoke from a fire. *Two days.* That's enough for me to carry out step two of the plan while I wait. "And good luck with the cheeseburger song."

"Thank you," she says seriously.

Step two: Grab his attention.

The most obvious strategy here would be to wait until my first peer mentoring session with Ares, but he hasn't reached out about a time and place yet, and I want his attention to be on *me*, not how badly I'm struggling with basic calculus. So instead I resort to my usual tricks.

In the cafeteria, I make a huge show of struggling to open

my water bottle, and hold it out just as Ares is passing. "Ares, can you help me with this?" I ask, smiling innocently up at him.

He just stares at me, those unnerving black eyes roaming from my face to the water, like it might be poison. I stare back, and notice the bruise blooming over his cheek. As if sensing my attention, he abruptly turns his head away. "My hands are occupied," he says, his hands in his pockets.

"I can help you with that, Chanel," someone calls out from the cafeteria line.

"No, let me help you," another guy from science offers, almost lunging for the water bottle in his eagerness to prove himself. "I've got it—"

"Looks like you don't need me for that anyway," Ares says, and walks right off, while four guys make a collective effort to twist open a water bottle cap.

In the library, when we're all meant to be studying, I move into Ares's line of vision and stand on my tiptoes before a bookshelf, stretching and straining to reach a book I'm never going to read in my life. After a few minutes of this, I turn toward him.

"Would you mind getting that book for me?" I ask.

He glances at the book above me. "That's the one you're looking for?"

I nod.

He still doesn't move but reads the title out loud. "*How to Avoid Stray Turkeys and Other Birds.* This is the book you plan on reading?"

"I'm scared of turkeys," I improvise. "I would very much like to know how to avoid them and . . . other birds. Can you . . ."

Before I've even finished talking, he starts walking away.

"What the—" I twist around in indignation. "Where are you going? Hey. *Hey*—"

But he's already gone.

In the corridors, I deliberately drop my wallet right by his feet and wait for him to pick it up for me. He doesn't. He merely glances down at my wallet, then up at me, his expression unimpressed.

"I know you're rich, Chanel, but I still wouldn't recommend throwing your money around. At least donate it to a charity or something."

By the time we head into gym for basketball, I'm desperate and more convinced than ever that Ares has been sent to destroy my life, with the fire or without it.

There's only one tactic I haven't tried yet, but clearly, I need to do something drastic—and soon.

I time my next step well. I wait until Ares has the ball in his hands—then I run up to him, arms lifted in defense, and in the half second before he aims to shoot, I knock my shoulder hard against his and pitch myself onto the gym floor.

I make sure to fall on my hands first. There's no cute way to land flat on your back, and the chances of actually hurting myself or gaining an unflattering bruise are too high for me to risk it. Once I'm down, curled up elegantly on my side in fake pain, I let out a dramatic yell, like an animal whose tail has just been stepped on.

Ares misses his shot and twists around.

Everyone else freezes. And then they all crowd forward, their concerned voices echoing off the vaulted ceiling.

"Chanel?"

"Oh my god, are you okay?"

"Wait, what happened?"

"Yeah, holy shit—that sounded painful."

"Look at her. She's shaking."

"Should we call an ambulance?"

Maybe my acting's too convincing. I quickly dial it down just a notch, restrict the trembling to just my lower lip, but make a mental note that I should really look into more acting opportunities, leverage my existing platform the way Rainie Lam has. I already know a number of up-and-coming C-drama actors, and some of them have so clearly only landed their roles because their parents are funding the drama or friendly with the director. . . .

"Chanel." The teacher's voice. "Chanel, can you sit?"

"I—I can try," I mumble, wincing as if in brave effort.

"Here. Hold on to me." Rainie grabs my elbow to help pull me up into a sitting position. I'm careful not to rise too fast, to make small noises of protest like it hurts just to move. Someone else—Bobby, I think—starts fanning me with his arms, which isn't super helpful from either a medical or an emotional standpoint, but the guy's heart is in the right place.

As I pretend to catch my breath from a nonexistent injury, clutching at my right ankle, more classmates gather around me like a funeral mass, their faces grave, their whispers somber.

"Don't worry, guys. I'm fine," I say in my softest voice, forcing myself to stare straight up at the fluorescent lights without blinking until tears form at the back of my eyes. Learning how to fake cry has been one of the most critical skills I've picked up over the years, perfect for occasions like these. The only time people are allowed to pity me is when I'm deliberately inviting their pity. When their pity is useful to me.

Ares steps forward through the crowd, his jaw tight. He stares down at me for a beat, looking torn between genuine concern and suspicion. "How bad is it?" The second he speaks, all the other voices drop away, everyone stopping to watch the exchange between us.

"Not that bad," I whisper. "I probably just need some ice from the nurse's office. I'll go there now—" I make a visible show of attempting to stand up, my face strained, my knees wobbling underneath me.

"Ares, can you please go with her?" the teacher asks.

He doesn't seem nearly as enthusiastic about this idea as most guys would. But he nods, and gestures for me to get on his back.

"I . . . don't think I can climb on like this," I murmur, glancing helplessly at my ankle.

He pauses. Appears to make up his mind about something. Then, without another word, he bends down toward me, sliding one hand under my waist, the other just beneath my knees, and lifts me up to his chest in a single movement until he's carrying me, bridal style, in the center of the basketball court.

The gasp that leaves my lips is exaggerated, but not entirely fake. His hands are hot and firm around my legs, and with my ear pressed against the thin cotton fabric of his shirt, I can hear his heart, its strong, insistent thudding, just a few beats too fast.

"This okay?" he asks, his voice reverberating into me. It sounds deeper from this position, raspier.

I shift a little, grabbing his neck to balance myself. "Yeah. It's okay," I say distractedly. This close, I can see just how fresh the bruise on his cheek is, the color still a bright reddish-pink. Had someone punched him? But who would have the nerve to?

I try to picture all the possibilities as he carries me across campus. I expect him to tire or at least slow down halfway, but his grip around me remains as steady as ever, all the way past the koi ponds and pagodas, across the running track and around the auditorium.

"So is there a reason you're suddenly everywhere I look?" Ares asks.

I glance up at his face, but he's staring straight ahead, his features giving nothing away. "Are you admitting that you've been paying attention to me?"

"Hard not to, when you keep popping up," he says. "What are you trying to do?"

My pulse skips. Is he on to me already? Does he suspect my plans? But I reply smoothly, "Nothing. I just think maybe we got off on the wrong foot, and I really feel like witnessing a freak supernatural event together was a great bonding experience—"

"I don't bond with people," he says flatly.

"Is that, like, your attachment style? Avoidant attachment?"

"No."

"Okay, right. Sure. Then what would you say your attachment style is—"

"Have you remembered any more details?" he cuts in.

"Details? About what?"

"The vision," he says, his voice strained.

I'd been prepared for this line of interrogation, and I've decided that the less Ares knows about what I know, the better. "Not really, I'm afraid. The fire was the only thing I saw. Just the fire and, like, a lot of smoke."

His eyes narrow. "Are you sure?"

"Why would I lie?" I ask innocently.

"Yes, exactly," he says under his breath, but his tone is accusatory, his fingers tightening around me. "Why would you?"

We've reached the next building, where rose petals and heart-shaped confetti still linger from the promposal at lunch—the third one so far today—and I sense an opening. The moment I've been working toward. We're alone together, I'm in a seemingly vulnerable position, and his arms are literally around me. Now's the perfect time to start slipping in hints about prom. "Did you watch the promposal?" I ask casually, nodding toward the petals scattered over the ground. "Wasn't it *so* cute?"

"Don't know," he says, looking about as interested in the subject as I do during my math lectures. "I wasn't there."

"Really? What about the promposal yesterday? The one with all the doves?" I continue with vigorous determination. *Come on,* I want to hiss at him. *Take the bait. Talk to me.* "I think my favorite was—"

"We're here," he says, coming to an abrupt stop outside the office door and setting me down just as fast. "I'll wait outside for you."

I snap my mouth shut, grinding the back of my teeth together. *Fine. Another time then.*

I limp all the way inside by myself, dropping the act only once the door swings shut behind me. Then I straighten and smile at the nurse, who I'm pretty sure has been working at Airington for as long as I've been here but somehow hasn't aged a year. I've been meaning to ask her about her skincare routine.

"Chanel! What's wrong?" She gestures for me to sit down on the ugly green couch, which is definitely older than both of us. "Have you been feeling lightheaded again?"

"Yeah, just a little," I say, embarrassed that she still remembers the last time I was here. I'd been fasting for two days straight under my mom's advice, and I'd thought I was fine until I stood up too fast after history class and the room suddenly swayed around me. I hadn't wanted to alarm anyone, so I'd walked alone to the nurse's office, white sparks dancing in my vision. She'd given me a large glass of sugar water and urged me to eat three full meals a day.

"You should really take better care of your body," the nurse says, shooting me a concerned look.

I nod along. I *do* feel lightheaded and nauseous, but for once, it's not because I'm starving myself. It's because of the boy waiting outside. Just thinking about him—how close he'd been, those unfeeling black eyes—makes me dizzy, makes my heartbeat pick up with sickening speed. It's like he's put some kind of curse on me.

I take my time sipping my sugar water, trying to figure out how I can better integrate him into my prom plans.

And then I think of it.

"What did the nurse recommend?" Ares asks when I find him out in the corridor.

I'm surprised he hadn't simply walked off while I was inside. Maybe he's not as much of a lost cause as I thought. "I'll survive, I guess, but she warned me not to carry anything heavy by myself. It's bad to put too much weight on my leg," I tell him, then sigh. "But like, I *really* need to go prom dress shopping tomorrow. Basically all my friends already have their dresses picked out." I sigh again. "What am I supposed to do? I won't be able to carry any of my shopping bags."

Ares raises his brows. "You're not expecting me to, are you?"

I take his rhetorical question and run with it. "Wait, that's *so* nice of you to offer—"

"I wasn't offering—"

"It would be *incredibly* helpful, and like, it'd definitely make up for the fact that you tripped me," I press.

He's silent. I have no idea what he's thinking, but after a beat, he folds his arms across his chest. "What time?"

7

CHANEL

The mall is busier than ever today.

I push through the crowds, past the happy, oblivious families and groups of best friends and carefree students, everyone else who isn't here on a mission, past hundreds of faces I don't recognize, looking for the one I do. The only one that matters to me right now, as unfortunate as this whole situation is.

Laughter bubbles all around me, voices bouncing off the glass storefronts and indoor fountains and escalators. A dozen different songs drift in and out from separate shops, the melodies all blending together, hardcore rap with slow, wistful ballads, the occasional English word sprinkled into the Mandarin lyrics to rhyme even when it doesn't make sense. I quicken my footsteps as I pass a couple locked in an embrace *way* too passionate for a Saturday morning.

Still no sign of him.

I'm starting to consider the horrible, nauseating possibility that Ares Yin has stood me up when I spot him outside the

Chagee store. He's dressed in all black again. As I watch, two girls sipping their new cups of milk tea do a double-take on their way out, then break into giggles. One of them starts to approach him, holding her phone out, no doubt ready to ask him for his WeChat.

"Ares," I call, marching forward.

The girl shrinks back, her face falling in disappointment.

Ares doesn't seem to notice any of this, or doesn't care. "How's the ankle?" he asks, tilting his head. It sounds less like he's concerned and more like he's testing me.

"Healing, but it still hurts," I say, making a point to slow my footsteps. "Thanks for coming."

He fixes me with an appraising look. "Maybe you shouldn't be shopping at all if your ankle hurts."

Is he trying to get out of this shopping trip before it's even started? I chew the inside of my cheek, trying to steady myself against the twist of panic in my stomach. If I'm being honest, I thought Ares would have softened up to me a little by now. According to my usual timeline, most guys would be professing their love to me and asking me to meet their parents.

And I don't have that much time left. Prom season is in full swing already, and almost everyone I know has their date for the night secured. If I want to change the course of my fate, I need Ares to ask me out—but right now he doesn't seem interested in asking for anything except the option to leave. "Well, you know what they say. Shopping is good therapy," I tell him. "I'll probably be healed by the end of today."

"I think you're confusing physical therapy with retail therapy."

"Same thing. Plus, the nurse said I was fine to walk."

He looks less like he's convinced and more like he can't be bothered arguing with me. "Well, then. Lead the way."

He follows me from one end of the mall to the other, then from the first floor up to the sixth. Past the bakeries selling oolong cakes and matcha Swiss rolls and vanilla canelés "house-baked fresh daily!" Through the cosmetics aisles offering live demonstrations on how to make your face look smaller with their latest contour palette. And into all the luxury stores, Chanel and Gucci and Versace, where the overeager sales associates offer us sparkling water and fragrance samples while they bring out their selection of dresses.

"I'll take all of these, thanks," I tell the sales associate after I've tried on seven dresses.

"You found your dress?" Ares asks.

"What? No, don't be ridiculous. Those are just for future parties or picnics," I say. The sales associate trots back with all the dresses wrapped in shiny bags, which she hands straight over to Ares. She must have assumed he's my boyfriend—a fact that pleases me more than I'd like to admit. "My prom dress has to be absolutely *perfect*. Come on, let's go check out another store."

Ares makes no further comment, but he carries all my bags dutifully, his sleeves rolled up, keeping in step with me.

"Oh yeah, do you have a suit for prom yet?" I ask him as we pass a menswear store, the window displays guarded by mannequins in smart blazers and ties. "We can pick something out for you too."

"No, thanks. I'm not going to prom," Ares says.

I stop walking. *"You're not going to prom?"* I repeat—too sharply, too panicked, my throat closing around my voice. He shoots me an odd look, and I try to school my horror into something more casual, like incredulity. He can't find out that my multistep strategy to save my house hinges around him going to prom with me. "But . . . but *why*? Everyone goes to prom."

"I don't get what the big deal is," he says with a shrug.

"It's a *very* big deal," I argue. "It's basically the most important event throughout all of high school. People at Airington dream about prom the way girls dream about their weddings. It's meant to be, like, this one perfect, grand, magical night you'll reminisce about in a retirement home fifty years later. It's your official coming of age. It's beautiful."

Ares considers this for a moment, then shakes his head. "I'm just not interested."

I stare at him in disbelief. There's something about the way he says it—completely unapologetic, direct, without catering to anybody else. I can't imagine ever doing that. I've been raised to feign interest, to show up and smile and act like I care about everything all the time, no matter how I really feel inside. "But you're literally nominated for prom king," I point out as I recover my pace. "By tradition, unless they have a major scheduling conflict or near-fatal accident, the prom king candidates *always* attend."

"By tradition, but not by law, right?" Ares says dryly.

"Okay, no, not technically, but—"

"And it's not like I asked to be nominated for prom king," he goes on in the same blunt, bored tone. "I didn't even know that was happening."

My blood heats. Ares's clear disdain toward prom doesn't just feel like a threat to my plans; it feels like an insult to everything I've built over the years. My networking, my scheming, my relentless, exhausting self-promotion, all so I could become prom royalty—a status that apparently means nothing to Ares. It's like when I spent weeks making paper-mâché flowers over the Christmas holidays, hoping they would lift my mother's mood. But when she'd spotted them sitting in a vase outside our spa room, she'd merely frowned and asked the ayi to toss them out. "Get me some real roses," she'd said, "or bring out the Swarovski flowers." Suddenly all my efforts had felt so stupid, so pointless.

But I can't let my frustration show, and I can't push Ares too hard about prom just yet. I'll only come across as obsessive and controlling, or highly suspicious. So instead I sidestep the subject and point to one of the boutique stores up ahead. "Let's go in there—it looks cute."

I say this as if I've spotted the store by chance, but I've frequented it enough times for the store manager and all the workers to know who I am—which is exactly why I'm tugging Ares inside with me. If I can't make him *like* me right away, at least I can try to impress him in a controlled environment. Remind him of how famous I am.

"Oh my god, Chanel Cao!" Just as I'd hoped, the store manager jumps up from the counter in the back section, where all the floral skirts have been mixed-and-matched with trendy lace tops and cropped pieces. She struts over, smiling wide. "Welcome, welcome. You came at *such* a good time—the season's newest dresses just landed yesterday. All one-hundred-percent real silk. There's this one dress that I know would look absolutely *gorgeous* on you. . . ."

I try it on in the dressing room, pleased with how the fabric falls over my body, how the crimson color contrasts my complexion, makes my skin look soft and smooth as milk.

When I step out, the store manager gasps in dramatic approval.

"Oh, you look *incredible!* Doesn't she look stunning?"

One of the shoppers stops browsing the racks and glances over appreciatively at me. "Could I try on that dress after her?" I overhear her ask.

Her friend lets out an envious sigh. "If I looked like that . . . I think I'd be happy walking around in a garbage bag."

I bite back a smile and do a slow spin before the floor-to-ceiling mirror, sucking in my stomach and subtly arching my back. I meet Ares's eyes in the reflection. He doesn't shift his gaze away, doesn't pretend to be fascinated by something else the way most boys do when they're caught staring. He simply stares right back, dark brows raised, as if to say, *Don't you want me to look at you?*

"Should I take this one?" I ask him.

He shrugs. "If you want."

"Is it pretty, though?" I press.

"You know it's pretty," he says, but I can't tell if that's meant to be a compliment.

"It's a very nice dress," I allow, scrutinizing my reflection. "The shape is perfect, and I love the color and all, but I don't like how the straps look. They're a bit too thick over here, on the shoulders, and the clasp makes it tacky. It'd be my dream dress if it had simple spaghetti straps." I turn to the store manager. "Any chance you could alter the dress?"

"We can't do any alterations, I'm afraid," she says.

I purse my lips. "All right. I'll get it as a back-up dress for now. Let me just take a photo to show my friends."

The store manager ducks out of the way as I raise my phone, angling it so that you can see the full shape of the dress—and Ares's unmistakable reflection in the mirror. Then I post it to my close friends story with the caption *prom things* and a tiny heart. Ares might not plan on asking me to prom yet, but it can't hurt to let people at school *think* he has, so that by the time he does ask—and he *will*, he must—we'll already be the perfect prom couple in everyone else's eyes.

The notifications flood in right away. Individual replies to my story from everyone in my circle.

omg????

CHANEL! IS THAT ARES YIN??!!!

girl what chapter did I miss??

spill. right now.

THE DRESS? THE MAN?!

please tell me you're going to prom with ares yin (and that you're getting the dress)

I fuel the speculation with just a few cryptic eye emojis.

"What are you smiling at?" Ares's voice sounds over my shoulder, much closer than I'd expected.

I hastily shove my phone away but keep the smile on my face. "My friends agree that the dress is pretty," I say, only a half lie. "Looks like our mission is complete for the day. Want to go grab food now? I know a *really* good spot—prepare to be amazed."

"I'm never amazed," he says, but he doesn't reject the dinner invitation outright, which I'm choosing to take as a sign that he's warming up to me.

"Well," I say, clapping my hands together, "that's about to change."

After Ares drops all my bags off at my driver's car, we step out together into the evening air. The sun is just starting to dip below the horizon, burning a brilliant orange as if setting the skyscrapers aflame.

We walk down the street in silence for a while, until it becomes clear that Ares isn't going to initiate a conversation.

That's fine. I've got it under control.

"So. Have you broken any bones before?" This is my go-to question. A classic. I've tried it out on at least ten different boys, and I've been continuously stunned by how well it works—even the most reserved of them will light up and tell you in vivid, heart-pounding detail their grand tale of heroism, the pain they suffered through and ultimately overcame, the drawn-out process of getting a cast, getting classmates to sign the cast, taking off the cast, and the long recovery afterward.

But Ares just nods. "Yeah. A few, I think."

"A *few*?" I echo. "Doing what?"

"Boxing matches," he says casually, like this is something everyone grew up doing.

My eyes widen with genuine surprise. "You . . . box?"

"My father signed me up for lessons when I was a kid," he says, and I note that this is the first time he's mentioned anything about his family—though, from the flatness of his tone, you'd think he was talking about a stranger.

"For self-defense?" I ask.

"No. That was never his priority. It was to protect . . ." He trails off, and his expression tightens, the muscles in his jaw hardening. Then he glances over at me. In an obvious attempt to turn the attention away from himself, he says, "Have *you* broken any bones before?"

"Just my pinkie finger. Like, four years ago."

"From doing what?"

I decide to just be honest. "Dancing."

He pauses. "And how does that work? Were you dancing with a hammer?"

"I was dancing in my bedroom," I admit. "I got a little too into it, and I accidentally hit my hand on the wall during one of the moves."

Something happens to his mouth then: the faintest twitch of his lips, like he's fighting to squash down any amusement. "I didn't realize dancing could be such a dangerous activity."

"Just wait until you see me dancing at prom," I say, which seems like the perfect segue—but before I can continue, something warm and furry brushes the back of my calves. I whip around to find a pair of wide, dark brown eyes gazing up at me. The animal's ears twitch. She wags her short tail back and forth with such enthusiasm it appears in danger of dislocating, her pink tongue lolling out to one side.

"A puppy," I say in delight, crouching down by the pedestrian lane.

The puppy draws closer at the sound of my voice, bumping her small, vaguely Labrador-shaped head against my knee.

"Hello," I murmur, letting the animal sniff my fingers, her wet nose grazing my skin. "Are you hungry?"

In response, the puppy wags her tail harder, now gladly licking away at my hand. I laugh and pat the dappled fur on her side, which is all the encouragement she needs to roll over, stretching out her belly for me to scratch.

I'm having so much fun playing with the dog that it takes a moment to notice how beside me, Ares has frozen, tension rolling through his body. When he finally speaks, his voice has none of its usual cadence or composure. "Get that thing out of here."

I stare at him, expecting him to be joking, but he's watching the puppy with real fear in his eyes. Even his breathing has shallowed.

"Ares," I say, unsure how we could possibly be seeing the same thing. "She's a tiny *dog.* She's friendly."

The puppy gives a little yap of agreement, but Ares flinches away, hiding behind me, his long fingers gripping my shoulders as though I'm a shield. I don't shrug him off; the sheer absurdity of the scene roots me in place. Ares Yin, the most dangerous and intimidating person I've ever met, who can make people part in the hallways just by glancing their way . . . is now hiding, trembling, from a harmless stray puppy.

"I didn't know you were scared of dogs," I muse aloud, unable to keep the incredulity out of my voice.

"Don't sound so judgmental about it," he says, eyeing the puppy like it might suddenly sprout fangs and attack.

The puppy in question stands up and pads forward, now sniffing around my shoes. Ares's grip tightens around my shoulders, and a thrill shoots through me. If I'd known that all it'd take to make Ares act this way—to rely on me, to seek me out for protection, to show vulnerability—was a puppy, I would have hired a dog actor.

"Get it away," he repeats, shrinking back farther.

This is my chance, I realize. My chance to be the hero, the princess in shining armor. "If I do, you owe me a favor," I tell him.

His voice is hoarse in my ear. "What kind of favor?"

"I'll specify later." I can't suppress my smile. "Hmm? Sound fair to you?"

"I don't—" The word falls flat as the puppy yaps again and bounces toward him. A choked sound escapes his lips.

"What was that?" I ask sweetly.

"Fine—*fine*. Just . . . send it somewhere else. . . ."

"Sure. But don't forget," I say, picking up the puppy. She curls instantly into my chest, nuzzling against the crook of my elbow, the warmth of her fur spreading through my shirt. I carry her along the street and set her down in front of a grocery store, where fresh strawberries and cherries are being sold in green plastic buckets bigger than my head. Then I buy a plain slice of bread for her, tearing it apart with my fingers and letting her eat it from my hands.

Once she's finished licking all the crumbs, the puppy lingers a few moments longer, as if to thank me, her watery eyes bright and round as the setting sun, before slinking off into the nearby bushes.

"Is it gone?" Ares asks when I return.

I'd been prepared to make myself comfort him, to build that fake emotional connection. But as I draw closer, I don't feel like faking anything. He's sitting on a stone bench, ankles crossed, his usually composed expression shadowed by embarrassment and the remnants of fear. His crow-dark hair is rumpled from the wind, strands of it falling into his eyes, his shirt smelling faintly, sweetly, of the cologne samples from the mall. The desire to comfort him rises up inside me without prompting.

"Yeah, it's gone."

"Thank you," he says, reluctant, but not insincere.

"No big deal. It's what I spend most of my time doing," I say. "Swooping in and saving pretty faces from monsters."

There it is again—the suggestion of a smile, forced back down before it can fully form, like he's annoyed by his own reaction.

"Hey, don't beat yourself up over it," I tell him.

"What?"

"Enjoying my company," I say. "It's perfectly normal."

He rolls his eyes and stands up, but this time, instead of following one step behind me, he walks right by my side.

★ ★ ★

"*This* is the spot?"

Ares stares around the barbecue stall and the tiny wooden chairs like he expects me to open up a trapdoor in the middle of the busy street, one that will lead to a proper restaurant, or just anywhere that doesn't cook its food right out in the open.

"What?" I snort as I drape my jacket over an empty seat to create a makeshift cushion. I motion for him to join me in the chair across the table, which he does slowly, angling his long legs so they don't bump against the wood. Everything here is small, squeezed to maximize profit. The table beside us is so close that I could easily turn my head and slide into the conversation happening between the two half-drunk college-aged guys there. I'm pretty sure one of them just got dumped, seeing as he laments every few seconds, between swigs of Qingdao beer and bites of grilled lamb, "I can't believe she just dumped me."

Most people fall in love with this city because it makes them feel important, being at the heart of everything. Or they love it for its endless opportunities, the cash flowing through the five-star hotels and dizzying plazas and live streamers on the streets to the skyscrapers in the financial district. Or the history, the hutongs that have survived the turn of centuries and the crimson-painted temples that have witnessed countless changes of seasons, white snow settling on their sparrow-wing eaves and melting again in the spring.

But I love Beijing most on nights like this: the thrumming crowds, the glow of the street stall lights, the lick of oil and salt in the warming air, the easy flow of conversation around me.

When I was in Australia, everything always seemed to close before the sun had even fully set beneath the horizon. More times than I could count, my friends and I would chat until we could tell the restaurant staff were impatient to leave, and then walk aimlessly through the suburbs.

Here, though, the whole city stays wide awake all the way until dawn, ready to offer you anything you wish for, so long as you know where to look. You could buy a heat pack and a strawberry plushie from the convenience store at three in the morning, or request red-date-and-ginger tea to be delivered to your door faster than it takes you to boil water yourself, or hail a rickshaw to the Olympic Village and wander around the glowing towers, because why not?

"It just . . . doesn't seem like your usual sort of style," Ares remarks, still staring, taking the place in: the hawkers in matching red caps and aprons crouching down to cook, the single LED light suspended over the grill, the smoke wafting into the night air, the ugly but eye-catching rainbow posters advertising the different skewer options in bold Chinese characters. *Squid, ten yuan. Lamb, five yuan. Chicken gristle, five yuan. Potato, one yuan. Leek, one yuan.*

I raise my brows to hide my satisfaction at his surprise. I'd deliberately chosen this place to show off how flexible I am, how at ease I can be in any environment. "You want to keep a man interested? You have to be unpredictable," my mother had advised me years ago. "Every time he thinks he has you figured out, reveal a different side of yourself."

"You think I'm incapable of eating something if it isn't prepared by a Michelin-starred chef and served on a golden tray?"

His gaze flickers back to me. "I didn't say that."

"You think my life is easy," I go on mildly, without accusation, as though I'm pointing out something as obvious and indisputable as the weather.

"I think," he says, "that your life is very different from mine."

"How can you be so sure?"

"I just do," he says. Then, after a beat, he adds, "I saw that interview you did."

"What interview?"

"The one where you were introducing all the items in your purse." He mimics me, holding up an invisible bag and retrieving an invisible object out of it. "'I always like to carry a spare necklace or set of earrings in my purse, you know, just in case I'm in a hurry to leave in the morning. I can't have zero accessories on, or else, like, I literally feel naked.'" He's teasing, but there's no real mockery in his expression, and that *does* sound like something I would say. It could even be a word-for-word reenactment of my interview, though I have no idea how he's managed to remember all of it.

"That interview was from years ago. How did you even manage to find it anyway?" I lean forward, resting my chin on both my hands. "Have you been googling me?"

He shrugs, shameless, not even bothering to deny it. "You're a public figure."

I don't know whether to be flattered or embarrassed by the thought of him deep-diving into every digital version of myself floating around on the internet. But it's proof that he's been thinking about me. That he's curious about me.

He goes on, "'There's this one necklace from a newly opened store in Shanghai that I just adore. I believe the brand's called JQ Jewelry, and all the necklaces are tailored according to your name and Chinese zodiac sign. I wear mine, like, all the time. . . .'" He drops his admittedly convincing impression of my voice. "Is that even true? Because I've never seen you wear a necklace like that before."

"No," I say with a snort. "My friend's family owns the brand, and she asked me to help them promote it in the video."

"So you lied." He doesn't sound like he's judging me, more like he's simply trying to understand my thought process.

"A white lie—barely even that," I reason. "A mild, harmless exaggeration, done only for the sake of friendship, and who doesn't love friendship? Well, I mean, maybe you don't."

He blinks, then huffs out a low sound of laughter. "Did you just imply that I don't have friends?"

"*Do* you have friends?"

"Your concern about my social life is touching."

"I'm just looking out for you."

His attention sharpens on me. "Why?"

I don't have a good answer for that, not without revealing the truth, so I play coy, lowering my chin and gazing up at him from under my lashes. "Why do you think?"

A cloud above us shifts, and a perfect slant of moonlight pools over his skin, lining the slope of his lips, the curve of those long, oil-black lashes. Time seems to slow, and I swear I can see the interplay of emotions on his face like light and shadow: suspicion, doubt, fascination, frustration. Then he breaks eye contact, pointing to the QR code printed above the posters. "Let's order first. I'm getting hungry."

After we add our items to the cart—twenty lamb skewers for him, with extra spice: two lamb skewers, two quail egg skewers, and two mushroom skewers for me, no spice and reduced salt—Ares gestures to his phone. "I'll pay," he says.

This is what I was hoping for, not because I care about the twenty-two-yuan skewers, but because it gives me the perfect excuse to protest, "No, no, I should get it. I was the one who introduced you to this place. It's only fair."

He shrugs, finishes scanning the QR code, stuffs his phone back into his pocket. "It's fine."

"I'll pay you back," I insist. "What's your WeChat?"

The most subtle of looks passes over his face, a kind of awareness, or amusement, maybe. I don't like it. It makes me feel entirely too transparent, like I'm standing on a stage and telling a joke when he's already read the punchline. "You want my WeChat?"

I've noticed him doing this. Always asking me questions that begin with "Do you want to?" or "Do you think?" without revealing anything about his own thoughts, what *he* wants. "Are you going to give it to me?" I ask, offering him a faint smile, suggestive but subdued.

"Depends how badly you want it."

"I do," I say. "I very badly want to pay you back. I hate owing people money."

That look again, this time paired with the tilt of his head. He considers me for a few seconds. "And how often do you ask guys for their WeChat?"

"Basically never. They're always the ones asking me," I say, more sulkily than I'd planned.

He studies me a moment longer, then reaches for his phone again, holding it out for me to scan.

Progress. At last.

I try not to look too excited as I add him. He accepts my friend request right away, and I click into his profile—only for disappointment to sink through me. Typically, just one cursory glance at someone's latest WeChat moments can tell you more about them than five in-depth interviews. Blurry pictures of a rave or a shirtless gym selfie or a caption about their *life-altering trip* to Bali? Basic fuckboy material. Well-lit photos of home-made egg-and-tomatoes or the natural scenery from deep in the mountains? More advanced fuckboy material. Glamorous shots of their silhouette against a hotel window or golf clubs or race cars? Rich fuckboy material.

But I have no idea what kind of material Ares Yin is.

His profile picture is a pure white square. His bio has been left totally blank, which I didn't even realize was something you could do. His Moments are visible for up to six months, but that's because he hasn't posted anything at all. Even his *name* is simply "Ares Yin." No creative capitalization or punctuation. Nothing.

"Your skewers are ready," the vendor declares, dumping them unceremoniously down on a paper plate in front of us, the skewers so fresh off the grill that you can still see the oil sizzling on the meat.

I grab one, biting the seasoned lamb between my front

teeth and sliding it slowly off the metal skewer, careful not to smudge my lipstick. It's so hot that I can barely even taste it at first. "So," I say, blowing on the rest before taking another bite. This time, I can't miss the salt and cumin powder slathered over the meat, the flavor bursting on my tongue. "How many girlfriends have you had?"

If Ares is surprised by the direction of the conversation, or the directness of the question, he doesn't let it show. "Define *girlfriend*," he says eventually.

My brows rise. "Many, then."

"That's not what I said."

"Either you've had too many, or they don't count because they were only hookups."

Another pause. "Define *hookups*."

Annoyance prickles along my skin like a rash. "I feel like you've got enough firsthand experience to know what the definition is."

His amusement seems to rise with my annoyance, an unfortunate pattern I've started to notice. He cocks his head. "And what makes you think that?"

"Because." I wave at him with the skewer like it's a mini dagger, the motion half threatening, pointing out the black wolf cut, the piercings, the noticeably lean stretch of his muscles beneath his shirt. His general aura, that dangerous, irresistible quality that's made half the girls at school lose their minds over him. "Just look at you."

"Thank you," he says.

"That actually wasn't a compliment."

"No?"

"No," I say firmly.

"Well, I've been with girls before," he says at last with a shrug. "Nothing serious, though."

I rip off the last piece of meat and let the skewer clatter onto the table. I'd thought that pushing an answer out of him would satisfy me, yet the rashlike sensation roots itself deeper, until even my insides itch with the knowledge. I'm not sure why it bothers me. It's what I expected, and I'd be extremely skeptical if someone of his age and looks claimed to have zero romantic experience whatsoever. Really, I should be pressing for more information, whatever will help me figure out his type and tailor my approach. But there's something nauseating about the prospect of being confronted with details. Imagining all the girls he's kissed, or undressed, or done more with.

"What about you?" he asks, his tone as casual as mine had been. "How many boyfriends?"

I cross my legs underneath the table and lean back. "Let me think."

"Are you counting?"

"Are you judging me?"

"No, not at all," he says, leaning back too. "You can have as many boyfriends as you want."

I feel another hot, irrational spike of rage. He sounds like he means it—like he truly couldn't care less if I were to tell him that I've been involved with every single guy in this city.

The truth is that I've only had two semi-serious boyfriends

before. The first had claimed to have "lost feelings" for me over the course of a summer, when he was in Italy and I was in Shanghai, and the second one had cheated on me with some girl he'd danced with at a nightclub. Apparently he'd been *so* drunk that night he didn't even remember who she was.

"I'm so, so sorry, Chanel—I swear I didn't mean to hurt you," he'd whispered when I found out, his eyes solemn and heavy with remorse, his hands spread out pleadingly. He looked like he was auditioning for the lead in a tragic play.

I had burst out laughing. I laughed so hard that my ribs ached. "Oh my god. You think you've hurt me?" I let my gaze rove over him before emphasizing, with relish, *"You?"*

He'd flinched back as if the word were a gunshot, sounding right next to his ear. The remorse was gone, replaced in an instant with distress, rising fast in pink splotches up his neck. This wasn't the script he had rehearsed with.

"Yeah, no, don't you worry about that. The problem here isn't that I'm heartbroken over you," I'd said with a snort. "The problem is much bigger. See, you *embarrassed* me. Publicly." I was already whipping out my phone to do damage control as I spoke. Luckily, I'd had the foresight not to post any pictures of his face on my accounts, but you could still see traces of his existence, proof to my followers that I was loved by a boy: a shadow splashed next to mine on the pavement, a second glass of Diet Pepsi on the dinner table, the flash of his shoulder at the park. I deleted all the evidence, leaving only the park post because my hair looked good in it.

When I glanced up again, he was staring at me like he was

seeing me for the first time. "I—I can't believe that's what you're upset about," he said at last.

"What else would I be upset about?" I'd asked coolly.

But I don't tell Ares any of this. I wouldn't have the chance to, anyways, because he finishes his last skewer and stands up.

"I need to head back," he says. "You want me to wait for your driver with you?"

"No, that's fine," I tell him. I can't stop second-guessing his intentions. Does he genuinely care about whether or not I get back home safe? Or is he just making sure I do so that I don't follow him? "You go ahead. I can wait by myself."

But there's one last thing I need to do. As Ares gathers up our used skewers and dirty napkins and turns around to toss them in the trash, I unclasp the custom-made Van Cleef bracelet around my wrist and drop it into his bag.

When he comes back, I'm already re-applying my lip gloss as if nothing's happened. As if I haven't just planted my bait.

8

CHANEL

Exactly ten minutes after Ares leaves, my phone buzzes over the table, Jamie's name lighting up my screen.

Perfect timing.

I hastily wipe the cumin powder and grease from my fingers, then pick up the phone, sandwiching it between my ear and shoulder. "Hello?"

"Okay, so, like, that took me way longer than I thought—the guy might as well be a spy or something—but I've got what you asked for," Jamie says.

Finally. My heart skips in anticipation. "Yes? Tell me everything you know."

"To start with . . ." She lowers her voice, and I brace myself, breath catching in my throat, waiting for the bombshell to drop. Maybe he's under witness protection. Or he's an assassin, if those even still exist in the modern world. Or he's on the run from assassins—"He's a Virgo."

"I'm sorry?"

"He's a *Virgo*," she repeats, like it's a life-altering revelation, no less significant than if she were to discover that Ares Yin was secretly descended from a royal family.

"Huh." I absorb this for a moment, and store the information for later. "Okay, I won't lie, that is kind of surprising."

"I also found one of the girls he supposedly had a fling with two summers ago," she adds. "Do you want to search her up?"

My body's reaction surprises me—the intensity of it, the immediate sour taste filling my mouth. I feel myself recoil, the muscles in my stomach clenching instinctively as if someone's just threatened to punch me. "Sure," I say, because this should be helpful. Finding out his type, whatever it is. It shouldn't bother me at all.

"Type in Suzy Liu, with three *U*s," she instructs. "Her profile's the one with her wearing a blue sundress on a balcony—you see it?"

I take a deep breath and do as I'm told. After a few seconds, her feed loads on my phone screen. Bright pops of color, flashes of smooth, sun-kissed skin, generic but aesthetic photos of picnics at the beach and brunches with friends, the neatest arrangement of freckles I've ever seen on a human being.

"She's really pretty," I comment in an attempt to be objective. I scroll slowly down through all fifty-seven of her posts, taking as much care as someone defusing a bomb to not let my fingers brush the Like button by accident. She's pretty in a different way from me—not overly dolled up, not trying too hard. Just subtle eyeshadow that suits her softer features and what looks like naturally wavy hair, fluffed by the ocean breeze. No fillers. No filters, even.

Is *that* what Ares is into? I make a note to start switching up my makeup style.

"What else did you find?" I prompt. "What about his family?"

"Right, right, I'm getting there," she says. "I had to ask a friend—well, that might be a bit generous, let's just say an old classmate—to dive into old hospital records, but they managed to find him. He was born in the States, in New York, and his mother was an economics professor."

"His mother *was* an economics professor?" I say, catching the past tense. "What's she doing now?"

A pause. "She's not doing anything now, because she's dead."

"Wait. What?"

"Yeah, she died giving birth to him," she says, not unsympathetically, but with the causal tone of someone rehashing the plot of a movie. "Kind of depressing."

I feel my heart clench. I almost don't hear what she says next, because I'm suddenly picturing Ares as a child. Alone. Helpless.

". . . and his father's based in Beijing, but he seems to fly out all the time. His father also has another son called Luke. The mother was a former assistant of his, but they never married, and she suddenly transferred to one of the company's other offices around the same time she would've been pregnant, so I'm assuming it was a one-night stand kind of situation."

"Luke?" I repeat. The name doesn't ring any bells at all, but I remember how Ares had trailed off before. "To protect . . . ," he'd started. Was that who he was talking about? Why his father had signed him up for boxing? "I didn't even realize he had a brother. He doesn't go to Airington, does he?"

"No. They filed a missing person report for him three years ago, and they still haven't found him. Qin, are you *sure* you want to be with him?" Jamie says suddenly. "Because, like, not going to lie, his whole family situation sounds super messed up."

I'm not sure of anything anymore, but there's this pull in my gut, a suspicion that I might have just found a critical piece to the puzzle I've been trying to solve since that first night. *Luke. Missing person report. Three years ago.*

But the more pieces I collect, the more terrified I am of how the picture will look once it's finally complete.

After I hang up, I walk down to the lake alone.

On the outside, the park appears so blissfully normal. The aunties heading home on their electric bikes, pink scarves wrapped around their necks to fend off the evening chill, their arms practically melded to the front handle underneath thick polka-dotted blankets. The more sociable aunties practicing the choreography for their courtyard dance routine, gossiping with each other about someone called Lao Wang and Xiao Li and their new son-in-law as they swing their hips and swish their fans. The old men huddled underneath the cool white glow of the streetlights. Navy caps on, sometimes a pipe dangling between their teeth, faces somber with concentration as they watch a game of Chinese chess unfold over stone boards, hands behind their backs except to point out an obvious move.

Then I arrive at the lake's edge, waiting. Watching. At first I can only see the moonlight pooling over the water, but when the moon reaches its highest point, the illusion of normalcy shatters.

I suck in a breath as the silver light ripples against the darkness, strange shapes emerging over the surface.

My heart strains against my chest, everything in my body suspended with both horror and hope. *Please*, I pray. I want so desperately to believe that the vision has changed already, that it'll show me dancing at prom instead, smiling up at Ares, crowns gleaming on our heads. That after spending all that time with him, after the way he'd watched me while I tried on the dress, after the puppy, and the dinner, there's a chance he'll come around. . . .

But then the shapes clarify slowly into the vision from my nightmares, and my stomach drops. Whatever I've done, it wasn't enough. It's still the same house engulfed in smoke and fire. The vision is even clearer than before. There are now two new figures in the periphery of the frame.

A middle-aged man with a crescent-shaped scar on his cheek, and a younger boy, standing next to him, his features twisted with panic. Maybe fourteen or fifteen at most. He looks familiar, though I'm certain I've never met this boy in my life.

The man looks familiar too, but in a different way. Like a face from a magazine cover or an old photo, someplace I've seen before . . . but where? He's around my dad's age, and from his suit-and-tie look, he would certainly fit into one of his circles. He could be any of the businessmen I've made small talk with at my dad's functions.

Maybe that, then?

I inch closer to the lake until my feet are perched on the very edge, trying to commit the man's face to memory—and to look for more clues, anything that will help me make sense of this.

But all I can focus on is the crimson moon, hanging in the sky like a blood-stained clock. A reminder that I have just a couple weeks left.

Mere weeks to completely alter my fate.

Mere weeks to stop Ares.

That night, I fall onto my bed, my stomach pressed flat against the duvet, and open up a new chat with Ares. Normally, I would wait longer after adding a guy on WeChat before messaging him, to avoid seeming too eager, but I can't afford to waste any time.

I stare at the blank square of Ares's profile, my thumbs hovering over the screen, my pulse thrumming. I shouldn't be nervous. It's just a message, and I've already planned out what I'm going to say, right down to the punctuation.

But I still find myself taking in a deep, shaky breath before typing out:

hey, have u seen my bracelet??

Then I quickly hit Send before I can overthink it.

I'm rewarded at once with the familiar chime of the WeChat notification. A grin flashes across my face—until I read his reply.

Just two words: *what bracelet?*

Not the most enthusiastic, sure. *But*, I reason with myself, *a reply is still a reply.* Now it's my move again. I can't reply right away, though—it would make it seem like I've been waiting around for him with my phone glued to my hand like some sort of lovesick loser without better things to do.

And I *do* have better—or at least more pressing—things to do. So I force myself to set my phone down flat on the pillow and head into the living room. I crouch down by the cabinets, rifling through them until I find what I'm looking for: our photo album collection. With an unpleasant pang that feels too close to nostalgia, I remember my dad's insistence that physical photos just *feel* better than scrolling through images on a phone screen.

I'd made fun of him for it before, but I have to admit that I'm glad to have the albums here, each of them neatly and methodically labeled by hand, the blue ink starting to fade in places. *Chanel Childhood Photos Ages 0 to 3. Honeymoon Trip One. Honeymoon Trip Two. Honeymoon Trip Three. Family Photos. Cao Yunchen's Business Photos 2015 to 2019. Modeling Photos 2015 to 2016. High School Photos.*

My fingers brush over the *Family Photos* album. I shouldn't, it'll only make me feel worse, but I flip it open to a random page, and my throat tightens painfully. It's a photo of the three of us right here, in this living room. Sunlight shining through the curtains. I'm still a chubby-cheeked baby, cradled in my mother's arms, and the house looks new. Cardboard boxes are open around us, packing paper and pieces of Styrofoam on the hardwood floors. Just moved in. My parents appear even happier than I remember. Younger too. So in love I can't fathom how it could've ended. But this house—it had been around to witness that love. It's the last survivor of their marriage, the last physical, tangible reminder that I used to belong to an actual family, a holder of our best memories and brightest years. To think of the house burning down, everything destroyed—

I swallow, and with a greater sense of urgency, I look through every single one of *Cao Yunchen's Business Photos*. The images blur together: my dad clinking tiny baijiu glasses across banquet tables, standing somewhat stiffly in a row of men his age. But none of them looks exactly like the man from the vision.

Had I gotten it wrong somehow? Only imagined that I'd seen him before? But I've always been good with faces and names. Kind of have to be, to avoid offending new fake friends at parties. And my instincts have never failed me before. . . .

I turn to *High School Photos* next. I'd assumed they were my dad's, but instead I find photos of my mother: enviably, irrefutably gorgeous even then. Raven hair shorter and her face a little fuller. Somehow makes her old school uniform look stylish, her tracksuit zipped down so that it hangs off one elegant shoulder. She's surrounded by friends in every single one, and I'm about to return the album to the cabinet when my gaze lands on a photo of her and a classmate—

"Holy shit," I whisper.

It's him.

The man with the scar on his cheek. Except it wasn't yet a scar when the photo was taken, but a fresh gash, still healing. There's a kind of awkwardness to him, sitting on the bench of a basketball court next to my mother, who's looking somewhere beyond the frame, mouth half open as if in mid-joke, not even noticing the camera. But he clearly has; he's staring right ahead, almost as if he can see through the lens to me right now, his face flushed. Three inches of polite distance are left between them, his body angled in her direction.

Suddenly I can hear my own blood pounding against my skull.

It's all connected somehow. The man with the scar. My mother. Ares. The teenage boy standing by the fire. But the few pieces of information I've gathered float around haphazardly in my mind; separate moving points without any clear lines between them. The more I discover about the vision, the more confusing everything becomes. And there's this hot, shaky sensation inside my stomach, the overwhelming feeling I'm missing something vital, but *what*?

The familiar chime of my WeChat notifications sounds from the other room.

I startle, my heart beating even faster as I drop the photo album and seize my phone. Ares has double texted. Well, I'm not sure it counts as a proper message—it's a single question mark, sent almost an hour after my last message.

But it still feels like a mini victory.

this bracelet, I tell him, and send him the photo I've preselected just for this. It's a selfie taken in a hotel bathroom, my hair wet from the shower, the lights turned low to enhance the shadows under my collarbones. I'm wearing my tightest tank top, posing with one hand against my cheek like I have a stylish toothache, my Van Cleef bracelet dangling around my wrist.

Then I wait.

Half an hour passes, then an hour, then two, giving me more

than enough time to search through every album for any other photos of the man. There's only one—a school photo taken of the entire year level, with every student's name and class printed in tiny font in the caption below. The man with the scar is standing on the farthest left, his shoulders hunched and his arms held stiffly as if he's trying to disappear from the frame. I trace my finger over the list until I find the corresponding name. *Long Ge.* Carefully I extract the high school photo and hide it underneath my jewelry box, then move the photo albums back into their original place, all while Ares leaves me on delivered.

At the five-hour mark, something flashes over the screen. I click into it, triumphant, disgustingly relieved. *Finally.* It must be a reply from him, it has to be—

A social media alert pops up instead.

Sixty thousand people have liked your post

I can't remember the last time I was so disappointed to be liked. Right now, it doesn't matter if a hundred thousand people like me when Ares Yin, the boy who holds my future in his hands, can't even be bothered to type out a reply.

"Oh my *god*." If it weren't for the vision, this would never be a problem. I don't obsess over boys. I don't give them power over me, don't even need to resist checking my phone for messages, because the temptation isn't there to begin with. I never think about them at night, never lose my cool. I only take calculated risks, but I guess there's a reason I keep failing my math classes.

Eventually I fall into a restless sleep with my phone on my pillow, dreaming of replies that never come and houses erupting into flames.

9

ARES

The blindfold seems like overkill.

Even after someone unties it, Ares has to squint into the darkness to get his bearings. He'd done his best to pay attention as Sangui led him through a series of twisted alleys, then deep underground, counting his own footsteps down the stairs, but otherwise, there'd be no way to tell where he is, or even what time of day it is.

A single, dying light bulb flickers above him, illuminating little except the empty boxing ring just ahead and the blood splatters on the floor.

He feels a frisson of fear. Sangui had refused to breathe a word about what to expect once they came down to the Cave, had simply grunted at him to keep walking. But what *has* he walked into, exactly?

"Welcome," Sangui says, tossing the blindfold over his shoulder, where it drops to the floor like a dead snake. "I'm sure you're eager to get started, so I'll keep it short. The Cave is run by Long Ge. By tradition, Long Ge will only appear at the Cave in person to congratulate the fight club's winner—whoever wins five rounds in a row—and offer them a favor."

"A favor?" Ares repeats, his head spinning with the possibilities.

"Just one," Sangui tells him. "Usually the winners will ask for money, or drugs, or a job through Long Ge's connections. Up to you."

This is why the vision had led him here, Ares realizes. He's almost certain of it. He can feel it deep in his gut, that he's closer than he's ever been before. Long Ge is the key to his brother.

"Don't look too excited," Sangui says. "If you want to join the Cave, there are two rules." He holds up his hand, covered in the same black glove he'd worn last time, and lists them off. "One, do as you're told. No matter what we tell you. And two, *never* fight outside the ring. You got it?"

Dread stirs in the pit of Ares's stomach, but he forces himself to nod.

"So if I tell you to punch, you punch," Sangui says, with a twisted smile that makes his face appear more foxlike than ever. "If I tell you that you can't fight back, you don't. Like right now."

That's the only warning Ares gets before Sangui shoves him.

His immediate instinct is to shove back, to defend himself, but Sangui's orders flash through his head. He can't fight back. So he lowers his fists and just takes it, the full weight of the attack, lets himself fall onto the cement floor, the impact so loud it echoes through his bones. There's a surreal, muted quality to everything as he lies there, barely breathing, his heart thudding in his ears. He sees the black flash of a boot right before he feels it, slamming hard into his rib cage.

Pain explodes through him.

He gasps out. He could reach up and seize the man's leg, flip him over. It wouldn't be so difficult—

But he can't.

"Don't fight back," Sangui had told him, and he needs to obey, needs to prove himself. Needs to secure his entry into the Cave and find his brother. And as Sangui raises his boot again, Ares squeezes his eyes shut. *Might as well let the pain come,* he thinks. Consider it a tithe; consider it punishment for losing his brother to begin with.

The pain does come, in a blazing blow to his stomach.

He doubles over, coughing, clutching at what will be a new bruise tomorrow. His mind scrabbles for logic, solid reasoning, something tangible to ground himself. He's heard of rituals like this before. Frat hazing. Pledging. Mental and physical tests designed to overwhelm you, to push you to your limits, see *just* how badly you want to join. And he wants this more than anything.

Maybe Sangui can sense it, or maybe he's simply grown bored of the kicking. There's only so much satisfaction to be derived from fighting someone who can't fight back.

"Get up," Sangui orders. His voice sounds funny. Distorted and too loud, like he's speaking into an old microphone.

Ares opens his eyes slowly, the single light bulb blurring in his vision until he can see five or six of them, floating over him. He flexes his fingers, steadying himself against the cold cement, even as his muscles scream at him to stay still. But a good boxer always gets up, no matter how badly it hurts. You don't let pain stop you. You don't let anything stop you.

"Wait here," Sangui commands.

He's stupid enough to hope that it's over, he's passed the test, when Sangui returns with what looks like a penguin mascot costume.

Ares blinks hard, willing the scene to make sense. Has he suffered a concussion?

"Cute, right?" Sangui says, throwing the fluffy penguin head at him.

He catches it just in time, the sudden movement sending another bolt of agony racing up his side. Wincing, he stares down at the penguin's cartoonish, long-lashed eyes, the cheerful yellow of its plush beak. It really *is* a costume, with the tiniest holes to breathe and see through.

Sangui grins at him. "Put it on."

"Are you kidding?" he says, then immediately clamps his mouth shut. Total loyalty. Total compliance. That's what Sangui had asked for. So he slides the penguin head on—it's heavier than he imagined, and the inside smells like cheap plastic—and looks toward Sangui for further instructions.

"How absolutely adorable," Sangui says, his grin widening. "Now, follow me."

Ares has to give credit where it's due: Sangui is creative with his methods of torture.

During the first few hours, he couldn't understand the purpose of standing on the side of a street in a penguin costume, other than for Sangui's entertainment. The only instructions he'd received were "Don't move from this spot until I tell you to." It had seemed absurd, but still simple enough.

But then the sun climbs higher and higher, bearing down

upon him like a drill, and more crowds surge through the old hutong districts, children running toward him, squealing, their little fingers sticky from their melting Popsicles or tanghulus. The influencers start showing up, accompanied by either hired photographers or well-trained boyfriends, and they block up the pedestrian lanes to pose next to him.

"Oh, the penguin is *so* cute," they coo, taking turns hugging him or grabbing his arms—well, his flippers. None of them even bothers to ask for permission.

His scowl is hidden beneath the penguin's smile.

Under ordinary circumstances, this would already be too much for him. He hates ridiculous costumes, he hates strangers, he hates taking pictures, and he hates people putting their dirty hands on him. But after the beating, he realizes that Sangui has concocted the perfect recipe for suffering. His bruised ribs ache, desperate for a reprieve, a place to rest. The heat is inescapable, trapping him inside the costume, his sweat stinging his open cuts. And he's gone so long without eating that he now feels nauseous from hunger. He can't stop himself from eyeing every single person who passes him with food: little glass jars of Beijing yogurt, crumbling brown sugar biscuits, fluffy pork buns, bags of roasted chestnuts . . .

He loses track of how long he's been standing there. His head feels too light, the weight of the costume too heavy, his knees buckling beneath him.

Don't move until he tells you to, he repeats to himself. He can see Sangui across the street from him, resting happily beneath the shade of an oak tree, cracking sunflower seeds between his teeth, and he feels a vicious bolt of resentment. If only he could hit back, he was certain he'd knock the man down in seconds—

No. Remember your brother.

Hold on just a little longer.

"How about over here, Chanel? The lighting's better."

He jerks his head up at the name as if he's been zapped awake. *Chanel.* Chanel Cao.

She barely seems real as she approaches him from the sidewalk, a man with a massive professional camera following close behind. Her hair burns gold in the light, bouncing over her shoulders in glossy waves. A glittering tiara sits atop her head, something that ought to look theatrical or even tacky—but somehow, on her, it's an elevated piece, a fashion statement. As if all the people who *aren't* wearing tiaras are the ones missing something.

He thinks involuntarily of the photo she had sent him last night. Was it a pretty photo? Objectively, yes. Was it a suggestive photo? This, he's less sure about. And if it *was*, what was she suggesting? Or did it mean nothing, and he was reading too much into it? Or is that exactly what she wants him to think? Another one of her tricks, concealing her true motives from him.

Either way, it had felt safest not to reply, to just wait until Monday and give her the bracelet at school. To not think about her at all.

Yet here she is, smiling up at him.

He's grateful, all of a sudden, for the stupid penguin costume. The freedom to just look back at her, absorb the full force of her smile without her knowing it's him.

"Yes, you should get a photo with the penguin," the photographer suggests. "You can add it to the end of your prom nomination post—it's cute, it's down-to-earth. Your fans will love it."

This man offering suggestions on how to appear down-to-earth might be the least down-to-earth thing Ares has ever heard. But that aside—is that why Chanel's wearing the tiara? For a prom photo shoot of some kind? He remembers the look in her eyes when she'd spoken about prom. *Gushed* about it, like it was all that mattered to her.

"Would you mind if I took a photo with you?" Chanel asks him. She's the first person who has. Her voice is sweet, gentle, and she doesn't immediately crowd in like the others, just waits for him to reply.

Ares manages to nod.

"Oh my god, thank you so much," Chanel says, still speaking directly to him. She steps closer and turns toward him, squeezing two fingers together to form a mini heart, the way idols like to pose. He experiences a terrible pang of self-consciousness, and he has to remind himself again that she can't see who he is.

The camera lens focuses on them.

Click. Click-click.

"Perfect," the photographer says. "I think we're done. You're going to look *so* gorgeous at prom—your date's a very lucky man."

Chanel just smiles, a close-lipped expression that could mean anything but gives away nothing, and Ares wonders if she has her date secured already. Tries to picture it, one of the guys from their class showing up to her house in a tailored suit and expensive cologne. Feels a strange twist in his stomach at the thought. Can't imagine why, it's not like *he* wants to be in their position. He'd already made it clear to her he wasn't going to prom at all.

"Hang on." Chanel motions for him to wait, then runs off to the milk tea shop on the street corner. She jogs with surprising nimbleness in her stilettos, her movements light and graceful as a fairy's; he almost expects her to leave glitter in her wake. A few minutes later, she comes back holding a large cup of lemon tea and offers it to him, ice cubes clinking inside the plastic. "Here. You must be hot in that costume," she says, still smiling.

It's a simple gesture, but Ares feels entirely unmoored by it. Chanel Cao doesn't just feed stray dogs—she feeds penguin mascots too? Or is this an act, more social media content for her to post to seem "down-to-earth" or thoughtful or whatever she wants her brand to be? Yet, when he searches her eyes, he can't detect anything except sincerity. And he *is* unbearably hot; he can feel the heat festering in his wounds, the sweat plastering his shirt to his back. His throat is so dry it hurts.

Cautiously, he accepts the tea from her. He's not defying any orders like this, he reasons. He hasn't moved from the spot where Sangui left him.

"Thanks again for taking the photos with me," Chanel says, and reaches up to pat his head.

Ares hadn't expected to find any semblance of comfort today. But for this one brief second, he forgets his pain, his hunger, his exhaustion, his humiliation, and lowers his head, letting himself lean in to her touch.

10

CHANEL

On Monday, I show up to school completely naked.

That's how it feels anyway. I haven't made such a drastic change to my makeup style in years, and my eyes feel bare without my usual heavy eyeliner, my face exposed without my pigmented blush and highlighter combo. My own appearance startles me when I catch sight of it in the dark glass panels outside the classrooms. Image is everything, I learned early on, but it still amazes me how manipulable image is. I could be someone else, a girl who runs through orchards and goes strawberry picking on weekends and actually *wants* to fall in love.

I'd set my alarm two hours early this morning just to experiment with the look, using the Instagram photos I'd saved of Ares's former fling as reference, all while feeling strangely sheepish, ashamed even, to be doing so much for a boy.

It's not as if I want to, I argued with myself the entire car ride. *It's only because of the vision. Once I secure Ares as my prom date and stop the fire, I won't have to care whether he's attracted to me or not.*

But at least my efforts don't go unnoticed, because when I catch sight of Ares in the hallway, he actually slows down. Stares at me, his dark eyes roving over my face.

"You look . . . different today," he remarks.

Not *quite* the compliment I was hoping for. "Good different?" I prompt.

"Just different," he says, neutral, and I feel a dull heat rise to my cheeks, the same choking, futile frustration that overwhelms me whenever I'm around him, as if we're actors going over a script together, and he keeps messing up his lines.

"Well, I felt like switching things up," I say with a shrug.

"But you weren't like this on Sunday."

"On Saturday, you mean," I say.

"What?" He frowns, like I'm the one who's mixed the dates up, then seems to remember something. "Right, Saturday. Two days ago."

Which is how long you've left me on read, I think bitterly inside my head. Nobody leaves me on read this long. No one. Even Erik Park, who I met only once at a Bulgari gala dinner and has been touring the world with his K-pop group, never takes any longer than three hours to reply to my messages.

The sheer *nerve* of this boy—

As if he can sense the direction of my thoughts, he reaches into his pocket and pulls out my bracelet. "I found this," he tells me. "It was in my bag."

I don't take it right away. Instead, I glance around, making sure enough people are passing by to witness this moment, before saying loudly, "Oh, *thank god*—I wasn't sure if it'd fallen into your bag or on the floor when I was trying on the prom dresses." Ares might not be following the script the way I want him to, but this is a show, whether he likes it or not. A performance for the girls crowding around the lockers, who nudge each other and exchange raised-brow glances and giggles. *Good.* If the rumors about me and Ares going to prom together hadn't been spreading fast enough after my Instagram story, this should do the trick. When I'd planted the bracelet in his bag, it wasn't just so I'd have an excuse to message him on WeChat later—it was also to serve as physical proof that I was with him outside of school.

"Don't lose it," Ares tells me, pressing the bracelet into my open palm. I try not to react when his fingers brush mine. It's a light touch, barely anything, yet it's as if all my nerves are made of electricity, dialed up to the highest voltage. His skin is smoother than I imagined, softer, despite his calluses. And there's a new ring on his thumb—silver, engraved with a dragon symbol, the metal a few degrees cooler than his hand.

He turns to go, and it's only then that I notice how stiffly he's moving. How he's carrying his books at an awkward angle with just one arm, as if afraid to put any strain on his other side. How he's almost limping, his gait slow and uneven.

"Wait," I call. "Are you okay? Are you . . . injured?" My voice rings out with genuine worry.

He glances back over his shoulder at me, like he's as surprised by my concern as I am. "I'm fine," he says.

"You sure?"

"Yeah." He pauses, then adds, "Remember that peer mentoring starts tomorrow. Make sure you prepare."

I'm aware that Ares had meant math preparation, and not mental preparation.

But I can't shake my nerves the entire afternoon, as if I'm getting ready for a first date with a celebrity—except I've done that before, and even then, I hadn't been anywhere near as restless as I am now. I plan out my hairstyle, my outfit, practice microexpressions and lines designed to charm. Revert back to my classic makeup style, because I need the confidence, and I feel more like myself with heavy eyeliner than without it. I pick out a café for us to study at, somewhere with a more casual atmosphere.

Nothing can calm me down.

As a last resort, I turn to my main form of therapy, which any qualified therapist would likely advise is very unhealthy: I search for my name online.

The first page loads right away, over a hundred different results, information pieced together from interviews about my early life, my mother and my father and my zodiac sign. Slowly I scroll through the photos, assessing each of them with utmost concentration, like a quality control analyst. The ones in the top row are all nicely photoshopped, my hair glossy and my makeup perfect, taken from magazine spreads or my own social media, but that's only because I made sure of it.

Last year, someone had uploaded a screenshot of me with my eyes half open, mid-speech at some gala; I'd immediately reported the image for "inaccurate information," which technically it was, because it was a super inaccurate visual representation of me. They took it down within two days, but even that had felt too long. The idea of anyone searching me up in that time and seeing those hideous photos made me want to claw my skin off.

When I've triple-checked that no more embarrassing shots have slipped through the cracks of the internet, I click on my most recent post. The photos were taken just yesterday in the old hutong districts, shots of me smiling in the sunlight, a tiara perched on my head, posing with a penguin mascot in the last one. The caption, drafted and edited multiple times in my notes app: *Honored to have been nominated for prom queen!!! voting is open now for airington students—link in my bio! love u all xxx*

It's me, but it's not. Chanel Cao, the brand. The girl you want to be—the girl even I want to be. And the comments float over the screen . . . she's *so* pretty, marry me, kiss me, Chanel, we love you so much, please don't ever die, you're perfect, you're an icon.

I try to view the whole thing with distance, as if I'm someone else, the way I do when I'm evaluating a selfie before posting it; sometimes I'll even close my eyes, wait for five seconds, then open them, as if I can trick my brain into thinking that my face is a stranger's face, and I can then determine, objectively, if it's up to standard.

And I'm satisfied, but the satisfaction is surface level, fleeting. Like those sugary drinks my mother hates that keep you full for maybe half an hour, then leave you even hungrier than you were before.

★ ★ ★

"Chanel. Are you paying attention?"

I look up at Ares's face, then back down at my notes on the café table. Slowly the black squiggles sharpen back into incomplete equations. "Sorry," I say, brushing my hair out of the way. "Please. Do go back to what you were saying about . . ." I pause, searching through my memory of the last ten minutes for something smart and math related, but end up only with my usual doom cocktail about Ares, prom, the vision. Even when he's right next to me, he's haunting me.

Ares raises his eyebrows. "Can you at least pretend to care about the topic for a second?"

"Sure," I tell him, sitting up straighter on the stool. "I believe it was . . . multiplication?"

"Multiplication," he repeats flatly.

"Or . . . subtraction?"

He shakes his head. If it weren't for the fact that he's pretty much been threatened into doing this by the school to avoid expulsion, I suspect he'd be packing his bag and marching out of this café right now. "I was teaching you about binomial probability."

"Right. Yeah. That thing."

"You seem distracted."

I grimace. *By you*, I want to add, but of course I can't. "I just feel a bit tired," I say, which is true. Ever since that first night at the lake, there's been a persistent throbbing in my temples, like I'm suffering through the world's worst hangover, without any of the fun of getting drunk. "Sorry," I say again, trying to sound like I mean it. "I promise I'll focus starting now—"

But before I can even look at the math textbook again, whispers float over from the table beside us.

"*Is that her?*"

"I swear it is."

"No, really. She looks exactly like she does in her photos."

I swivel my head toward the voices and identify the trio of girls who'd been loudly snapping photos of their strawberry crepe cake earlier. They were very committed too, with one of them tapping the whipped cream with her spoon, while the other carefully poured the chocolate sauce over the plate, and the third stood up on her chair to find the perfect angle. But now they've completely forgotten their cake to gawk at me.

"Do you really just have fans everywhere?" Ares asks, following my gaze.

"I can't help that I'm famous," I say as the whispers grow louder. I'm fairly certain one of them is taking a video of me, from the way her phone is angled.

Ares rolls his eyes. "Well, it's not helping you concentrate on math. Maybe we should study somewhere less . . . public. Like the school library—"

"Libraries put me to sleep," I tell him. "I'm not exaggerating," I add when he throws me a disbelieving look. "One of the longest naps I've ever taken was at the back of a library."

"What about your house then?" Ares suggests.

Everything in me seizes, panic striking my stomach. He can't find out where my house is, or else he'll recognize it from the vision. And he'll know where to go to burn it down. "My mom's filming this new variety show at our house," I lie on the spot. "It's even more chaotic than the café. How about your house?" My prom plan flashes through my head. *Step eight: Get invited to his house; hook up there.* I'd been meaning to work my way up to it, but math tutoring could be the perfect excuse to secure an invite, and once I'm there . . . The idea of hooking up had seemed pretty straightforward when I first conceived my plan, a purely strategic move, but now it sends a jolt of something hot and wild and electric up my spine. Like anticipation.

Ares hesitates, then checks the time on his phone. "I'll . . . let you know," he says, distracted. "But I need to head off in a few minutes."

"Where to?"

Either he hasn't heard me, or he's avoiding the question on purpose. "Come on," he says, tapping the notebook spread open between us. "Let's try this equation one last time before I go."

11

ARES

Ares stares down at his first opponent.

A man, but just barely, with weak stubble and stooped shoulders and badly dyed straw-blond hair, the black roots already starting to peek out like weeds. College-aged, if he even goes to college. Heavier than Ares is, which could be a problem, but he knows from experience that it could also mean he's slower.

The man stares back, his teeth bared and yellow, his fists raised. On his thumb, he wears the same ring Ares had been given upon initiation: rusted silver, a dragon carved into the band.

"Last chance to place your bets," Sangui calls out from the shadows of the Cave.

"I'm going with the new boy," someone says.

"*That* kid? Nah, his face is a little too symmetrical," someone else remarks.

This earns him an obnoxious cackle that echoes off the grimy walls.

"What's a symmetrical face got anything to do with it?"

"A face like that hasn't been messed up enough. Means he hasn't seen enough fights," the second man speculates.

"Or it could mean he's never lost," the first one points out.

"Well, I never lose my bets," the man retorts.

"Yeah, right. You lost just the other night."

Jeers and laughter sound around Ares, more voices rising, arguing, calling out names, mixing with the loud rattle of mahjong tiles from the floor above.

Ares keeps his eyes straight ahead. As his opponent lowers himself into starting position, he wonders, briefly, what brought the man through Beijing's outer city, into the twisted alleys, down the steep steps here tonight. What kind of favor he wants from Long Ge—if it's hard cash, or a job, or if there's someone he needs to find, like Ares.

But he doesn't let himself wonder any more than that. He doesn't want to know whether the man standing before him has a mother waiting for him at home with a bowl of steaming beef noodles, or whether he's struggling under the weight of hospital bills for his little sister's surgery. He doesn't want to know anything that might make him hesitate to shove the man onto cold concrete and split his skin open, because even a second's hesitation could mean losing, and he can't lose.

A bell rings to his left.

Ares breathes in, steels himself, and charges.

From the very beginning, he's on the offensive. *Always punch first.* Old advice from his boxing coach, though he hasn't attended a proper boxing lesson in a while now. Doesn't have time for them anymore, and doesn't care for official competitions and prizes—nothing compares to what the fight club can give him if he wins.

His first punch lands with a solid, satisfying *crack*, and he immediately chases it with another punch to the stomach. If he can just keep punching, keep going no matter how wounded he is, keep drawing blood without giving his opponent a second to recover, he can win. He can separate his brain from his body, step outside himself for the duration of the match.

It's not him in the fighting ring. That's what he tells himself. It's not his fist driving itself into the man's face. It's not his knuckles splitting open yet again upon impact. It's not his blood filling his mouth with rust when the man punches back.

He's above it all.

He's only distantly aware of his arms moving, though it's as disconnected from him as a video-game character on a screen. Like Street Fighter—that was Luke's favorite game. Luke would always race to it at the arcade, and every time he lost, he would beg for another match, and Ares would humor him, emptying all the tokens in his pockets. . . .

"*Wocao*," the man curses, doubling over as Ares knees him bluntly in the stomach.

He shoves his opponent to the ground, pinning him down by the neck, trying not to feel the blood pulsing underneath his nails, the muscles straining around the man's throat as he gasps.

A countdown begins.

"Three . . . ," the crowd chants. "Two . . . one . . ."

And finally Ares comes back to his own body. To the pain throbbing in several different places, his own labored breathing.

He wipes the sweat trickling down his jaw and stands up, even as a sudden wave of exhaustion threatens to sweep him off his feet.

From the corner of the room, Sangui steps out, fully tatted arms crossed over his chest. He catches Ares's eye and gives him the briefest of nods before declaring to the room: "Ares has won this one."

The crowd explodes into yells and hoots of triumph and outright gloating ("And you said his face was too symmetrical—you're just jealous yours isn't!"), and as dirty money is passed from hand to hand, Ares staggers off alone.

In the dingy backroom, he slumps onto the bench and mechanically inspects his wounds, the way you might inspect a car for faulty parts.

A sharp prickling in his left arm rudely calls for his attention.

He identifies a gash the length of his thumb. Sighs. Reaches into his pocket for some tissue, then dabs at his own blood. He clenches his teeth around a hiss, knowing that any noise from him would reach the ears of the men outside, and it would only invite ridicule, rather than pity.

His pain means nothing to them.

To anyone. His own father wouldn't care if he saw him this way, though that would require him actually visiting Ares, which hasn't happened in over a year. Their only form of communication these days is through his father's monthly bank transfers. One hundred thousand yuan each time, more than enough to cover his school fees and his groceries. He shouldn't complain.

The door creaks open, and Sangui ambles his way inside, whistling some old opera tune. His expression remains indifferent when he sees Ares bleeding.

"That was decent for a first match," he says in his chain-smoker's rasp.

"Thanks," Ares mutters. He doesn't feel like talking, but he also knows better than to ignore the man who'd let him join the Cave. His new membership here is his only connection to Long Ge—and his little brother, by extension—and he can't mess things up. It's this connection that he's planning on using to approach Long Ge at the nightclub tomorrow, just like he'd glimpsed in the vision. Maybe, if Long Ge sees the ring on his finger, the dragon symbol marking his loyalty, he'll be willing to hear Ares out. Ares knows that until he's crowned victor and secures his favor, Long Ge is unlikely to reunite him with his brother—but if he could just get a new photo of Luke, a one-minute phone call, any updates about Luke at all . . .

"Just four more matches to go," Sangui says, leaning one shoulder against the wall. "Next one is in three nights. Make sure you win."

Before the fight tonight, Ares had overheard whispers that Sangui had been involved in some kind of elaborate kidnapping scheme gone wrong, under the orders of a big director at Longfeng Oil. The details were brief—this clearly wasn't fresh gossip—but he gathered that the mission had left Sangui with nothing, or else the man wouldn't be here. Nobody would be here if they had a better option. The whole place reeked of resentment, of jaded people who had been slighted or lied to and now had to resort to wronging others to make up for it.

"I will," Ares says, holding the man's gaze. "I'll win it. I'll win the round after that too."

"Let's not get too cocky now," Sangui says, rubbing a speck of dust off his gloves.

Ares has never seen Sangui without his black gloves, and he's starting to suspect that they're artificially attached to his body, or maybe even a part of him. He imagines Sangui combing his dyed orange hair every morning with those stupid gloves on, or washing a bowl of grapes, or brushing his teeth. He imagines Sangui climbing out of the womb with the gloves plastered to his tiny fingers, the doctors' shock and confusion as they tried explaining the phenomenon to Sangui's family.

"Is something funny?" Sangui asks, his eyes narrowing.

Ares presses his lips together. "No."

"Better not be." Sangui glances down at the floor, where Ares's blood has splashed across the cement in three dark drops, glistening like wet ink. "Oh, and wipe that up before you leave. The floor's dirty enough already."

Ares walks home alone.

It should only take ten minutes, but his injuries are slowing him down, and as the adrenaline from the fight seeps out of his bloodstream and the night breeze stings like salt on all his open cuts, he can feel the panic kicking in. Not that the panic is ever really gone. It just lies dormant, skirting the edges of his thoughts.

When it's particularly bad, like tonight, it compromises his ability to breathe. He knows that *technically*, he can't just stop breathing out of nowhere. That he has a pair of functioning lungs. That there's more than enough oxygen outside, with the oak trees lining the street, the city spreading out wide around him.

But then he'll think about how fast time is passing, and how he might never find his brother, will never get the chance to make things right, and no matter how hard he tries to inhale, it's like the air ends up trapped in his throat. His lungs seize, drawing nothing in.

He has to pause beside a traffic sign, one hand gripping the metal pole to support himself, lightheaded and gasping like the man he'd almost strangled earlier. Karma, maybe.

Then a boy on a bike rides past him, slow enough for Ares to glimpse his face under the streetlights. His heart stops.

Luke.

It's him, it has to be. The unruly black curls that never stayed put, no matter how hard you brushed them, the soft, boyish features that always made elderly women grin and pinch his cheeks, the wiry frame. He's even wearing the same shirt— white cotton, a graphic logo printed on the back.

"Luke," he calls out into the night, almost choking on the name. He feels nauseous with hope, his pulse thrumming violently.

When the boy doesn't turn around, Ares starts running, his worn sneakers slapping the concrete. He pushes himself faster, tearing down the street, narrowly avoiding crashing into a Meituan courier who swears at him. Every step sends a judder of pain through his bruised ribs, but he ignores it. He's well trained when it comes to ignoring pain.

"*Luke!*" he calls again, his voice echoing in the cold night air. "Wait, it's me—Ares."

And finally, finally, the boy squeezes the brakes, the bike wobbling before he nudges the kickstand down with one foot. He lifts his head and—

It's not him.

Ares's stomach drops, the disappointment so crushing and complete it feels like he's lost his brother a second time.

The boy stares up at him, wide-eyed and clearly unnerved, and as the haze of hope clears, Ares can see how stupid he'd been. Yes, the boy does bear a resemblance to his little brother—but he resembles his brother from *three years ago*. In his head, Luke has become immortal, his appearance permanently frozen on the day he ran away from home, when in reality, he wouldn't be a little kid anymore, but a teenager. The version of Luke from the vision is older, taller, his features so hollowed out and somber that Ares almost hadn't recognized him when he'd first peered into the lake.

"Were you calling after me?" the boy asks.

"Sorry," Ares says. He swallows, wipes the sweat from his forehead. "I thought . . . I was looking for someone, and I thought you were him."

The boy blinks. "Okay, that's okay." He hesitates, maybe sees the naked desperation on Ares's face, and adds: "Do you need help looking for him? Maybe . . . if he goes to school in the area, my friends might know—"

"No," Ares says, feeling more and more stupid by the second. "But thanks."

"Okay," the boy says again, and glances up at him one last time with something like concern—though he isn't sure if it's for the boy's own safety, or Ares's sanity—before righting his bike and riding away.

Ares stares after him for a few moments longer, his chest hollow, then slowly continues limping down the street.

12

CHANEL

"Do you like someone, Chanel?"

I lower my phone and glance up at my mother in surprise. "What?"

She doesn't look back at me. She's too focused on her reflection as she carefully twists another lock of sleek black hair around the curling iron, the fumes of her heat-protectant spray wafting out through the open bathroom door. "I said, is there a boy you like?"

"Oh my god, Mom. No," I say quickly. I'm not lying, I shouldn't *need* to lie, but my stomach does a funny little twist as Ares's name flashes through my mind. "Why would you think that?"

"You've been acting a bit . . . odd this past week," my mother says, letting the curl fall over her ear, perfectly framing her cheekbones for whatever party or gala is happening later tonight. "You changed your makeup, you keep zoning out, and you've been glued to your phone all morning."

Heat rushes up my skin in a guilty flush, as if I've been caught doing something unseemly. "I was only texting a friend," I say, but I'm fully lying this time. I'd been checking—in futile, embarrassing hope—to see if Ares had messaged me. Ever since he took off from our brief math tutoring session yesterday afternoon, he hasn't bothered acknowledging my existence again. Not even to like the new, carefully curated series of photos I'd posted on WeChat before breakfast.

"As long as it's actually just a friend," my mother says, setting the curling iron down on the counter to fluff out her curls.

I've watched her get ready like this so many times—in awe every single time, wishing I could be half as beautiful—that I can predict what her next step is. Before she reaches for her perfume, I hurry over and fetch it from the cabinet for her, hoping to cut the conversation short. "This one smells really nice," I tell her. "Very floral."

"Sometimes I think it's a little too floral," she remarks, then continues without missing a beat. "If it *isn't* just a friend, then you need to be very careful not to get attached, Chanel. The worst thing you can do is waste your heart and time and youth on some boy."

Another funny twist, low in my belly. "I know."

Don't get attached. It's just one of my mom's many rules for men, rules she's laid out for me over the years.

You get a man by attracting him, not by being good to him. If you're good to him, he'll only take you for granted.

You can praise the things a man does, but you shouldn't praise *him*. Praising the services he offers will encourage him to keep doing nice things for you. Praising him will only make him cocky.

He has to *think* that you like him, but you can't let him *know* you like him. If he's already confident about how you feel, he'll see no point in trying to win you over.

The most fundamental rule of them all is simply: *Don't fall in love.* Because once you do, you might as well be handing over a knife and turning around, defenseless, exposing all the soft, vulnerable flesh of your body for them to draw blood.

"I really don't like anyone," I emphasize, maybe a little too loudly, as if I'm trying to convince myself as much as my mother.

But her warning blares like sirens inside my head all through-out the day as I find myself looking for Ares.

He doesn't show up until the very last period, where he walks in with a pronounced limp and a cut on his lower lip. He was already injured after the weekend, but these injuries are new. Which is deeply concerning. Not that I'm concerned about his well-being or anything, but it's concerning because it's suspi-cious. There's still so much about Ares I don't know—how he's acquiring these injuries, where he goes after school, what he wants from the vision. And if he's not going to tell me himself, I have to find out another way.

So after the bell rings, when everyone's waiting for their driver to pick them up, I stop Ares outside the classroom.

"Hey, Ares, can I borrow your phone for a second?"

He lifts a brow. "Why?"

"I really need to call my driver, but my phone's dead," I tell him, holding my phone up to show him the black screen as proof. I actually have a backup phone that's fully charged in my bag, and two power banks always at the ready for filming content, but he doesn't need to know that.

Ares hesitates, then shrugs and hands his phone over. "Sure."

I have to be quick. While I pretend to enter my driver's phone number, angling the screen so he can't see it from where he's standing, I pull up his maps. My eyes flick through his location searches, and my pulse quickens as I land on the most recent one. Club Sixty-Eight Hours.

Finally, a bit of luck. Because if there's one place where I might actually have an advantage over Ares, it's my father's nightclub.

13

ARES

Ares has never been inside a nightclub before.

He's sure that if he ever volunteered this information, people would treat it with suspicion or even just straight-up disbelief. He *looks* like the kind of person who'd frequent this kind of place, proven by the other late-teen to early-twenties guys trickling through the neon-lit doors, into the pounding heart of Club Sixty-Eight Hours.

They're all dressed the same, with their double piercings and expensive undercuts and the glint of silver jewelry hanging from their necks, their arms around giggling girls in strapless tops and thigh-high boots. He need only hover at the periphery of any group, and he'll blend right in with them. So it's easy to follow them inside, made easier by the fact that the bouncers here clearly don't give a shit. They offer him the most cursory of glances before waving him forward. They haven't stopped anyone to check for ID, and from the bored, nearly stoned expressions on their faces, he doubts they would, unless someone were to waltz in wearing a middle school uniform. Maybe not even then—he's just spotted two women in tight white tops and plaid schoolgirl skirts, and he can't tell if they're actually that young or trying to look it, but nobody else appears worried about their legal ages.

Red strobes flash like warning signs down a winding corridor, which opens abruptly to a dance floor, already jam-packed with bodies.

He's never been inside a nightclub before, but it almost feels like he has, because everything here looks exactly like the scene from the vision. The club name glowing neon pink above the bar counter. The posters advertising its special new Blue Lagoon cocktail, available today. Cheap black sofas crowding the corners, where people are draped over the cushions, pouring drinks and playing cards and laughing at nothing. Massive screens curving upward over the walls, distorting the senses, abstract streaks of light flowing over them like lava. The painted lanterns strung above the DJ booth, the electric candles inside them offering a modern touch, something Chanel Cao might pick out from a catalog.

The place reminds him of hell, although it actually *could* be hell: the inescapable heat, the thick smoke filling the air, the amber glow around the bar counters, the stench of stale alcohol mixed with bland cologne, the press of strangers' bodies far too close to his own.

Now that he has his ring and the bruises as stamps of loyalty, this might actually work. If he can find Long Ge, he's out, and never coming back.

As he cranes his neck, scanning the dense dance floor, something sharp and hard taps his elbow. He jerks away out of instinct and sees the long acrylic nails first, encrusted with gems, then the pale fingers and an oval-shaped face, slightly greasy with make-up or sweat. Some girl he's never seen before.

"Shuaige," the girl says, or shouts it rather, in order to be heard over the heavy rattle of music. "Guo lai gen wo wan'er ya?" *Come hang out.*

"No, thanks," he half shouts back, already looking past her.

"Why? Are you here with a girlfriend?" she asks, and even though he hasn't glanced back at her face, he can hear the pout in her voice.

"I'm busy."

For some reason, she takes this rejection as encouragement to wrap her nails around his arm, pulling it too close to her, and she speaks directly into his ear, her hot, beer-tinged breath fanning his skin uncomfortably. "Too busy to dance with me?"

He wonders if it would be rude to just shrug her arm off. "I don't dance," he says. It's true, and he doesn't seem to be the only one. Most of the people out on the floor aren't really dancing but standing around, scrolling through their phones, only remembering to bob their heads a little when the beat drops. A few are playing some sort of game where they keep holding up their fingers and screaming numbers out at each other like they're in an extremely drunk math tournament.

"We can do other things, if you're not up to dancing," the girl says, her nails wrapping tighter and sinking into his skin like claws.

He pretends he doesn't understand the suggestion.

"You don't come here often, do you?" the girl continues, her persistence almost inspiring. "I'd definitely remember your face."

His eyes flicker to her with new interest. If she's a regular, then she might have seen Long Ge around before. "There's this man I'm looking for," he says, cutting to the chase. "Early forties, short hair, glasses, square face. Has a scar about this big—" He makes an estimate with his thumb and index finger. "On his left cheek. I've heard he comes down to this club a lot. Do you know him?"

The girl purses her lips. "Maybe."

"Maybe?"

"I don't remember right now," she says coyly, her small, glitter-dusted face giving away nothing except desire. "But I might later, if you dance with me."

He has no patience for her teasing, not when his stomach sits tight and heavy as cement and the awful remix thudding through the speakers is making his head hurt, but he can't think of a better option. "Okay," he says, resigned and hating himself and this whole situation. He clenches his jaw and lets her lead him down to the grimy, crowded floor, completing his descent into hell.

But if it means bringing back his brother, there are far worse places he would go.

14

CHANEL

I was fifteen when I entered my first nightclub.

My father was the one who took me inside Club Sixty-Eight Hours before the official opening. He owned other nightclubs, but he wanted this to be special, and like any good businessman who understands his target demographic, he sought out my opinions on everything. What did the *young people* want these days? What was trendy? What wasn't? He let me look around and took notes when I pointed out things that could be improved. I loved that he took me seriously, that he cared enough about what I thought to let me decorate the place. He strung up the painted lanterns I'd picked out from a catalog, moved the DJ booth when I asked him to, and cleared room in the back for influencers to take photos under the neon signs.

It's been almost a year since I last came, but everything is just as I remember.

I love it here.

I love how the blend of darkness and drunkenness around

you takes the edge off your self-consciousness, and it doesn't matter if you look a little stupid because everyone does. The girl dancing next to me is going all out with the theatrics, one hand clutching her chest and the other raised over her forehead like she's an actress in a Shakespearean tragedy, her eyes squeezed shut with emotion.

I keep an eye out for Ares as I let myself sway to the melody, slowing down my movements when the track switches to Eric Chou's "Unbreakable Love."

And the room swells with noise, heat, energy. And the flickering dots of light in the ceiling expand into constellations. And the music pulses in my ears like a heartbeat, alive and vivid and miraculous, and I hum to the chorus like it was written just for me.

The DJ cycles through more songs, Jay Chou for the nostalgia kick and all the latest trending tracks on Douyin, and there's the fizzing sweetness of the cocktail on my tongue, the warmth of bodies moving next to mine, the cool sweat beading over my forehead, and I'm wonderfully aware of myself in this moment. How I look from the outside. I'm eighteen, I'm beautiful, I'm desirable, I might just be the best thing you'll find tonight—

Then I see Ares with another girl on the dance floor.

It feels like someone's poured freezing water over my body. My throat tightens as I watch them together. She's pretty, but she doesn't look like his type. Still, he isn't pulling away when her hands roam across his chest.

A bitter taste fills my mouth.

I'd suspected that Ares had come here tonight with a specific goal in mind, something related to the vision, but what if he's actually just here *for fun*? To dance and hook up with strangers and get drunk off his face?

"Hey." Some guy my age sidles up to me. Muscular, tanned, handsome in a predictable way. He's blocking my view of Ares. "Have we met before?"

I start to tell him no, I'm not interested, but then he steps forward and Ares looks over at just the right time. Our gazes meet. I can't clearly see his expression, but all that matters is that he's looking.

The guy says something into my ear right as the bass drops, something I'm assuming is meant to be seductive but just sounds like *radishes*.

"What?" I ask.

He tries again, straining his voice over the music. "Ravishing! You look absolutely ravishing! Like one of those—" He waves his hands about, his face scrunching in concentration. "*Artworks*," he concludes decisively, looking very proud of himself for thinking of it. "Those artworks you might find in one of those . . . museums!"

"Thank you?"

Encouraged, he plods on with vigor. "And your hair! Your hair is marvelous hair. It's so very curly and shiny and—"

"Let's just dance," I suggest, to spare the both of us, circling my arms around his neck as I move my hips.

It's only because Ares is watching that I let the stranger kiss me, sloppy in a way that reminds me of how dogs lick their owners' chins. I keep my eyes open, my attention sliding right past the boy whose mouth is currently smushed against mine, his lashes fluttering with one-sided pleasure. My gaze locks with Ares's across the dance floor.

An electric shock zips up my spine. I deliberately arch my back, encouraging the boy to come closer, which he's all too happy to do. I don't look away from Ares, and it doesn't matter that we're dancing yards away from each other, that someone else's hands are on my waist. It's as if we're the only ones here.

But then Ares seems to spot someone else on the other end of the club. He quickly untangles himself from the girl and begins to push his way forward, his movements hurried. As I push off my overeager dance partner, I follow the direction of his gaze and my heart stops.

It's the man with the scar on his face. My mom's old classmate.

The man from the vision.

Suddenly I get the strangest feeling of stepping outside my body, of seeing the three of us, me and Ares and the man, all connected in inexplicable ways, as moving pieces on a timeline. What happens from here, how these pieces fit and clash, will have unthinkable ripple effects on the future.

But if both Ares and the man are present at the fire in the vision, then the man could be an accomplice of his. Maybe, I realize with a lurch of horror, *tonight* is meant to be the night where they plan it out together. I have to stop Ares from reaching him. Need to distract him, somehow—

An idea springs into my mind.

Acting drunk is a subtle, sophisticated art that, like any other art, requires practice and dedication. It's difficult to get right. You either risk overdoing it, slurring your words too much and tripping all over the place and completely embarrassing your-self, or not doing it with enough conviction, in which case you might as well not do it at all.

The first time I'd ever gotten drunk, it had been a deliber-ate choice, just to see what I was like. I'd made sure I was in a safe, controlled setting—at home, with nobody else around, god forbid I made a fool of myself with any eyewitnesses. I'd broken out an old bottle of my mom's pinot grigio from the cabinet, poured too much of it into a Swarovski toasting flute, plopped onto the couch, and downed it like it was grape soda.

I recorded myself the whole time, and when I sobered up, I played it back, watching it closely like an audition tape for a dream role.

So I know exactly how to act now, pretending to drink from the little red cups the nightclub waitresses are offering, stumbling across the dance floor to Ares.

"Hello," I slur, blocking his way. "Didn't expect to see you here."

Ares's eyes flicker from me to the man at the back of the club. "I don't have time to talk—"

"What, you're leaving already?" I pretend to take another long swig from the cup, even though my lips are pressed tight, allowing only a thin trickle of wine down my throat. "But I just got here."

"That has nothing to do with me," he says, his jaw hard. "Aren't you already here with someone?"

Right on cue, the guy from earlier finds his way to me. His large hand grips my waist roughly, pulling me to his side. Ares's eyes narrow.

"What are you doing?" the guy says. "Let's keep dancing."

I blink. Smile at him, even though I want to gag. "Yeah, okay. Let's dance. I love dancing."

His hand inches up my rib cage. "You sober?"

"Yeah," I say, giggling. "Super sober. Super super sober. I have amazing alcohol tolerance. Could have, like, ten of these cups—" I hold it up like it's a trophy. "*Ten* of these, and not feel a thing!"

The guy's eyes gleam. "Okay, good—"

"Dude, she clearly isn't sober," Ares snaps.

"She just said that she is," the guy says. His hand is still moving over my body, and beneath my performance, I feel the first prickling of fear, the urge to slap his hot, heavy hand away. When his fingers slide even higher up my waist, I stiffen, fighting to keep the fear from my face.

Ares's eyes whip from my expression, then darken as they focus on where this man has grabbed me.

In a flash, Ares seizes the guy's wrist, yanking it away from me, and shoves him back so far that he almost crashes into the people dancing behind him.

I stare, stunned, my heart beating too fast. I feel for a moment actually drunk, like everything is tilting upside down and spinning away from me, out of control, like maybe this isn't real. Because my impulse is to go to Ares. Stay close to him. Turn to him for safety, when I should know for a fact that he's the most dangerous person in this club, in this whole city, even.

"What the fuck, man?" the guy yelps. But maybe he sees the threat blazing in Ares's face, because he doesn't try to approach me again. Just shoots Ares a glare and slinks off into the crowd.

Ares whirls back to face me, and I try to adjust my expression, to affect nonchalance. "Is this how you always act when you're out?"

I shrug. "Thought you said it has nothing to do with you."

He releases a low breath. Searches over my shoulder, his features tight with concentration, his brows furrowed. "Where is he?" he mutters.

"Isn't it such a coincidence that we're both here," I say cheerily, pulling his attention back to me, just in case the man he's looking for hasn't gone far enough away yet.

"Is it really a coincidence?" Ares asks.

"What do you mean?"

Smooth as shadow, he surges forward, trapping me in place. My body is suddenly frozen, my breaths constricted. "You know, Chanel, I'm starting to think you want something from me," he says, his voice like silk, the warmth of it bare inches from my cheek, everything about this moment terrible and forbidden and obscene.

"I—" The word rises and dies on my tongue.

I'd promised myself this wouldn't happen. I'd been determined not to let him affect me.

But no amount of self-awareness or self-control could possibly protect me from Ares's proximity: his face, lovely and hypnotic, hovering over mine; his long hair the glossy pitch-black of a crow's wing; his dark eyes burning as though lit from within.

My head swims.

Dimly, I recall the road trip my family had taken in Australia, the long coastal drive down from Sydney to Melbourne. At night, a kangaroo had suddenly hopped out onto the road, right in front of a passing truck. "Run!" I'd wanted to scream at it. "Get out of there." But it didn't move. Simply stared, wide-eyed at the blazing headlights. It had seemed so stupid to me at the time, that the animal would just *freeze up*, stay in place like a lump of rock while the truck hurtled toward it.

Turns out that in practice, I'm not much better.

None of my limbs remember how to cooperate.

Then Ares pulls away, breaks eye contact, and shame spikes in my veins alongside a strange, disturbing pang of regret.

"I'm going to call you a car," he says. "You should go home and sober up."

I start to protest when I hear a terribly familiar voice—

"Chanel?"

No. Not him.

There's no way he's here. Out of all the places in a city as crowded as Beijing, out of all the nightclubs he owns, the meetings he could be attending, the overpriced restaurants he could be dining at, the business partners he could be shaking hands with . . . the odds were meant to be in my favor, but then, nothing's really working in my favor these days.

Part of me wants to pretend I didn't hear him. Flee out the exit, down the fire escape, let him wonder if he'd hallucinated the whole thing. Except it's too late.

He's already pushing his way through the crowd toward me, practically indistinguishable from the other middle-aged men prowling the area to escape the boring comforts of domestic life and feel young again. His hair has been dyed black—too black, you can tell right away that it's fake, like a botched nose job. And his button-down shirt is wrinkled around the collar. My mom never would've allowed him to leave the house like that. "Let me fix this for you, or else your employees are going to think you've been living in the wild," she'd tut, reaching around his waist to smooth out the fabric while he laughed. Guess his mistress doesn't have the same concerns. Maybe he even likes that about her.

Bile bubbles in my throat.

I haven't seen my father in months. The last time we were face-to-face like this, I'd screamed at him and shoved him out our living room door and possibly thrown a purse at the wall. I regret that—not the yelling or the throwing, because he deserved it. I just wish I'd done it with more dignity, in a cooler manner, without the ugly tears and the pathetic little hiccups at the end of my sentences. Since then, I've come up with a hundred different, wittier, harsher lines I should've said, instead of just "Why? Why did you have to do it?" Over and over again, like a child demanding to know why the sky was blue and the moon was round some days but not others.

"You know him or something?" Ares mutters in my ear. I'm not surprised by his confusion. People tell me I look like my mom all the time—a few have even confused the two of us before. "You gave your daughter all your modeling genes," they'd joke. But most people can't see the resemblance between me and my dad, which is generally agreed to be lucky.

"Not very well," I say.

"Chanel." My father stops one foot away from me, and

pauses, his eyes narrowing as he takes in Ares. I can only imagine what he's seeing: his only daughter, at a nightclub in a skimpy skirt, her arms around a boy her age who looks like he goes around breaking hearts for the fun of it. A boy who looks dangerous. "You . . . shouldn't be out so late," he says at last, shouting to be heard over the music in some futile attempt at fatherly authority. "It's a school night."

A school night. I almost laugh in his face. Like that's the most pressing problem here. "I was just about to leave," I tell him coolly and lean closer to Ares, stroking the back of his neck with my fingertips, my lips curving into a smile. "With him," I add, unable to resist the urge to upset him, this man who ruined our family and now has the audacity to act like he cares if I'm not in bed by curfew.

Ares stiffens, too surprised to push me away. His gaze darts from me to my father, back to my face. *Please, just go along with it,* I urge silently, letting the desperation show in my expression. I'll pay for this later, I'm sure. But as far as he knows, I'm drunk out of my mind, so I can't be entirely blamed for how I'm acting.

"And who is he?" my father demands, frowning at Ares. "Does he go to your school?"

"Maybe," I say with a shrug. "Maybe he's my boyfriend. Maybe he's just some random guy I met at this club ten minutes ago who I really, really like. Who knows?"

My father's frown deepens, and a blue vein surfaces just above his temple. "Be careful, Chanel. Guys like that . . . he might take advantage of you—"

"Or I might take advantage of him." I wrap both my arms

around Ares's neck, draping myself over him like a satin cloak, my lips mere inches from the sharp line of his jaw. I can smell his cologne, a scent I'd previously associated with smoke but now reminds me more of burnt caramel. A pleasant scent that briefly masks the sweaty odor of bodies from the dance floor and the bitter tang of booze.

For a second I forget I'm even acting and inhale again without thinking, nuzzling up to him.

"Are you *drunk?*" my father chokes out, his complexion visibly pale, even under the flashing lights. But he doesn't seem as pissed off as I'd hoped. He looks more worried than anything, which sends a new wave of nausea sloshing through my stomach. If he were really worried about me, he could've thought twice before ruining our family. "This is not okay. You need to call your mother and go home right now—"

"Yeah, yeah," I cut in loudly, sliding my hand down the planes of Ares's chest. "I already told you, I'm leaving. Come on," I tell Ares, without meeting my father's eyes. "Let's head over to your apartment."

I don't mean to glance back over my shoulder. But I can't help it, and in that brief moment of weakness, I see two versions of my father at once, like one image superimposed over another. There's the man who held my hand on the first day of kindergarten and taught me how to swim, and the man who left my mom sobbing on the kitchen floor, who's proven that nobody, no matter how much you love them, can be trusted not to hurt you.

The before and the after.

Then I twist around and head out the exit, vowing silently that this was the last time I would ever let myself look back.

It's a little easier to breathe once we're outside.

I wrap my coat around myself, drawing the cool air into my lungs while Ares opens his phone to request a DiDi. The moon hangs in the black, wind-whipped sky, and the Yintai Centre Tower rises up on the horizon, glowing like a lighthouse from a cliff peak, guiding late-night stragglers home. If I listen hard, I can still hear the music thumping inside the nightclub.

"What's your address?" Ares asks.

I'm about to tell him, when I remember I can never let him see my house. My stomach heaves at how close I'd been to ruining my own plans. A split second of carelessness, and my life could be destroyed.

"Number five Xiang Jiao Hua Yuan," I tell him. It's *technically* my house, but it's one of my mom's investment properties, located fifteen minutes away from where I actually live.

Ares types the address in. "Should be here in three minutes," he says, glancing down at his phone, then up the near-empty street.

"Thanks," I say, remembering to slur my words.

Headlights blaze through the dark as the DiDi approaches. It's one of those seven-seat, extra-comfort electric cars people usually hail on the company dollar, and even though it's a small thing, my chest twinges at the thought of Ares taking care to select the most luxurious ride possible for me.

He helps me into the leather back seat, holding one hand up

over the doorframe so I don't bump my head, his other hand steadying my waist. When I'm all settled, he reaches over me, the muscles in his arms flexing as he grabs the seat belt and tugs it across my body, strapping me in. I wasn't expecting him to be so gentle, so patient. An unexpected shot of emotion blazes down my throat like whiskey. I swallow, overcome by the strange urge to cry. It's not even sadness, exactly, just a feeling. I feel so much right now that I'm terrified it'll all leak out of me and there'll be nothing left.

Which is my excuse for why I seize his wrist when he slides into the seat next to me. He stiffens in surprise, but he doesn't pull his wrist away. He just lets me hold on to him, like how a child might hold a stuffed toy tighter to their chest after waking from a nightmare.

"So that was your dad," he says after a moment.

"Unfortunately," I mutter.

"Right. I was looking at him and wondering to myself, *Who does this guy think he is, walking around like he owns this place?*" He shakes his head. "Who could've guessed that he actually owns the place?"

Despite myself, I cough out a small laugh. "Yeah, who could've guessed." As the car speeds down the road, I briefly squeeze my eyes shut. "You must think I'm a total bitch. Talking to my own dad like that."

"I'm sure you have your reasons," he says.

When I open my eyes, I'm surprised to find that Ares looks sincere. It unlocks something inside me. Loosens my lips. "Sometimes I want to forgive him. I really do. But then I'll feel so guilty for even *thinking* about forgiving him, like I'm betraying my mom or something. I just feel shitty either way."

"Did he . . . ," Ares says carefully. "I don't want to assume, but he—"

"He cheated, yeah. Found out just last semester," I say, and realize as I do that he's the first person I've told about it since Alice, and that had been half an accident, since Alice had already found out on her own. I'm meant to be keeping the divorce a secret, but maybe I had more to drink than I recall, or maybe there's something strangely addicting about holding Ares's full attention for once, the way he's watching me, like he really cares what I say next, because I can't seem to shut up.

"And obviously, before that, he did everything he could to hide the evidence of the whole affair and make up all these lies, but you know what? The funny thing is he didn't even need to go into all the trouble, because my mom was doing all the lying for him. She lied to herself better than he ever could." I lean my heavy head back against the leather, woozy and mildly nauseous.

"If he returned home late, she'd accept the vaguest explanation that he'd been held up at a meeting. If he was drunk off his face for the third time in a week, she'd simply excuse it as him doing whatever he needed to bond with clients, and she'd say, 'Look how hard your dad's working to make money—he doesn't even like drinking that much.' She assumed that all his friends were guys and he never corrected her. She ignored the lipstick stains on his shirt and believed him when he said that the perfume on his skin was actually the new air diffuser at the office. She said nothing when he supposedly had to travel to Hangzhou on a business trip again, even if he'd just gotten back from there. . . ."

In my head, I can see myself like someone on a TV screen, sitting down with my mom to deliver the news.

"I know it hurts to hear," I'd told her softly, reaching for her bony hand, covering the eighteen-carat diamond ring that had been featured in multiple women's magazines, widely shared and salivated over on the internet. My mom loved finding opportunities to show it off, using her left hand to grab things even though she was right-handed, or fluttering her fingers when she was giving love advice to her friends. But now all I could feel were the cold, sharp edges of the jewel digging into my palm. "I'm so, so sorry, Mom. But you have to—"

Her face had twisted, and she'd yanked her hand away from me, her eyes blazing. "Stop. I don't want to hear it."

"If he really loved you, he would never—"

"He *does* love me." She'd said it with such vehemence I almost lurched back. "He does, he does, he does—" And then her voice cracked, and she made a horrible, choked sound, like she'd been fatally wounded.

I was terrified. This was the same woman who wouldn't let herself laugh too hard at a joke because it would give her wrinkles. The woman who had found a poisonous spider on her shirt while filming a variety show in Australia, and still managed to keep her cool, knowing the cameras were on her. "Mom," I tried to say. "Mom, it's okay. We don't need him. You've got me—"

"I wish you'd never told me," she sobbed. "Why did you have to *tell* me? I could've . . . It could've worked out—I could've been happy and kept loving him. . . ."

"Why would you want that?" I asked, genuinely confused.

"You don't understand," she said, rocking back and forth. "You don't."

And that was when it hit me.

You could have everything. You could be a literal supermodel with perfect proportions and lips that are always glossy. You could be sweet and generous and the kind of girl who bakes banana bread on weekends and smiles at babies in prams. You could be talented and clever and patient and wise and you could offer up all that you have without complaint. You could bring the entire world to the table and you might not even ask him to bring anything, not even leftovers, only that he sit down at the same table and stay, but he would still break your heart.

"That's really fucked up," Ares says.

I blink at him. He's not offering condolences or solutions or advice. He's not watching me with sympathy. But for some reason, hearing the words stated outright like that makes the ache in my chest more bearable. Like finally receiving a diagnosis for a pain that's been eating away at you for years, even if there is no immediate cure. Having someone say, yes, it *is* fucked up, you're allowed to be sad about it.

"I'll survive," I tell him, and in this moment, I feel so hopelessly, disgustingly tender toward him that I rest my head against his shoulder. For the remainder of the car ride, neither of us moves.

After Ares drops me off outside the uninhabited house and leaves, I call my driver to take me back to where I should actually be.

My own home is empty too. I stand there in the living room

for a few minutes, feeling the sadness burn holes in my stomach, listening to the clock tick, the only sound in the silence. It was never this silent before.

When my father still lived with us, he made his presence known. He was almost always on the phone, either finalizing the agenda for a very important meeting or hosting a very important meeting or debriefing someone after the very important meeting. Like many of his CEO and CFO friends, he didn't believe in the concept of business hours. After all, what was the point of work-life balance when your work *was* your life?

You could hear the voices of his employees straining to hide their resentment toward him for making them wake up at six to go over their marketing campaign a third time. "That's such a great idea, Cao Zong," they'd chorus. "Yes, we'll run the numbers. No, we haven't heard from Huang Zong yet—"

And you could hear my father talking over them, his voice ringing with urgency and echoing throughout the house, because apparently running a business meant that everything was urgent. "Huang Zong makes a good point, but if you had any business sense, you would understand . . . Do you understand? It's complicated. . . . We can't overcomplicate it. . . ." Sometimes I was convinced he wasn't even speaking in full sentences, just throwing out random words that were meant to sound serious: *Thursdays, fifty-five thousand, the annual meeting, twenty percent, from a long-term perspective, manufacturing, the market, the next financial quarter, index . . .*

He'd been doing this for so long that I could have written out his speeches for him by the time I was thirteen. I knew all his techniques. He liked to reference a recent online trend to make it seem like he was still young and up-to-date (even though he relied on me to explain it to him the night before), and whenever he felt his audience's attention slipping, he liked to throw in an anecdote or two about me. That time I burned my finger on the curling iron became a long-winded, somewhat confusing segue into how the consumer experience mattered above all else.

I used to complain, half jokingly, about it to my mom.

"Sometimes it feels like I live in an office building," I'd remarked one night, shutting the door to the kitchen, though it barely muffled his voice on the other side of it. My father didn't have a dedicated home office. Or, rather, *every* room was his office. On a number of occasions, I'd seen him take his laptop and phone with him into the bathroom.

"He's just very passionate about his work," my mom told me. "He's always been like that, ever since I met him. Don't you think it's inspiring, hearing all his speeches to his employees?"

When my parents first got married, some people had speculated that my mother was only after my father's money and resources. But I could tell, in those moments, just from the way she spoke about him, that she truly loved him.

That's what scares me the most, looking back on everything now: The love was there, it had felt *real*—and all it had gotten my mother in return was the worst heartbreak of her life.

15

CHANEL

The call comes at five in the morning.

That's how I know it's bad news, even before I pick up. Good news respects your schedule—it lets you sleep in and do your hair and choose your outfit for the morning. Bad news doesn't really care about any of that, since it's going to ruin your day anyway.

"Oh my god, Chanel, I'm so sorry," Jamie says immediately into the phone.

"What?" I say, rubbing my eyes, wrestling against sleep for clarity. "What are you talking about?"

"I saw the news," she says.

"What news?" I ask, sitting upright now, already pulling open Baidu. My fingers quiver over the phone screen and I keep typing my own name wrong, but it turns out that it doesn't matter because it comes up automatically in the trending searches. It's in the top three this morning. I stare at the little red fire symbol next to the headline, the one that's only used for the hottest topics.

BREAKING: Coco Cao files for
divorce from Cao Yunchen

It takes me three tries to read through the full article. Maybe it's some sort of automatic self-defense mechanism kicking in, but my brain refuses to absorb anything on the page. The words keep blurring together on the screen, skipping out of reach, until I make myself sit down with the phone balanced on my knees and stare at the sentences a stranger somewhere wrote about the most personal pain I've ever experienced.

After twenty years of marriage, nightclub owner Cao Yunchen and model Coco Cao have officially called it quits. A close source to the Beijing-born billionaire has revealed that the pair split up in late December of last year.

This news may come as a shock to those who have been rooting for the power couple since their famously extravagant fairy-tale wedding, which was reported to have cost over $25 million. Gift bags alone were heavily sponsored by luxury brands and valued at $20,000 each, including an all-expense-paid, week-long vacation to Sanya, with some bags resold after the event for $100,000. An estimated three hundred of the total two thousand guests were fellow celebrities.

A number of eagle-eyed fans from Coco Cao's official fan club, however, have said there were signs early on. Coco Cao was first photographed without her wedding ring outside Sanlitun on January 28, though it later appeared in the series of selfies she shared on Weibo on February 4.

Fans have also connected the divorce to Coco Cao's recent

noticeable weight loss. While she is known for her tall, slender figure, fans expressed their concerns after photos of the supermodel in a low-cut gown at a Bulgari event went viral, noting her "sickly" complexion.

Other sources claim that the couple has become increasingly hostile as legalities proceed, to the point where they're no longer even speaking to each other. Rumors of Cao Yunchen cheating with a much younger woman continue to circulate.

Their only daughter, eighteen-year-old Chanel Cao (@chanel.cao), is currently in her final year at Airington International Boarding School. She's reported to be living with her mother, though she was spotted entering her father's nightclub, Club Sixty-Eight Hours, last night.

Neither Coco Cao nor Cao Yunchen has publicly commented on the divorce.

More articles keep popping up. They're delving deeper into my family history, connecting the dots, concocting their own theories about why it happened. My parents' marriage is now a museum with a full tour and free entry. My childhood photos have now become the face of the Great Tragic Divorce.

I slam my phone down on the bed, my blood pounding in my ears.

The timing feels too close to be a coincidence. Had someone spotted me at the club last night? Had they witnessed my fight with my father? Is that why they're leaking the story now?

Or could it be some kind of extreme effort to sabotage my prom queen campaign?

If so, it's working. At school, the news has clearly made its way around already. People still say hi, but there are a hundred unspoken questions tucked into that single word, questions I know they're all dying to find out. *Is the news true? How long was your father cheating on your mom? When did you first realize?*

From all the pitying glances I'm getting, you'd think somebody in my immediate family had died in a freak accident. But underneath their pity, I can sense their glee too.

Finally. Proof that my life isn't so blessed, that I'm not so absurdly, outrageously lucky, that I don't get to have everything. They'll go to bed and remind themselves that yes, I might be enjoying the nice cars and the luxury handbags and the TV appearances, but do they *really* want to be me, knowing my dad cheated on my mom with someone closer to my age than hers?

It's a blow to my reputation, and I don't know how I'm supposed to recover from this. I can feel my vision of myself as prom queen—perfect, beautiful, admired—starting to disintegrate at the edges, slipping further and further out of reach. Even if the fated fire hasn't happened yet, my life seems to be going up in flames already.

Maybe my prime is already over, the way every actor or singer must have a peak and inevitable subsequent downfall. Maybe my life will never be as good as it once was.

There's a hot prickling sensation in the back of my eyes, and I'm blinking fast to make it go away when Vanessa Liu stops me in the hall.

We're the kind of friendly where we beam and wave at each other and stop to compliment each other's hair or complain about our classes, but we would never actually hang out together on weekends.

She's staring at me now, sympathy swimming all over her face as she clasps my hand. "How *are* you holding up?" she asks.

I remind my lips how to smile. "Oh, I'm fine," I tell her.

"No, *really*. It must be *so* hard." She keeps this up for a while, with her spoken-poetry-style emphasis on random words, as if everything suddenly becomes profound when your parents' divorce is splashed all over the news. "Are you *all right*? Do you *need* anything? Because if you *do*, I'm *here* for you—you can talk to me at *any* time."

"Thanks, girl, that's super sweet of you. But I am fine. *Really*," I add in the same tone she used.

"I just can't believe it," she says, apparently still not done with this conversation. "I'm shocked. I'm so shocked—were you shocked? I mean, did you *know*?"

I'm trying to figure out a quick escape when someone taps my shoulder. I twist around, braced for another half friend to pry into my life under the guise of concern, but instead I find myself staring up at Ares.

He holds my gaze for a beat, his lips slightly parted, his head cocked as if to assess something.

And all at once, everything from last night rushes back to me. The confessions I'd made in the darkness of the car, the way I'd nuzzled against him. He had been so patient and gentle with me, and I'd been so grateful for it that I had let my guard fall. But now, in broad daylight, regret burns sour in my throat like a nasty hangover. Could *he* have been the one to leak the story?

"Can you help me with something?" Ares asks.

Vanessa's brows shoot up with a new sort of curiosity. I don't think Ares has asked anyone at school for help before.

On any other day, I would be thrilled by this, the fact that *he's* the one seeking *me* out. Proof of progress, a rare sign that he's interested in me. But I hesitate and eye him warily, my mind still combing through all the information I'd slipped to him yesterday, trying to connect it with the article, to calculate the chances that he's the culprit. "Okay," I say at last.

He leads me away from the countless pairs of eyes, down the corridor and into an empty Chinese classroom. The door clicks shut behind him, and he stops under the display of crimson paper fans we'd folded for the spring festival.

I drop into the teacher's chair and cross my ankles to keep myself from fidgeting. I can't believe it's still morning. It feels like a decade has passed since I woke up.

"Chanel," Ares starts to say. "Are you—"

"Did you leak the story?" I blurt out.

He had been walking toward me, but he comes to an abrupt halt, his eyes widening with confusion, then surprise, before hardening. I realize at once that I've asked the wrong question, made a fatal mistake.

"Why would I do that?" he asks, visibly affronted.

"I—I don't know." I swallow the lump in my throat. Even though the windows have been left ajar, the classroom feels too hot, too stuffy. "To embarrass me? To ruin my reputation? To make money off the story? Because you don't like me?"

With every word that comes out of my mouth, the muscle

in his jaw winds tighter and tighter, until he takes a step back, shaking his head. "Jesus, Chanel," he says. "I wasn't aware you had such a low opinion of me."

"It's not you, personally," I hurry to say, to somehow explain it's less that I don't trust him, and more that I don't trust *anyone*, but I can tell the damage has already been done.

"I was just going to check to see if you were okay," he says slowly. "But if you don't want to tell me anything, that's fine."

"Wait," I say, reaching for him, as if I can reach through time and reverse this whole conversation, but when I grab his arm, he flinches like my very touch burns him, his jaw clenched. I pull back, humiliated, blinking fast, trying not to let my hurt show.

Without another word, he turns to go, as if he can't stand being in this room with me for even one more second.

Come back, I'm tempted to call after him. *I didn't mean it.* But my pride is already lying in pieces at my feet.

The door slams shut after him, and in the following silence, I draw my knees up to my chest, feeling sick. I'm almost impressed with how badly I've fucked everything up. My classmates all pity me, my chances of winning prom queen are lower than ever, and I've just single-handedly shattered whatever goodwill I've built with Ares over the last week.

Being at school is awful, and being at home is worse.

I barely have the energy to drop my schoolbag down on the doorstep before falling onto the couch, my head angled to avoid smudging my makeup on the cushions.

I could blame the news, all the things netizens are saying about me and my family, but there's this feeling that's been festering inside me for a while now. Maybe from the day I found out about my father, or maybe even earlier than that, but it used to be easier to ignore. It's duller than despair, but heavier. Less the specific, cutting pain of an open wound, and more the vague discomfort you feel when you're running a fever, your head woozy, everything too bright and too loud and disproportionately draining.

I don't really understand it. I only know that the thought of the near future—of having to climb out of bed, put on my makeup, brush my hair, go to school, talk, smile, scheme, eat but not too much, work out tomorrow and tomorrow and the tomorrow after that—fills my chest with such dread that it practically pins me down.

Get up, do something, I urge myself.

Do something.

You're running out of time.

But the prickling sensation I've been trying to ward off all day sharpens into a burning, and I taste the salt of tears. At least I'm alone right now. Couldn't bear to let anyone at school see me this way—they all love being around me when I'm happy, the life of the party, not when I'm too deep inside my own head.

The key turns in the door.

My mom steps inside—or staggers, more like, kicking off her boots by the door with none of her usual grace. When she removes her sunglasses, I notice the mascara smudged around her eyes, the tiredness in her face.

I quickly wipe away my tears and pad over to her. "Mom? Are you okay?"

She doesn't say anything for a long time. "Yes, I'm fine," she replies at last, in a distant, strained voice. But she continues to move as if in slow motion, setting down her bag, then her keys on the marble counter, then the cream-white gift box in her hand. "I think I might sleep early tonight."

"Okay, yeah, that's a good idea," I say, desperate to make myself useful. "Go get some rest—is there anything you need, though? I can order you some chicken vermicelli salad for dinner first. Or some herbal essences for a bath—"

"No, that won't be necessary," she says. Then, still in the same strange voice, not really looking at me, she asks, "Did you see your father yesterday?"

I freeze. "What?"

"In one of the articles." Her expression is impossible to read. "It said you went to his club last night, and he was present. I'm a little surprised, that's all. I suppose I wasn't aware that you two were still in touch."

"I'm not," I rush to say. "I haven't spoken to him since you . . . And I bumped into him by accident. It was a pure coincidence—"

"You bumped into him at the club he owns?" she says mildly, turning into the living room. I hurry in after her, my stomach twisting. "You needn't sound so defensive, Chanel. If you wanted to see him, you have the legal right to. I do, however," she goes on, an edge to her words, "advise that going forward, you are more careful about your behaviors in public and what people might say. When you're out and about, you're not just some random teenager, you know. You're Chanel Cao. You represent this family. Anything you do reflects not only on you, but me as well."

All I ever do is think about what people might say, and I'm exhausted. But my throat closes over the protest. "I'm sorry, Mom. I promise, I'll be more careful."

She presses her lips together. "You have to be." A pause. "Did anyone at school ask you about the situation? You didn't say anything, did you? You can't trust them, *any* of them—not even your friends. Who knows which one of them will go blabbing to the press?"

"I didn't," I say. "Really."

She nods, but I know she isn't satisfied. She never is. "I'm going to shower," she says, walking away.

I hurry to clean up after her, storing her boots away, straightening out her coat and hanging it properly so it won't be wrinkled tomorrow. Then I pick up the gift box. Some kind of care package. All of my mom's favorite face masks and lip products and teas are inside it, with a printed-out message tucked inside the wrapping paper. I'm about to store it away when I glimpse the sender's name, and my heart stops.

Dear Coco,

I've been meaning to get in touch for a while. I was very sorry to hear the news about your marriage, and I sincerely hope you're doing okay. Please be kind to yourself, and do let me know if you'd ever like to catch up. This is my new number: 13610439745.

Kindest regards from your old friend,

Long Ge

The sensation of pressure building inside my head, my chest, the buzz of dread. Like standing alone on a shore, helpless, watching the tsunami come in, the sheer force and scale of it infinitely greater than I am. It feels absurd to even try to stop it, but then I hear the creak of the bathroom door from the other room, the hissing of the shower curtain being drawn. The spray of water.

If I don't do anything, my mom will be—

Can't even think it. I have to act, now. Trembling, while the shower is running at full blast, loud enough to muffle my voice, I call Henry.

He picks up immediately. "I was just about to call you," he says. "I would have done so sooner, but I've been in meetings with my father the entire day."

"No, no, that's fine." I'm barely aware of myself talking; I keep staring at the name written on the card, the skin on my face numb.

"I was looking into drowning out the article about your parents from the trending searches on Weibo," he continues, and this might be one of the things I appreciate most about Henry Li: He's not the kind to offer empty words of reassurance. He offers practical solutions.

"How long would that take?" I ask.

"Well, here is the thing." He pauses, and I hear the frown in his voice when he says, confused, "Strangely enough, someone's drowned out the top result already."

"Like, there was another scandal?" I ask.

"No," he says firmly. "It must be the work of bots. The number of clicks, the speed at which the new articles have risen to the top, and the nature of the comments all suggest that someone had paid for it. Organic engagement simply doesn't work this way."

"Maybe it was my mom's agency," I say.

"Maybe," he allows. "If that is the case, then they're doing an excellent job. Still, if there's anything I can help with—"

"You can," I tell him. This seems to be all that I'm doing nowadays. Asking for things from people, pleading, close to begging. "There's a man in the vision. Long Ge. He's going to be here, when my house burns down. And I might have just found his phone number."

A drawn breath. "How?"

"He gave it himself. Apparently he reached out to my mother right after he heard the news about the divorce. Sent her this giant gift box that he likely ordered online. If I give you the phone number, delivery date, and the gift box brand, would you be able to help me track down the sender's IP address?"

"Yes, not a problem," he says, and I've never felt so grateful to be friends with one of Beijing's most accomplished tech prodigies. "Leave it to me."

16

ARES

Ares had naively believed the week couldn't get any worse.

He thought he'd already hit his lowest point at school, when Chanel had accused him of selling her out. He can see it even now. The distrust in her eyes, the bitterness in her tone, just when he was starting to believe he meant something to her, something real. And as if the whiplash from the accusation wasn't enough, she'd grabbed his arm right over his newest wound, and he'd felt the hastily done stitches rip, an awful, tearing sensation that made him shudder. Had barely a second's chance to react before he hurried out of the room, determined not to let her see the extent of his injuries. He was bleeding through his school uniform by the time he reached the bathroom, trying to staunch the flow with paper towels.

His arm still burns right now.

But the pain pales in comparison when he remembers what day it is. The day everything went wrong, the day that marks three years exactly since he last saw Luke.

Three years since they all went out to eat at Luke's favorite burger restaurant. It was always Luke who told their father what he craved, and that was always the place they went. Ares simply followed, like he was doing now, two steps behind his father and his brother as they headed toward the entrance, where the menus were plastered to the glass doors, advertising their newest chicken-salt curly fries and cheeseburgers in several sizes.

The dog had bolted out of nowhere.

That's how it seemed, anyway. Just a blur of dark and brown fur, a snarl that echoed down the street, and then the dog's hot breath on his wrist before the creature sank its fangs in. It happened so fast that he barely had time to register the pain, only a horrible, bone-crushing pressure.

He didn't scream.

He was too stunned, almost incredulous—he had just been *walking*, hadn't he? He'd been deliberating whether to buy the double or triple cheeseburger. How could he be bleeding because some wild creature had attacked him? Why hadn't anyone stopped the dog?

Then his survival instinct kicked in, and he jerked back from the animal, gasping. The animal appeared to have lost interest anyway; it licked the fresh blood on its chin and sniffed the air, its ears perking up. Then it bounded off in the direction of the roast-pork store opposite the restaurant.

"Are you hurt? How are you feeling? Look at me." His father's voice, trembling with worry.

Ares collected himself, determined to put up a brave front and assure his father he was fine, but when he lifted his head, his father wasn't even looking his way. He had pulled Luke to the side to protect him, and was now crouching down in front of his little brother, scanning his perfectly unscathed face while Ares stood there alone, blood trickling down from his fingertips.

"Don't be scared, erzi. The dog's gone now," his father said, squeezing Luke's shoulder, still without even a glance at Ares.

Now the pain was really here, pulsing like white-hot electric shocks through his arm. He didn't know if he was supposed to wrap something around the bite or leave it alone or try to clean it. A lump pushed against his throat. He wanted, embarrassingly, to burst into tears, but he hadn't cried since he was a little kid. He wasn't going to start now.

"I think Gege's injured," Luke whispered, and only then did his father turn around.

His father frowned over at him, and Ares strained to detect some glimpse of genuine concern. Pity would be fine too; that wasn't asking so much, was it? You could even pity a stranger in pain, or a movie character on a screen. But his father's jaw was set, his face hard. "You should go to the hospital to stitch that up," he said at last. "Wouldn't want to get rabies."

"Right. Yes," Ares said. He felt somewhat lightheaded, like when you were only running on three hours of sleep but pushing your brain to work anyways.

"You can call yourself a DiDi, can't you?" his father said. It wasn't really a question. "We'll meet you after lunch."

With his uninjured arm, he fumbled for his phone, and the lump in his throat hardened until he couldn't even swallow. His fingers kept slipping over the keyboard, the pain making it hard to focus. *Wrong password. Try again. Wrong password. Try again.* He hissed under his breath. His father was walking away already, holding Luke's hand, talking about trying the new curly fries.

Wrong password. Five attempts left. And then the terrifying words circled his mind like a threat: *hospital, rabies, stitches.* He didn't want to think about any of that right now. He just wanted to go home.

He did, eventually, after the lonely visit to the hospital, where everything smelled like rubbing alcohol and sickness and stale final breaths. "Where are your parents?" the nurse had asked him while she stitched him up, and he lied about his father traveling for work. Even at a time like this, he rushed to his father's defense.

"Almost done," the nurse told him. He couldn't stop staring at the needle threading through his flesh, couldn't stop thinking about how fragile humans really were.

It was almost midnight when he staggered down the corridor, his arm throbbing. He passed by Luke's bedroom—the biggest en suite, with a wrap-around balcony, the walls covered with science and car posters. The kind of bedroom he would've dreamed of having as a kid, but he'd been forced to squeeze himself into a tiny cot back at his grandparents' house, which creaked every time he moved.

Luke was still awake. He was sitting comfortably on the couch, licking a boba ice-cream bar Ares bet he'd stolen from the fridge when their father wasn't looking. Not that his father could bear to get mad at Luke for it, even if he found out.

And Ares felt an ugly emotion rising, rising up in him.

Luke lifted his head and spotted him in the doorway. Blinked those innocent eyes at him. "Gege. You're back—is your arm okay?"

"Yes, it is," Ares said stiffly. He waited for that resentful, self-pitying feeling to go away, but the longer he stared at Luke—perfect, adored, sheltered, angelic Luke, his half-brother—the stronger it grew, until it was impossible to ignore. He hadn't meant to think the words, let alone say them, but suddenly they were stumbling out of his lips. "You know, it's funny. Our father really doesn't give a shit about me."

Luke stopped licking the ice cream. His eyes widened. "Yes, he does," he said, which was somehow more enraging than if he'd simply agreed.

"No," Ares snapped. "He doesn't. He only cares about you—"

"That's not true," Luke said. "He loves us equally. All fathers love their sons equally, that's what my friend said—"

"Not our father."

Luke's nose scrunched up in confusion. "But—"

"Jesus, can you just leave me alone for once?"

Shock flashed across Luke's face, as if Ares had suddenly reached out and struck him.

Ares made himself leave before he could say anything else. He continued on his way to his bedroom at the very end of the corridor, already regretting the conversation. He should've just kept his mouth shut. Luke was still a child, it wasn't his fault. *Tomorrow*, he thought, once he had the energy and his arm wasn't hurting so terribly. Tomorrow, he'd apologize to Luke and tell him he hadn't meant it. He'd make blueberry pancakes and draw a smiley face in maple syrup the way Luke liked it, as compensation, and he'd take Luke to the arcade to play Street Fighter, and things between them would be okay.

But the next morning, Luke was gone.

17

CHANEL

I squint down into the bluish glow of my phone screen, scanning the address Henry had sent me earlier in the afternoon, even though I've committed it to memory already.

Then I glance up, checking the street signs in the unsettling darkness. It's quiet except for the sound of my own ballet flats, chosen for discretion over fashion. Wherever this place is, it's so isolated that there aren't even any lights to illuminate the way. Nobody else around to rescue me or even witness it if I were attacked and screamed for help—

I try to shake the thought away, even as the back of my neck prickles with foreboding, the night air uncomfortably cold against my skin.

Be careful, Henry had texted. *Don't do anything impulsive.*

got it lol, stop worrying so much, I'd replied. *it'll age u*

Nothing impulsive. Because this isn't an impulsive decision— it's a necessary one. To save my mom, to find out what Long Ge's deal is.

I stop outside a rusted door, marked faintly with what looks like graffiti spray. The symbol of a dragon. Another glance at the address. Then I draw in a deep breath and push the door open.

The first thing I hear is the clatter of mahjong tiles, mixed with voices from below. I move as lightly as I can, my flats padding down the stone steps, noticing as I do that they're stained with something dark red, something that resembles blood. A chill shudders through me, but I don't turn back around.

The next set of doors open up to a fight ring.

For a moment, all I can do is stare. There's a crowd already gathered in the cavernous, dimly lit room, the same kind of crowd you might find lurking around populated tourist areas, waiting to pick pockets and scam you for everything you have.

Then I spot the boy stepping into the ring, and my heart freezes in my chest.

It's Ares.

He's here, somehow, standing just a few feet apart from a man twice his size.

A bell rings, and the man lunges at Ares like a wild animal. Before I can properly react, can even process the fact that Ares is *here,* at the same place Long Ge had sent the gift box from, Ares darts out of the way, swift on his feet, and shoves the man from behind. The man stumbles to his knees, and Ares closes in immediately, grabbing the collar of his shirt to hold him there while he strikes at his ribs. The man grunts, squirming free long enough to aim a swing at Ares.

Misses.

Tries again.

They exchange kicks and jabs like boxers, but it's nothing like a professional boxing match. It's unregulated, ruthless, nothing off-limits. The only goal seems to be to knock the other person flat to the ground, whatever it takes, however much they break or bleed.

I can't tear my eyes away.

Ares has always been intimidating, but in action, he's *terrifying*. A chill shudders through my body. His gaze is utterly unfeeling as he swings his fist straight into the grown man's face with a loud *crack*, punches again and again, his hand coming away stained with crimson.

Fresh blood gushes from the man's broken nose like running water.

One final, solid punch to the stomach sends him tumbling straight to the ground, where he lies, eyes bulging and gasping like a fish, struggling to rise again. I clap a horrified hand to my mouth, my stomach turning. I'd thought I was already aware of how sheltered I was. Well protected, privileged, comfortably shielded from the world by my parents' money and connections.

But it's only now that I realize *just* how sheltered I am. I've never even witnessed true violence before. I've never seen this amount of blood outside movie screens and hospitals.

The crowd starts counting down, their voices bouncing off the gray walls.

"Five . . . four . . . three."

Ares looms over the man, both his fists still raised, ready to attack should his opponent crawl back onto his feet again—but he doesn't need to worry about that. The man seems to have given up, his limbs splayed over the concrete, his eyes shuttering closed.

"Two . . ."

So *this* is what Ares has been doing. This is why he's been showing up to school with new scrapes and bruises. It feels like a missing puzzle piece slotting into place, but it's still not enough for me to construct the full picture.

"One."

Half the crowd erupts into cheers, while the others shout out in protest. But all their faces are flushed, bright with bloodlust. As the man is dragged off to the side, leaving a trail of red behind him, the spectators turn to each other and start chattering excitedly. I catch the words *winning streak* and *sure bet*, but none of it makes any sense.

My gaze slides back to Ares, who remains standing at the center of it all, alert and erect, his breathing barely labored. Even though he's just won, there's no trace of pleasure or triumph in his expression. Only a kind of grim satisfaction, the look of someone on the verge of completing an almost impossible task.

I don't understand it, don't know why he's here, but now I'm more certain than ever that it's connected to Long Ge. Everything is connected to Long Ge.

Before Ares can spot me, I step back, slipping into the shadows of a narrow corridor. There must be more clues. Information I can find. I make my way carefully down until I reach the end, where there are only two rooms—storage, to my left, and to my right, a door marked with the same dragon symbol. My fingers close around the doorknob, but it won't budge.

Locked.

As I'd anticipated.

I slide one of the bobby pins out of my hair and bend it carefully into a pick, sticking the end into the lock. I work as fast as I can, listening for footsteps, my heart slamming in my chest as I wriggle the pin, trying to find the right angle, until I hear a soft *click*.

And just like that, I'm in.

The room looks like the world's most depressing office. Windowless, a single standard desk and chair, no decorations whatsoever. I work my way through the drawers, sliding each one open, not even sure what I'm looking for. I rifle through bound folders, contracts, sheaves of statistics, hundreds of documents for what seems like dozens of different companies—

Until I come across my mom's face.

I suck in a sharp, horrified breath. My pulse is beating so loud in my ears that I'm terrified it'll give me away, that it'll echo all the way down the corridor and those men will hear it and come running. Trembling, I pick up the photo of my mom from the bottom drawer. She's smiling in full glamour, her already gorgeous face edited to look flawless. I vaguely remember seeing it before; it's from an old campaign for a perfume brand, taken years ago.

But it's not the only photo of her.

The entire drawer appears to be some kind of secret shrine dedicated to my mom. Newspaper clippings, extracted from over the decades. Magazine covers. Paparazzi shots of my mom crossing the street in Shanghai, waiting at the airport, sipping a lemon water outside a café I recognize, lounging on a beach with a shawl draped over her body to prevent any unwanted tanning, the camera zooming in so far you can see the sunscreen smudged on her nose. A torn page from what might've been a textbook or yearbook, my mom's handwriting curling over it: *Have a good holiday, Long Ge! I hope we're in the same class again next year.* An old hair tie. A single origami star, not even folded very well, one of the corners dented. And letters, the first few written on yellowing essay sheets, the type teachers hand out at school, with the gridded lines starting to fade, the more recent ones written on glossy letterhead paper. But they all begin the same way.

Dear Coco . . .

Dear Coco . . .

Coco . . .

I used to hate studying before school—used to dread coming to school at all—but ever since the teachers put us in the same revision group, I find myself excited to wake up. . . .

Have you ever stared at someone and wondered how it's possible that the universe could be so kind to them? To give them not only extraordinary beauty, but also such a warm personality, a lovely laugh, effortless charm. . . .

I get this funny feeling in the pit of my stomach every time I think of you. . . .

Forgive me if this comes across as overly forward, but your existence lends meaning to mine, which I can only take to be a miracle, as I'd always thought of the world as a cruel, inherently meaningless place. . . .

I wanted to extend my congratulations on your first runway walk. It comes as no surprise whatsoever that you've made it in the modeling world.

Do you still remember me? I know it's been years, but I can't stop thinking about you. . . .

Sometimes I find myself revisiting the route I took to school. You only walked with me that one time to help carry my books while I was limping, but it was, truth be told, the best day of my life. I honestly wouldn't have minded if my ankle had remained twisted, just to give me an excuse to walk home beside you. . . .

Thank you for the wedding invitation. I hope you'll forgive me for being unable to attend. . . .

I can't stand it anymore. You're too good for him. I'm sorry, but you are. He doesn't deserve you, he's never deserved you. But right now, you're also too good for me. I understand that. Give me three years, Coco, and I promise, I'll be good enough. I'll provide you with everything he does and so, so much more. If he buys you a mansion, I'll buy you two, with a hedge maze and a tearoom like you always wanted. If he buys you a luxury handbag, I'll buy you the whole brand. If he flies you out in business class, I'll fly you out on a private jet. I'll make the entire city bow down to you.

I have to stop reading to breathe. A hot, tingling feeling spreads through my scalp, like there are invisible insects crawling all over me.

Long Ge. My mom. Of course she's had her share of admirers, men consumed by their love for her, sick in the head with it. Like that stalker who'd broken into our holiday house in Sanya last summer and was sitting right there on our couch when we came in. Or the one who had gotten a photo of my mom's face tattooed on his back.

But this level of obsession is unlike anything I've seen before.

"Xiao meimei, did you get lost on your way to the nail salon or something?"

I startle and hurriedly drop the letters back into the drawer before I spin around, coming face-to-face with two leering men. I take in their bruised knuckles, their rough features and week-old stubbles, and instinctively reach into my purse, my heart pounding.

Still, I make myself smile at them. Try to keep my cool. "I was just waiting for a friend."

"Ah, you got a friend here?" One of the men laughs and steps forward. He's three heads taller than I am, perfectly blocking the doorway. "We can also be friends."

My clammy fingers close around the glass of my perfume

bottle. "No, thanks," I say mildly. "My friend might get jealous, you see. I'll wait for him outside."

But the man only steps closer. He smells like the train station—like cigarettes and ramen powder and unwashed clothes. "Why don't you stay a bit longer?"

"That's fine," I say as firmly as I can.

He acts as if he hasn't heard me. He looks me up and down in a way that's as familiar as it is nauseating. Then he reaches for me, and I pull out the perfume bottle and spray it wildly, my eyes squeezed shut, knowing I've aimed in the right place only when I hear his grunt of pain. I open my eyes to find him doubled over, clawing at his face and coughing—

But his friend is still standing, and his eyes narrow at me.

"That wasn't very nice," he says.

I hold my perfume up like a gun and press down again, but nothing happens. I try one more time, my throat tight with desperation, my fingers trembling so hard that I almost drop the perfume bottle. *Shit*. The nozzle is jammed.

All my thoughts are lost in the sound of my own scream as the man corners me, seizing me by the wrist. I try to squirm away, but it's futile. I don't stand a chance, and he knows this. He yanks me to his side with such callous force that I fear he's dislocated a bone, and I've never been so terrified, never been so mad at myself for getting into this situation in the first place, and I'm so fucking screwed—

There's a flash of shadow, the heavy *thud* of a collision.

Ares slams the man down, pinning his squirming body in place as if he's nothing but a worm in the dirt. There shouldn't be anything graceful about this, the crunch of bone and the splash of blood and gasps of pain, but Ares moves with all the streamlined grace of a natural fighter, a wolf determined to clamp its jaws down on its prey.

Then he lifts his head, his blazing eyes locking on mine. "*Go*," he says. "Run."

I do. I turn on my heel and run and run and I don't stop until the stitch in my side makes it physically impossible to keep going. I'm halfway down the block, panting, my head spinning, the stench of blood in my nostrils, when Ares comes to find me.

His pale skin is flecked with red, the color as vivid as new paint. A few loose strands of hair, come undone during the fight, tumble over his eyes. He looks ready to tear down the building back there with his bare hands. Ready, and capable of it.

I'm struck by a sudden sense of déjà vu so intense it almost knocks the breath out of me. I've witnessed this before—this very moment, the alley I'm standing in, the way he's walking toward me. *The vision.* Between the news about my parents and Long Ge, I'd forgotten about it.

But before I can flee from the scene, Ares corners me.

"What were you doing in there?" he demands, his eyes pitch-black, blazing with some emotion I can't parse. Something darker and more complicated than anger. "Did you follow me?"

This seems like a better, easier explanation than revealing what I've found out about Long Ge, so I nod. "I'm sorry, I was just curious—"

"What were you thinking? Do you know how dangerous that was? Do you know what would've happened if I hadn't come in time, if they had—" He cuts himself off, breathing fast. "This isn't a fucking game, Chanel. These men won't hesitate to run a knife through a living person; it doesn't matter how rich or famous or well-connected you are. Your name won't protect you in a place like this. If anything, it only makes you more vulnerable. Honestly, it's a miracle you're not dead."

"But I'm fine," I say, dazed, almost dizzy. "I'm not hurt or anything."

"You're not hurt," he repeats. Without another word, he moves so fast that I gasp, reaching for my arm. But despite the rage simmering through his frame, the knife's edge of his words, his grip is surprisingly gentle as he lifts my arm up, turning it over. "If you're not hurt, then what the fuck is *this*?"

It's only then that I notice the purplish marks around my wrist, stark as ink. They must be from when the man grabbed me earlier.

"Not badly hurt," I amend weakly, pulling my arm away from him. The new bruises have already started to throb, but I barely even register the pain. It feels like the sky and ground have been reversed, like everything's upside down. In the vision, I would have sworn that Ares was the one who'd hurt me. But then, the vision had never shown him attacking me, only the bruises on my wrist, the anger on his face. So has the vision changed, because I've managed to actually change Ares's feelings toward me? Or had I simply interpreted the vision wrong in the first place? "Really."

He stares at me, long and hard. A drop of blood trickles

down his neck, staining his shirt collar, but he doesn't seem to notice it, or maybe he doesn't care.

"You should be more worried about yourself," I tell him.

"Who said I was worried about you?" he says flatly.

I'm almost tempted to roll my eyes. "Okay then, you should *only* be worried about yourself. Let's go get you cleaned up. Where's your house?"

"I don't need you to—"

"I'm actually not offering, I'm asking. I'll call the car now," I say, holding out my phone for him to enter his address, which he does, albeit reluctantly, jaw clenched. "Oh, and . . . Ares?"

"What?"

"Thank you," I whisper.

His face softens, and even with all that blood on his cheeks, the immediate change it makes is stunning. Like watching ice thaw in a sudden blaze of heat.

I flick the light switch on inside Ares's apartment, illuminating an almost empty living room. There are only the bare necessities: a muted gray couch, a single dining table with two side chairs. No houseplants or decorations or pictures in frames. I've been inside hotel rooms that felt homier than this.

After I help Ares down onto the couch, I head over to the kitchen, find a towel hanging over the dishwasher, and wet it under the tap. Then I pass it wordlessly to him.

"Do I look too scary like this?" he asks, his mouth curving with grim amusement.

"You don't scare me," I lie, unable to stop myself from staring as he runs the towel over his cheeks, his collarbones, the hard line of his jaw, wiping off the dried blood splatters. The white fabric comes away a dark, dirty red.

Then he lifts his shirt up over his head.

"Oh my god," I whisper, horror lurching to my throat so fast I think I might be sick. "Oh my god."

"Thanks. That's how most girls react when I take off my shirt," he says dryly.

I'm too stunned to even respond to that. I'd seen the fresh bruises on his knuckles, the flashes of split skin. But it's so much worse than I thought. Half his side is mottled deep purple and yellow, new wounds acquired faster than old wounds could heal. Long gashes snake down his torso, and even the spaces beneath his collarbones are marked by angry red crescents that look awfully like human nails. There seems to be no inch of muscle that's been left unscathed. I can't imagine how it feels. Can't imagine how he's managed to get up in the morning and go to school every day like everything's normal when it must hurt to even breathe. It hurts just to look at him.

The back of my nose prickles, a sharp, sore pressure that builds up to my eyes. "Oh my god, Ares," I say again, my voice breaking.

Ares stares at me, more confused than I've ever seen him. "What are you doing?"

"What do you *think* I'm doing?" I sniff.

"You're . . . crying? But . . . why?" He studies me a moment longer, then pulls me down to the couch next to him. Softer, quieter, he says, "Is it because of what happened earlier? I know that must've been scary. . . . I promise it won't happen again. I won't let them hurt you." He strokes my hair as he speaks, his touch so gentle that it's disorienting. It doesn't seem possible that those same hands had broken a grown man's nose tonight, had ripped two people away from me and thrown them to the concrete. "You're safe now."

And despite everything the vision had warned me of, I do feel safe. Safer than I should reasonably feel. "That's not . . . It's not because of that," I whisper, dabbing my tears with the corner of my sleeve. I motion toward the cuts across his torso, all that raw and ruined flesh. "It's . . . this. I don't like it. I don't like—I don't want you to be—I can't stop picturing . . . I mean, doesn't it *hurt*?"

He freezes.

Something flickers across his eyes, which are almost pitch-black in the low light, his pupils dilated. "My pain," he says slowly, like he's struggling to understand a new, abstract concept in class, "means something to you?"

The answer is a given, but the problem is that I don't know what exactly it means.

"Of course it does," I say.

"Of course it does," he repeats, like he still can't quite believe it.

The tears are falling faster than I can wipe them away. "Fuck, now my makeup's ruined," I say on a shaky breath, half laughing at myself.

"You still look pretty," Ares says matter-of-factly. "You always do."

My heart stumbles over itself like a drunken fool trying to find the exit, but there's no escaping this feeling. And so when the air shifts between us, when his eyes flicker down to my lips, I lean in.

In the past, kissing was a pleasant pastime at best, a chore more often than not, and a disgusting, deeply regrettable ordeal at worst. There have been occasions where I'd kiss a boy simply because we'd run out of things to talk about, and we were both already sitting there, so might as well. I had perfect control over myself. It was like I could disconnect my body from my mind; I could calmly plan out my breakfast or outfit for the next day inside my head while I drew them closer to me.

But something in me fractures when his lips graze mine.

My mouth parts on its own accord and I shift forward, letting my knees spread until I'm straddling his torso on the couch, every possible inch of skin pressed together, and still, it isn't nearly close enough. My nails sink into the muscles in his shoulders as I kiss him, wild and breathless and stunned by the intensity of my body's response to him.

Is *this* how it's supposed to feel? Like hunger? Like the world's on fire? Like I might be losing my mind?

He grips my leg with the kind of sureness that only comes from experience, and violence blazes through me at the thought of him touching any other girl this way, even if it was before we ever met. I run my nails down his back like I can keep him there, just keep him, make him mine. A breathless sound escapes my lips, and for once I'm not faking it. If anything, I'm holding back, clenching my teeth to stifle a gasp when his hands slide to my upper thigh.

My head is spinning, or the room is. I only stop when I taste the rust of blood on his lips and I remember, dimly, too late, that he's injured, but his fingers find the nape of my neck and he pulls me down to him again.

"Keep going," he says hoarsely.

"But . . . you're bleeding—"

"Doesn't matter." His voice is rough, the rasp of flint.

He kisses me harder, and I think I've done it, I've figured out a way to keep the future at bay, because time seems to halt. There's only the two of us, his heart thudding against my chest. I bite gently down on his lower lip and he makes a sound deep in the back of his throat, the most vulnerable and unraveled I've ever heard him, and his hands are everywhere but still not enough—

It almost hurts to break away from him.

Not because I want to, but because I need to leave him wanting more. It's the most basic of rules when it comes to attraction: Never give him everything at once, or else there'll be nothing for him to fantasize about, no point for him to keep chasing after you. It's just as well. If I were to keep going any longer, let him hold me tighter, run his hands even farther down my body, all those rules might just dissolve from my mind.

He opens his eyes slowly. There's the briefest moment where his features are relaxed and his guard is down, where I glimpse what he might be like when nobody else is around. Then his expression smooths out, and he releases his grip on my hair with just enough reluctance to make me consider kissing him again.

Silence passes between us like a truce. This is new. Uncharted territory.

"Do you want to watch something?" he asks after a beat, nodding at the TV.

The casualness of the question surprises me. As if it's just any ordinary evening, as if we've long fallen into the habit of making out on his couch, and he hadn't narrowly escaped being beaten to death mere hours ago. As if he isn't still bleeding right now.

"Okay," I say, matching his tone.

He leans forward to grab the remote, barely wincing when the movement pulls against his wounds, and settles back down next to me, his arm draped around my shoulders. He starts to flip through the five-second previews, but my eyes land on a familiar logo in his Continue Watching history.

"Wait. I was on that variety show," I say, pointing at it. "You were watching me?"

He pauses, his hand still on the remote, and appears on the brink of denying it, then relents. "It came up on my recommended list the other day and I was . . . curious," he admits. "I only saw one scene."

A thrill races through my blood. *He was curious about me.* I'd thought that my chances of winning Ares over had pretty much evaporated after I'd accused him of leaking the divorce story, but after tonight, maybe my chances aren't so bad after all. But it feels like more than just a victory, more than relief that my plan to save my own future is working. It feels almost like a type of pressure building inside my chest, a complicated heat and weight, like his body on mine minutes before.

"Let's keep watching it, then," I say.

He raises his brows. "Really? You want to watch yourself?"

"What, do you think that's incredibly narcissistic of me?" I ask, grinning.

The corner of his mouth rises, like he can't help himself. The closest to a smile I've seen on him. "I already knew about your narcissism, though your shamelessness is refreshing." But he clicks into the show anyway.

As the opening theme plays, I lie there with my head nestled against his shoulder, the blue glow of the TV screen flickering in my peripheral vision, too comfortable to move. It's so easy to pretend the rest of the world away like this, everything blurry and secretive and vaguely intimate. I can smell the perfume in my own hair, mixed in with the lingering notes of blood, hear the loud thudding of his heartbeat.

"You flew to Paris just for your birthday?" Ares asks as a scene of me strolling down the Champs-Élysées flickers to life on the screen.

"Yeah. It looks nice, right?" I say. The cameras continue to follow me throughout the weekend: stopping to take photos in cobbled alleyways, sun on my shoulders, floral sundress billowing around my ankles, smiling through perfume-making classes and private cathedral tours. Then the actual birthday party at a luxurious restaurant with a panoramic view of the city, me showing up with my hair done, in a custom-made dress, holding a brand-new Chanel purse I'd been eyeing for months, while a group of girls—all gorgeous, all my age—gathered around me. "But like, I barely knew any of those people."

Ares frowns at the screen, where one of the girls is loudly gushing over my dress. "Those aren't your friends?"

"Nope. It was just for the show," I say, shrugging. "All those girls are the daughters of CEOs and fashion designers and entertainment company founders. The director of the variety show and my mom created the guest list. I didn't even know who was coming."

Ares doesn't say anything to that, but he grabs the blanket from the other end of the couch and covers my bare legs with it and holds me tighter.

The shot cuts to a lychee cream birthday cake from Holiland, my name written out in chocolate and pink swirls in the center. And though I'm used to seeing myself on screen by now, it's still strange to be presented with the edited version, cropped by the camera, and remember how it had felt to live inside the frame.

I'm grinning like I'm competing to be the happiest girl in the universe, blowing out the candles, and then cutting through the cake with a shiny gold knife. "That's the part I was looking forward to the most, you know," I tell Ares. "The birthday cake. It'd been ages since I'd had cake or any kind of dessert."

"And? Was it good?"

I shake my head. "I didn't get to taste it. Right before we all went to sit down, my mom reminded me that we were still filming for the next few days, and if I had any sugar, I'd end up looking bloated. So I did the trick where I was like, playing with the icing using the fork—see what I'm doing there?—but when

the camera moved away, I'd simply put the fork down. What?"
I can sense Ares staring at me, and I tilt my head toward him. It's difficult to read his expression, but something glimmers in the depths of his eyes.

"You should have had some," he says, his voice quiet. "You deserve birthday cake."

I blink in surprise, the pressure inside my chest expanding until it nearly resembles pain. It's so unexpectedly sweet, so *sincere*, that I don't know what to say, except . . . "Thank you."

We finish the episode in silence, but I'm barely watching anymore. Instead, I run my fingers absently through his hair, over the hot shell of his ear, the cool, metallic edge of his piercings, and I let myself pretend for just a little while that the boy lying beside me isn't fated to ruin my life.

18

ARES

His legs are numb when he wakes.

He glances down, frowning, his thoughts still half hazy, and finds Chanel Cao asleep on top of him. Suddenly he's wide awake, the events of last night trickling in like the pale sunlight through the curtains. The fear that had pierced his lungs when he first spotted her at the Cave, stumbling home together after, the kiss that tasted of blood and cherries, the unreality of seeing her grab towels from his kitchen like she belonged here, like their lives were irrevocably tangled. He must have dozed off at some point—he isn't sure when, which is . . . strange. He normally struggles to fall asleep to the point where his body shuts itself down from physical exhaustion, and even then he'll spend much of the night tossing around, waking every hour or so with a start and struggling to relax again.

Yet the last thing he remembers is closing his eyes, and now this:

Chanel, her dark hair spilling over her shoulders, her head

resting on his stomach. There's no blanket around either of them, but he isn't cold at all, not with her body pressed so close to his.

She breathes slowly, her features soft, her lashes dark against her skin, her makeup smudged and beginning to fade. He never imagined he would get to see her this way, and only in comparison does he realize how alert she always is. Always scheming, calculating, showing off her best and brightest sides.

So while the pins and needles in his legs are starting to feel more like a thousand tiny daggers, he holds himself very still, careful not to shift his weight on the couch. He doesn't move at all until she stirs, her eyes fluttering open.

"Morning," he says.

She seems, briefly, surprised to see him there. She looks around at the room, then down at herself, and sits up, swinging her legs off the couch like a gymnast, lithe and soundless. "I need a new shirt," she declares.

"What for?"

"Because," she says calmly, "there's blood on my dress."

So there is. He hadn't noticed it last night, but in the brilliant light of day, his eyes draw down to the rust-red stains in the white fabric, the bloodied fingerprints that have dried like a morbid pattern around her waist. Criminal evidence of everything that had happened to them, and between them.

"Sorry," he says, meaning it. "Was the dress new? I can wash it for you."

"Oh no, you can't wash this dress. You can't actually clean it at all. You're not even really supposed to wear it outside—it's very delicate, this fabric."

He frowns. "What's the point of a dress you can't wash or wear?"

"It's fashion," she says, like that explains it. "Though this was from last spring, so it's about time I retired it anyway."

He opens his mouth. Realizes that any questions he asks now will only lead to more questions, and that he really isn't interested enough in the world of clothing to find out. "I'll get you a shirt," he says instead.

In his bedroom, he rifles through his limited selection of T-shirts and tank tops, all black and dark gray, no branding or logo or even a splash of color on any of them. The opposite of Chanel Cao's closet. He picks out his newest shirt, his favorite one, and heads back out into the hall—

Then freezes.

She's standing with her back turned toward him, her dress lifted over her head. He catches a flash of her shoulder blades, elegant and symmetrical as butterfly wings, the moon-white skin between them, the smooth indents at the base of her spine, before he averts his gaze, his blood beating too hot and thick through his veins. The shirt is crumpled in his hand, and he's wondering if he should just set it down somewhere and leave when he hears her footsteps approaching.

"You're allowed to look if you want," she says casually, her dress falling with a faint rustle onto the floorboards behind her. She makes no attempt to cover her body as she steps into his line of view and takes the T-shirt from him. "What?" she asks, her gaze fastening on his as if daring him to break eye contact. "Don't tell me you're suddenly shy."

"I was trying to be a gentleman," he says, and is aware that the quality of his voice has changed.

Her brows arch. "Didn't seem that way last night."

She's slow to put his clothes on, bunching her hair up and pulling it free from the collar. As he'd expected, his shirt is far too big for her, the short sleeves hanging loose around her arms and the hem falling past her bare thighs.

The sight of it makes him want to do something awful and irrational, like kiss her again.

"Think I can pull this look off?" she asks him, gesturing to herself.

The answer slips from his tongue: "You can pull anything off."

She rolls her eyes, but she's clearly biting back a smile. "I know. Where's the bathroom, by the way?" she asks, stepping past him. "I'm going to get ready."

"It's first to your right, down the hall," he says. "Do you have your things?"

"Yeah, I bring my makeup bag everywhere with me."

He contemplates the possibility that he's still sleeping, that this is all a dream, as he watches Chanel Cao get ready from the bathroom doorway.

She ties her hair at the base of her neck with a ribbon. Sets her phone down on the bathroom counter, scrolls through her Spotify for a good few minutes until she stops at the right playlist, presses Play. An upbeat Chinese pop song he's heard at a restaurant before blares through the tiny speaker. Then, shoulders moving naturally to the music, she dumps the entire contents of her makeup bag out on the other side of the counter, letting the mascara and eyeliner and other pencil-like products he doesn't know the names of spill over the marble.

He watches her dab mysterious white powders onto her skin, cover the lines under her eyes with a brush, then carefully draw the lines again with a darker brush. That seems to be the pattern here: erasing the shadows around her nose, then retracing it. Blotting concealer around her eyelids, then smearing a dusky brown dust on top of it. He doesn't understand it, but there's something ritualistic about the whole thing, and oddly intimate too—witnessing Chanel transform into Chanel Cao before anyone else can see her.

So he continues watching, mesmerized, careful not to even breathe too loud.

She takes her time, her movements sure and deliberate, her eyes focused on her reflection. Both sharply aware of herself and unselfconscious in a way that he's come to realize is rare for her.

When she's almost done, she frees her hair from the ribbon, runs her fingers through it to comb and fluff it out until it falls over her shoulders in glossy black waves. Uncaps the Chanel No. 5 perfume bottle, adjusts the nozzle, and spritzes it behind her ears, on the pale underside of her wrists, at the hollow of her collarbones. He can smell it from here, the floral curl of jasmine and the warm vanilla notes beneath.

Two fresh bruises bloom like small violet flowers against the skin just above her chest. She seems to notice them too. She doesn't try covering them up, but rather tugs the collar of her shirt down an inch farther, tracing over the bruises with her fingers. His blood quickens at the memory of his lips there.

Then her gaze swings to him in the mirror.

"You want to help me?" she asks, in the voice of someone offering a once-in-a-lifetime deal he'd be a fool to miss out on.

He pauses with one foot over the threshold. "Help you how?"

"With this." She holds up her lipstick. Before he can choose his answer, she hoists herself up onto the counter, legs dangling off the side, her back pressed to the mirror, and beckons him forward. "Come here."

Maybe the answer was never his to choose. He isn't aware of himself stepping forward, crossing over the cerulean tiles, but it's like he's moving in a trance. The nearer he is to her, the stronger her perfume grows, enveloping his senses.

She spreads her knees out, letting him walk closer still.

An invitation. A trap.

Definitely the latter. The second he's positioned before her, his eyes level with hers, she grins like a cat and wraps her legs tight around his waist. An involuntary breath escapes his throat, and he's fighting hard to keep his expression level, to not notice the heat and pressure and weight of her body when she shifts against him to rebalance herself on the counter.

"Hmm? Something wrong?" she asks, her mouth bare inches from his.

"Course not," he says, and accepts the lipstick like a challenge. It's practically a foreign object in his hands, but he unscrews it, lifts it up to her chin. She purses her lips, waiting, baiting him. Now it's her turn to watch him, and he hears himself swallow as he traces the edge of her full lower lip, his heart beating far less steadily than his hands are moving. It wouldn't be so difficult to remain calm if he didn't remember with such aching clarity the softness of her mouth from last night.

"You're good at that," she says, twisting around to examine his work once he steps back.

He's pleased that she's pleased. Feels the sickening, pathetic urge to do anything to please her more.

She smiles up at him. Then her eyes fall on the paper half tucked into one of the bathroom drawers, and her body goes still. "What's this?"

"Oh, that. It's just a design," he says, taking it out to show her the sketch of a crescent moon. "I'm getting it tattooed. . . ." With a start, he remembers the vision he'd seen in the lake. Him and Chanel together at a tattoo parlor, her sitting down beside him. His pulse quickens. He'd feared that his chances were ruined after what happened at the Cave yesterday, that he was further away from finding Long Ge than ever. If they don't let him go back, he'll never be able to win the final matches and secure his favor. But is it possible that this is how things were meant to fall into place? Chanel showing up last night? Coming back home with her, and waking up to this?

Chanel leans closer to study the sketch. "It's pretty."

"Do you want to come with?" he asks, and he feels the *rightness* of the question as he asks it, a sense of forward motion, the gears of time turning and clicking. The future will come true. He will make it come true, using the vision as his blueprint, his map, guiding him to his brother.

"Where?"

"The tattoo appointment," he says, hoping he doesn't sound

too eager. "It's next week . . . I don't know if you'd be bored, though."

"You really want me to be there?" she asks.

I need you to be there, he thinks, a little desperately. *For whatever reason, you being there is a crucial part of the vision.* "Yeah. If you're interested, I mean. I'd like that."

"Okay, sure," she says. "Could be fun."

"Cool," he says, and realizes belatedly what it sounds like he's asking her for. A date. A proper date with him. Which he guesses it is, in a way.

She's quiet for a moment, maybe realizing the same thing too. Then, "Did you really mean what you said last night?"

"About what?"

"That it wouldn't happen again. That you wouldn't let anyone hurt me," she says. "Does that include yourself?"

"Of course. Why would I ever hurt you?" he asks, confused.

"Yeah," she murmurs, half to herself, it seems. "Why would you?"

For the first time, he feels a frisson of fear. On the outside, nothing has changed. She's still smiling up at him, her makeup fresh, her dark hair tumbling over her bare shoulders. But there had been a shift just now. A glimpse of something moving underneath Chanel Cao's perfect, polished surface, like a creature flitting beneath a moonlit lake. It should send him running, but he's strangely compelled to inch closer, dip his hand into the cold waters, see what's really there. Even if it bites him.

"Are you okay?" he asks. It's the wrong thing to say, not the question he meant.

"I'm fine. I'm just thinking." Her voice is light, so light that it seems to detach itself from her and float right over him, revealing nothing of the intricacies of her mind.

"You sure? I mean . . ." He pauses. He has this encroaching feeling that he's upset her somehow, brushed against a nerve without realizing. It normally wouldn't affect him so much; he's used to people being upset with him, or disappointed, or angry. He normally wouldn't pursue the topic with such desperation. "Are you tired?" Again, the wrong question. But he doesn't know how to ask her outright: *Did I say or do something wrong? Could you stop pretending for just a moment, and let me know you as you truly are?*

She blinks those large, liquid-lined eyes up at him. "I'm not tired at all. I slept very well last night."

"Okay," he says, but he still can't shake the sense that he's missing something.

19

CHANEL

The key to any successful viral marketing campaign is that you can't lose momentum.

It doesn't matter if one of your videos went viral once; if you aren't quick to follow it up with something else, people will lose interest. They'll forget why they saved the video in the first place, they'll move on with their lives, their attention will be stolen by another trendy brand or hot influencer with shiny teeth.

The same goes for Ares. I knew I had his attention when we were kissing the other night. I could tell that he desired me, if only for that moment. But it has to last beyond the moment, especially with prom happening in just over a week.

So the morning after I come back from Ares's apartment, I text him:

we still need to decide on a place for math tutoring btw

Half an hour later, he texts back.

We can do it at my place?

A ridiculous, triumphant grin bursts over my face, and I have to take a breath and restrain myself from agreeing too fast. This is exactly what I wanted, what I had hoped for. If Ares and I start hanging out regularly in private at his apartment, I'll be closer to my target than ever.

yeah ok, I text back, after a reasonable amount of time has passed, then stare at our brief text exchange, my stomach already flipping at the thought of seeing him alone again. I never thought I'd be this giddy over the prospect of math tutoring.

Part of me is almost afraid that it's too good to be true, that he'll change his mind and cancel. But he simply sends me his address again and confirms the time. So the following evening, when the light leaks out of the sky and the moon rises over the city, my driver drops me off outside his building.

Before I leave the car, I do a careful evaluation of my reflection using my phone's front camera. Hair is fluffed: check. Lips are glossy: check. No lipstick on teeth: check. No smudged mascara: check. Skirt is rolled up, shirt collar pulled down: check, check.

He's already waiting for me down in the foyer. From the moment I walk in, his gaze sweeps over me, taking me in with the kind of quiet, scorching intensity that makes me feel zipped open, makes my blood burn like lighter fluid.

"Hey," he says. "You ready?"

"Yeah, I'm always ready," I say, in a voice that sounds like it's fighting a bit too hard to be casual. Because none of this feels casual at all. Not when he's leading me inside by the wrist, his thumb brushing over where my pulse point is, and I wonder if he can detect how my heartbeat changes, how all the cells in my body reorient themselves to him. It's only a physical response. A good thing, so I don't have to fake my attraction to him to carry out my plan.

I don't even have to think about pretending when he walks me into the living room. I slip my shoes off and lift my head, expectant, waiting for him to kiss me, for his fingers to find the small of my waist and pull me in—

"Where are your books?" he says.

I blink. "Huh?"

"Your math textbooks." The corner of his mouth twitches. "Why, were you planning on doing something else?"

"No," I say quickly, ducking my head so he can't see the flush spreading across my cheeks. I'm usually good at predicting what guys want, and when, but Ares keeps throwing my rhythm off.

"Let's study over here." He helps spread a freshly printed worksheet out on his kitchen table, slides into the seat next to me, and jumps into the first question without any preamble. To give him credit, Ares isn't a bad math tutor. He's surprisingly patient and to the point, and doesn't overcomplicate concepts. The one time I'd asked Henry Li to help me with math, he'd introduced three entirely new theories and referenced so many obscure mathematicians that I'd ended up more confused than I was in the beginning.

But with Ares, the random numbers and symbols actually start to make sense. He walks me through every step, and works the questions out with me until we've completed half the practice worksheet from our last math class.

"Yes, exactly, like that," he says approvingly when I solve an equation on my own for the first time, and I feel a surprising rush of pride. "Now, try this one. It's trickier, but the basic rules are the same."

I manage to sit through a whole hour of this before I can't concentrate any longer. All I can focus on is the loud, incessant ticking of the clock in the kitchen, a reminder of the time running out. There's been *way* too much productivity tonight, and not nearly enough physical proximity.

"My neck's sore," I grumble, dropping my pen.

Ares casts me a faintly amused look. "You want a break?"

"I think I need one. Like, seriously," I say. "There's a huge knot in my muscles."

"Really?" he says, still with the same amused expression, like he's humoring me.

"You can feel it." I grab his arm and, when he doesn't resist, guide his hand to the base of my neck. "Here."

"Right here?" He presses down, his fingers finding the exact place where my muscles are bunched too tight, and as he starts to massage the spot, the soreness melts into a pleasurable ache.

A sigh slips through my lips, and I find myself leaning almost automatically into his touch. "That feels really good."

"Does it?" His voice is a low murmur, and then he grabs my chin, lifting it up toward him. His gaze is scorching. Pure heat. Radiant and deadly and impossible to resist. "What about this?"

And then he's kissing me, and every rational thought burns away. I rise from my chair, my back against the table, and his hand curls over the corner so it doesn't dig into me when he presses closer. It's perfect. It's so perfect I can't believe this is only the second time it's happened. I'm used to having to teach guys how I want to be kissed, like offering assembly instructions for furniture: *Move this part here, be careful with this, repeat this step.*

But somehow, Ares knows exactly what to do.

Knows to tug my hair a little, just firmly enough to make me gasp against his lips. Knows to push me against the table until there's nowhere else to go, no possible way to be closer, kissing me the entire time with such urgency it knocks the breath out of my lungs.

I don't realize how much control I've surrendered, how eagerly I'm kissing him back, until he pulls away without warning. When I try to close the distance again, he deliberately moves just out of reach, teasing, grinning down at me like the devil himself. "You didn't answer me," he says.

"I—what?" I ask, the words loose as wine on my lips. God, I sound drunk.

His fingers thread back through my hair, holding me there. "Does this feel good to you too?"

I manage to make a vague noise, the most that my pride will allow. "Mmm."

"What's that?" He moves his hands down to my neck, and a violent shiver courses through me, terror inseparable from desire, dread twisted with anticipation. I don't know if I'm scared of the way he's touching me, slow and reverent, or if I'm scared that he'll stop. "I want to hear you say it again."

"I hate you," I mumble, but maybe what I really mean is: *I hate the effect you have on me. I hate that my own body won't listen to me when you're around*. Because I'm still reaching for him, my hands moving over his chest like I'm trying to find an answer, my mouth open and waiting for him to kiss me again.

His eyes gleam. His lips are swollen, his long, crow-black hair still rumpled from where I'd run my fingers through it. "If this is how you act when you hate me," he says, glancing down at my hands on his body, "then I wouldn't mind if you hated me more."

But he stops taunting me and pulls me back to him, and I can't think of anybody I hate more, just like I can't think of anything else I'd rather be doing.

Our study sessions continue over the next few days, each one running longer than the last.

By the time we finish all the practice questions on Wednesday, it's already midnight. My math textbooks have been left lying open on the table, and we've migrated to the couch, where I'm draped over his chest like a blanket. He's writing something on my back with one finger, his touch soporific and so light that it tickles. The living room is warm, peaceful. Through the sheer curtains, I can see the few scattered squares of orange and pale blue light glowing from the other apartments. How many of them are staying up to prepare for a presentation, like my father would, or study for a test, like I'm sure Alice is right this moment? And how many are seeing a bad idea all the way through, like me?

"What are you writing?" I ask him sleepily.

"Guess," he says, drawing out a horizontal line at the base of my spine.

I close my eyes, which were falling shut anyway, and try to focus on the sensation, the strokes of each character. But instead I find myself listening to his breathing and wondering when that became such a familiar sound, like the song of sparrows at dawn or the sound of footsteps outside my bedroom.

"Can't guess," I mumble. "Just tell me."

When he speaks, I can feel the reverberations in his throat. "Then it's a secret."

"You keep a lot of secrets."

"So do you."

I can't deny it, so I stay quiet. Or I try to, but my stomach chooses to interrupt the silence by growling loudly.

Ares laughs. "Are you hungry?"

I'm starving. Have been for the past day, or the past thirteen-something years, if I'm being honest. I would never usually admit it, except I'm already on a horrible streak of making exceptions, and it's as if my brain has lost the ability to think beyond what I would like *right now*, in this very moment. Ares has a strange way of rooting me to the present, when all I should really be thinking about is the future, the vision, the fire. "Yeah. A little," I say.

"I'll cook you something."

"What?" My eyes open again. "Right now?"

"Yeah," he says, sitting up, the front of his tank top creased from the weight of my head.

"But it's way past dinnertime," I say, lifting my legs off his stomach and swaying slightly before I rise to my feet. Despite my half-hearted reasoning, my mouth is already watering at the idea of food. Real, substantial food, not the plain salad I forced myself to choose for lunch. "I didn't even know you could cook."

"Well, don't expect a feast. I'll be quick," he adds. "You can just stay here."

I follow him into the kitchen anyway and lean one shoulder against the fridge, quietly observing him. He works his way around the cabinets with the ease of someone who cooks for himself all the time. He grabs four ripe red tomatoes, a few thin stalks of green onion, sprigs of coriander. Washes them thoroughly and sets them out on the counter. Cracks three eggs into a bowl and whisks those with one hand while he reaches for the salt.

He *is* quick. Soon he has the tomatoes peeled and sliced on the juice-stained cutting board, the water bubbling in a pot, the range hood humming over the stove.

"Okay, turn around," he tells me.

"Why?"

"I have to add the special ingredient, but nobody's allowed to know what it is," he says very seriously.

I gesture to myself. "Not even me?"

"You're the only person I've ever made this for, except myself. So no. Not you," he says.

"You better not poison me," I say dryly, but I cooperate by turning and fixing my eyes on the dozens of magnets on the refrigerator door. There's no pattern or aesthetic to them: a porcelain cat licking its paw, a postcard-worthy miniature painting of the Great Wall, a wooden carving of a bamboo grove. "Where are these from?" I ask him, pointing to the magnets.

"All over the place. Tourist shops. Random malls. Train stations. I was obsessed with collecting them when I was, like, seven." Then, casually, in the same breath: "And just for the record, I'm not going to poison you. Has anyone ever told you that you might have trust issues?"

"I wouldn't have trust issues if people weren't so hard to trust," I say.

From behind me, I can hear the crinkle of plastic as he tears something open, the tap of chopsticks against the edge of the pot when he stirs. If it were anyone else, they'd probably counter this, make a moving little speech about how there's an abundance of good in the world and I should open up my heart and stop being so cynical, but all he says is, "That's fair."

When the egg-and-tomato noodles are ready, he brings the bowls over to the breakfast nook, where a single striped sofa is fitted against the wall.

"Careful, it's hot," he warns, setting my bowl down before sliding onto the sofa next to me. He hands over a pair of chopsticks and motions for me to try it.

I blow on the noodles to cool them, then take a small, tentative bite. Then another. Then another, much more generous bite. Then I give up on trying to look elegant and tie my hair into a ponytail, leaning all the way forward to slurp the noodles straight from the bowl. "Wait, this is really good," I say in surprise. "Like, *really* good." The eggs are perfectly fluffy, the sour kick of the tomato juice balanced by the fresh fragrance of chives and some kind of spice. It's a familiar flavor. I've finished half the bowl when I realize: "Is your special ingredient . . . ramen powder?"

The corner of his mouth ticks up. "Possibly."

I snort. "Okay, I feel like I shouldn't give you too much credit, but this might actually be the best use of ramen powder I've ever tasted."

"You should eat more, then," he says. "You can have some of mine too."

And maybe it's the way he looks in the soft kitchen light—the angles of his face less imposing, his eyes more of a liquid gold than their usual midnight black, his hair mussed and falling over his brows—or the fact that my stomach feels full for the first time in forever, or the drowsiness addling my brain, but I feel a curl of something hot inside my chest. Something adjacent to desire, but heavier, more destructive.

"So what else can you make?" I ask, determined to ignore the feeling.

He shrugs. "Your usual dishes. Pork ribs, wontons, stir-fry, scallion pancakes, braised chicken wings, a bunch of different soups. I learned to cook for my brother, so . . ."

I latch on to this tiny piece of information, the rare glimpse into his family life. You'd think he was born out of a void and has lived alone ever since, looking at his house now: no portraits, no second set of headphones, no traces of his father's existence. The only spare mug in the kitchen is the one I've been using when I come over. "You learned to cook just for your brother?"

I ask, treading carefully, like someone approaching an easily startled bird in the woods.

"He was a super picky eater," Ares says, his gaze distant now, like he's looking through the air into time itself. "It was his only problem; he was the perfect child in every other way. My father hired about twenty different chefs, and none of them lasted longer than a couple months at our house. So I thought I'd try it myself—I searched up tutorials online and experimented with different dishes until I made something my brother liked.

"I remember this one time, I made him Coca-Cola chicken wings, and he ate twelve of them in a single sitting. My father was so happy that night. He was only happy when Luke was happy. It was the first time he ever complimented me."

"He's lucky to have you," I say softly. "You're a good brother."

Something tightens in his expression, and the look on his face makes my throat constrict. The guilt there. The intense self-loathing, so stark and tangible it could have been carved into his features by a honed knife. "No," he says, but he seems more to be talking to himself. "No, I'm really not."

Then, as though becoming fully aware of my attention, that dark, wretched look falls away, a cool mask sliding into place. He clears his throat and shifts back in his seat. "You think you're prepared for the math test tomorrow?"

I let him change the subject. "I don't know. I guess my math mentor has been pretty decent."

"You're pretty decent too," he says.

"In general?"

"At math," he says, then pauses. "In general, you're . . . more than decent."

"Are you flirting with me, Ares?" I ask.

I'd hoped to make him smile, but I'm still surprised by the sheer pleasure and relief that floods through my body when he does. As if a single smile from him could mean that much. "You always think everyone's flirting with you."

I fix him with a coy look. "Well, most of the time, people are." And then, ever so casually, I add, "I mean, I've had ten guys ask me out to prom already." I haven't brought up prom since last week, and I watch him carefully for his reaction, but there is none.

"Oh? And what did you say?"

"I haven't agreed to go with anyone just yet," I tell him.

"I see," he says. That's all. Not even a perfunctory question about who's asked me out.

My heart falls. It doesn't seem wise to press him further tonight—it's late, he's exhausted, he's in a strange mood after bringing up his brother—but I'm gripped by the terrifying possibility that all my efforts so far to change his heart have only endangered mine. And with the night of the blood moon looming, I can't help feeling like I'm walking directly into flames.

20

CHANEL

When I walk into the math classroom, Ares is the first to notice me.

"Good luck," he mouths.

I nod and try to smile like it's no big deal, but the truth is that I can't remember the last time I felt so tense before heading into a test. There were no nerves beforehand, because I knew how I would do: badly.

Now it's different. Now there's a chance that I might *not* do badly, that all the time I threw into this, all those study sessions, might not be for nothing. Basic economics, really. The greater the investment, the more desperate you are for returns. And maybe there's also a part of me that wants to prove to myself—and to Ares—that I can do this.

I slide into my seat, then double-check all my equipment before zipping everything up in the Gucci cosmetic case I've been using as a pencil case. Around me, everyone is arranging their calculators or looking over their notes at the last minute, their pencils and rulers spread out on their desks. A few people swallow audibly when Ms. Hoang starts making her way around the room to pass out the tests.

When she approaches me, she stops and sends me a stern look over the thick blue frames of her glasses. "I hope you do well, Chanel," she says as she hands over the test booklet.

"Thanks," I say, my stomach clenching.

This would be so much easier if I were actually smart. I remember the days before Alice left, when I'd glance over and see her studying on her side of the dorm room, her head down, her pen moving in a blur across the page. She'd earned the title of Study Machine for a reason—in fact, I was certain that even machines couldn't compete with her. I had no idea how she did it. *How do you stay so focused?* I wanted to ask her. *How does your brain manage to work so fast? How do you just always know the answer?*

But I can also imagine Alice's voice inside my head now, full of warmth and conviction. *Remember that you're Chanel Cao. You're iconic. You can do anything.*

I take a deep breath and write my name down carefully in the top corner, with my signature loops around the *C*s and a little heart after the *O*.

Then I flip the test open to the first page.

Our results are released the next day on Airington's school bulletin board. Out of habit, I search for my name at the very bottom, but it's not there. Not in the second or third last row either, and I'm just wondering what the hell I'm meant to do if I actually fail this class when I spot my name in the middle row.

"Oh my god," I whisper.

"*Chanel*," Ms. Hoang calls, making a beeline for me down the corridor. "Oh my goodness, excellent, excellent work on the test. Your improvement is incredible."

"Wait. Are you serious?" I ask, trying not to sound too excited. "There wasn't a mistake with the grading?"

"No, you did wonderfully." She smiles at me. It's the most a teacher has ever smiled my way for reasons actually related to school, and not because I was flattering them.

"Thank you," I say, grinning, unable to believe it. Everything suddenly feels malleable—possible. Changing people's impression of me, changing myself, changing fate. The future. Why not?

"Guess your math mentor was pretty decent after all." Ares's voice floats over from behind me. "Good job."

"Okay, but you can't take *full* credit," I say, turning around.

He offers me the hint of a smile. "No, I definitely can't."

"Are you impressed?"

"I was already impressed by you," he says, and the strange thing is he sounds sincere.

And as I stare at him, smiling, basking in his approval and my own small victory, I think: *I might love you*. The horrifying thought emerges almost as a physical sensation, like a sudden stitch in your side or a muscle cramp. It's the first time this has ever happened, and I try to convince myself it's fine, it's not fatal, it'll just go away if I ignore it—

But over the following days, the thought keeps coming back.

In the leather back seat of the car, the windows rolled down, as Beijing's night scenery rushes by in a blur of dazzling lights and motorbikes. There it is, insistent, terrifying: *But I love him.* At Sephora, when I'm testing out the latest lipstick shades in parallel, shiny strips on my forearm. Shanghai rose, heartbreak mahogany, dark espresso, and—*I love him.* At the gym, determined to run until the burning in my calves sears away any sentimentality in me, but even then, I can't outrun what I'm feeling. At the spa, while a woman with gentle hands cleanses my skin of any impurities and massages my temples slowly, a towel wrapped tight around my torso, sage burning in the corner. "Empty your mind," the woman advises me. "Relax. Breathe in. Let everything go—"

But I love him.

For worse, I love him. And that doesn't change anything. It doesn't even matter what *I* feel. What matters is how *he* feels, whether *he* likes me or not; that's what my entire future is riding on, not fairy-tale fantasies.

I tell myself all of this. Yet—

When he texts me the time and address for his tattoo appointment on Saturday, I catch sight of myself in the mirror, and it's hard to convince even myself that my excitement about spending time with him is solely for strategic reasons. My eyes are wide and aglow, my cheeks flushed as if the summer heat has come in early. I don't look like a master manipulator laying out traps to defeat her enemy. I look like a foolish, hopeful girl about to go on a first date. The kind of girl who gets her heart broken too easily.

If it weren't for the motorcycle, I probably would've missed the tattoo parlor.

Whoever chose the location seems to have done it on a whim—it's smack in the middle of a random narrow street, removed from any malls or offices or subway stations. The only other discernible spots nearby are a store selling nightgowns that would've been considered last-season ten seasons ago, and a wine bar that looks like it might sell its last bottle and die any night now.

Even the entrance to the tattoo parlor is half obscured by the shade of a willow tree. I'm about to walk right past it when I spot the handwritten sign hanging off the neck of the motorbike like a price tag.

Book your tattoo appointment today. Room 2301, second floor.

A cartoonish arrow points toward the glass front door.

"How did you even find this place?" I mutter to Ares as I follow him inside. A steep set of stairs leads us upward, the buzz of tattoo needles growing louder with every step. The air has that strange chlorine smell to it, like what you might breathe in at swimming pools—something chemical and distinct and slightly plastic, tinged with the lingering scent of cigarettes.

"I found the tattoo artist first," Ares explains. "Spent half a year comparing different portfolios and reading reviews from old clients and figuring out the style I was after. There was another artist I wanted—his work is pretty cool and all, and the way he draws the ink is like traditional calligraphy, but he's based in Shanghai."

This, I'm realizing, is the kind of person Ares is. Someone

who'll get a tattoo as soon as he's able to, but thinks it over and puts in the research long beforehand. Someone who does everything for a reason. Someone who cares, underneath his general air of nonchalance.

"Thanks for coming, by the way," Ares adds in an offhand tone, pausing on the top step, his gaze on me. "Not that I needed the company but—it's nice you're here."

Again, that horrible hope, unfurling inside me: *Maybe he's getting attached. Maybe he genuinely likes me. Maybe he won't hurt me after all.* "I'm glad I'm here too," I say lightly as I move past him. "Couldn't miss an opportunity to see you in pain."

His voice trails after me, edged with amusement. "You say such romantic things sometimes."

"Only to you."

"Yeah, that can't be true," he says dryly. "What about all your other guys?"

"What other guys?" I ask, leaving it an open question on purpose. I can't have him thinking I've already lost interest in anybody else—that'll only make him cocky—but he also needs to think he's special.

Everything brightens on the second level. My imagination had been embarrassingly limited to the old mafia movies my father watched; I'd pictured flickering neon lights and small, shadowed rooms and dingy curtains drawn over leather beds. Instead, I'm surprised to find that the tattoo parlor reminds me of the hair or nail salons I usually go to. Modern, spacious, with clean white walls and potted plants settled over the shelves.

The tattoo artist pauses the game on his phone when he sees

us, his eyes widening slightly as they land on me. A flicker of recognition—not uncommon. Maybe, hopefully, he follows me on Instagram, or, the worse scenario, he's read the news articles about my parents. But he's polite enough not to ask about it, just springs up and leads us into a private room. He introduces himself as Zaizai, a strangely endearing name at odds with the tattoos rippling over his muscles and his full beard.

As he prepares his equipment, he grins over at me. "You here to support your boyfriend?"

It's a simple question, but it sends my thoughts spiraling in a hundred different directions, scattering into a hundred different breathtaking possibilities. I can't just say the truth when I don't even know what the reality of us is. *Boyfriend* feels too normal a title—made for couples who can stroll hand in hand through parks and go on coffee dates and kiss without the threat of supernatural visions looming over their heads. Couples who can plan out their futures together without plotting against each other. But *friend* would be wrong; it's too casual, too light, failing to account for the fact that he's bitten bruises into the tender skin on my neck. *Crush* is too flippant and middle school, and *mortal enemy* might be a tad too heavy to drop into everyday conversation.

Everything between us feels hazy and undefined, like the rippling light of the moon on water.

"He doesn't really need my support," I say, glancing over at Ares to assess his reaction. His expression appears very deliberately neutral. "He's got great pain tolerance. I'm just here out of curiosity."

"You have great pain tolerance?" Zaizai asks Ares. "That true?"

Ares shrugs. "Guess we'll find out, won't we?"

Zaizai busies himself applying a layer of Vaseline to the skin under Ares's collarbone, and then sketches out the same tattoo I saw in the vision. "This is what you wanted, yes? Any adjustments you'd like me to make?"

"I can't really see it myself from this angle," Ares says.

"Here, I'll take a photo for you." I grab my phone and snap a few photos in rapid succession, holding it up for him to review. But when I'm done, I don't delete them; instead, I save the photos to set as my lock screen wallpaper for later. Just another little detail to feed the dating rumors at school about me and Ares; proof that I'd been right beside him for a milestone as significant as his first tattoo.

"I don't know," Ares muses, turning to me. "What do you think?"

But I'm distracted by how the sunlight streams through the window and touches his jaw, the look of simple concentration on his face. For a second, he isn't the boy who'll set my future ablaze, but a boy I might've bumped into by chance on the lake banks. Just a boy with long hair and soft lips and quick, steady hands.

"Why are you asking me?" I say.

"Because," he says, "I trust your opinion."

"I'm not, like, a tattoo expert or anything."

Before Ares can reply, Zaizai grins. "Of course your boyfriend's going to care whether or not you think it looks good."

Ares doesn't say anything to confirm or deny it, but as Zaizai cleans the needles, he glances over at me, a private, amused look just between us, smiling with one corner of his mouth, almost shy.

"In that case, yeah. Yeah, it looks good," I say, and think to myself, *Wouldn't it be nice if we weren't destined to ruin each other?*

Briefly, I let myself imagine it: a future that doesn't end in flames.

A future where happiness isn't just possible, but simple.

I show him my favorite Italian restaurant, the one in Chaoyang District, with the sunlit terrace and stunning views of the city and three-star Michelin rating. We order too much food for just us, eager to try everything, and he helps me brush my hair out of my face when I lean forward to eat. Pushes the door open for me on our way out. Holds my purse while I carefully reapply a layer of lip gloss. All of this, without me having to even ask for it.

When my mom's away on another business trip, we spend the evening indoors, the sheets draped over our bodies, my cheek nestled against his chest. His laptop is propped up at the edge of the California King bed, and we pick out a drama from last year, the kind that's so terrible it's good. We take turns making fun of the characters' wardrobe choices and the wildly outdated depictions of China. But I'm only half watching anyways, because I'm gazing at him, tracing out the black lines of the tattoo under his collarbone. A perfect crescent moon. In this future, a moon is just a moon. It doesn't mean pain. So I love that tattoo, just like I love everything about him: the crisp American curl of his accent, the way his dark hair falls over his eyes and he has to push it back when he's in the middle of talking, the way he swears under his breath in seven different languages, the way he walks down the street like he owns it, the rotation of plain black and gray sweaters he wears, the pair of sunglasses he carries around everywhere with him, even when the sun isn't out.

But then the tattoo needle whirs to life, forcing me back to the present, the reality of us. Because he isn't *really* my boyfriend, and I can't let my guard down just yet—not when the blood moon is less than a week away.

21

CHANEL

Once every couple of weeks, my mom will host one of her famous parties, and our house will become *the* local attraction. But this is her first party since the news about the divorce broke, and she's gone all out on the decorations, as if the sheer lavishness might distract guests from the fact that her cheating ex-husband is no longer in the picture. An actual ice sculpture of a swan has been set up by the grand piano, and the legs of each table have been wrapped with a gold-edged bow, the surface decorated with a clear glass vase containing a single lily stem or peach-blossom branch.

If my mom hadn't put so much effort into hosting and absolutely insisted that I stay, I wouldn't be here tonight. With only a few more days before prom, before the fire, I should be spending every waking moment with Ares, trying to make him love me—not wandering around a room filled with C-drama actors and billionaire entrepreneurs and culture-shaping boy-group singers.

I pass by Stella Yao, who first became famous through a

romance drama when she was in her early twenties, and then again through a surprisingly popular variety show featuring once-famous female celebrities over the age of thirty. Her raven hair is pinned up to show off her emerald earrings and ballerina's neck, and she's swirling her champagne around and around in its flute without drinking it while she chats with a younger, lesser-known actress.

"I think it's good for me, at the end of the day," she's saying, in the overly authoritative voice of someone who's trying to convince herself as much as everyone else. Has probably tested this line out loud in front of the mirror before coming here. "I haven't been single since I was fifteen. And so I never figured out who I really was by myself. Now, I have all this freedom—I can do whatever I want, like . . . like—" She pauses, thinking hard, then triumphantly jerks her glass forward so fast that champagne sloshes out of it. "Like *gardening*."

"Oh, yes, gardening," the other actress says. "Gardening is great. Always wanted to get into it."

"Same—and now I can. I have this list of flowers I'm going to start planting—I want roses and daffodils and magnolias. I could plant fruit too! Grow my own little patch of raspberries . . ."

"That's wonderful, Stella," the other actress says, playing her part. "I'm so happy for you. Raspberries! How exciting."

"Yes, at the end of the day, this really is for the best," Stella repeats, as if she's arriving at a startling new conclusion, rather than circling back to an old one. "A blessing in disguise. Everything happens for a reason, as they say."

The actress nods politely and sips more of her champagne until they're joined by a young singer, who's been riding a wave of success all throughout the winter and is clearly there in search of praise—which comes right away.

"Oh my god, Wenwen, I've been listening to your new album and let me tell you, I *cried*," the actress gushes.

"I cried too. No, I sobbed. Your voice is so beautiful," Stella says, the two of them in an open competition to see who can be more gracious and generous and prove themselves totally unbothered by this shiny newcomer.

"I'm just *so* happy for you and all your well-deserved success," the actress continues, not to be outdone.

To these people, happiness is a brand, a status symbol to be paraded around like a Bugatti. Happiness doesn't mean anything unless it's visible to others, proof that they did everything right and that they're better than everyone.

It's exhausting. And strangely, it makes me miss Ares. How honest he is, how *real* he is, in a way that none of the people here seem to be. If I were with him right now, I wouldn't have to pretend, wouldn't have to fill awkward conversations with fake niceties and listen to conversations that aren't interesting or laugh at jokes that aren't funny. I could simply be a girl, not Chanel Cao.

As the party wears on, bite-sized dishes come out in gleaming trays, carried by pretty waitresses in tailored qipaos. There's golden scrambled tofu laid out on delicate lotus flowers; taro pieces dipped in melted sugar and stretched into the shape of hearts; yolk-stuffed buns and flaking nut-filled pastries decorated to resemble swans, with sesame seeds for eyes and custard swirls for wings; glazed sea bass and tender lobster bites laced with saffron and bright, edible flowers.

And beside each plate and platter is a silver strip of paper, containing a line from an ancient Chinese poem—something about peach blossoms and the fleeting seasons and an isolated mountain hut.

Little gasps and appreciative murmurs sweep across the room, and even from here, I can make out the gleam of satisfaction in my mom's eyes. This is her goal, to throw a party deemed luxurious by those already accustomed to luxury. To impress the most impressive. To be seen as living a lucky life, which is more important to her than whether or not her life is something she actually likes.

I flit between cliques and tables, a glass of apple cider in my hand, making meaningless chatter about how school's going and the restaurants in Paris I'd recommend and how fun Krystal Lam's concert in Shanghai was and did you hear about this new eyeshadow palette? I'm impressed by my own acting skills, how perfectly put-together I look. The girl reflected in the black marble is smiling wide, like this party was thrown just for her, her red lips matching her red-bottom heels.

". . . can't believe it's been three years already! I still remember you as a little kid—but you're basically a woman now." The middle-aged man smiling down at me must be the fiftieth or sixtieth person I've spoken to tonight. Stout and balding, he's wearing an outfit that's utterly uninteresting, except for the diamond belt fastened around his middle. Every time he shifts position, the precious gems sparkle, their light dancing off the marble pillars. *Tuhao*, my mom would call him behind his back—a term for those with an astounding amount of money and a shocking lack of taste. My mom's worst nightmare is getting lumped into that category.

"Yes, well," I say as enthusiastically as possible. Though his name escapes me, this tuhao is the business director for one of my mom's sponsors. It's important that I leave a good impression.

"You must be very strong," he goes on.

"Sorry?"

"What happened with your mother . . ." He clucks his tongue. "A shame, a shame."

"We're doing just fine," I assure him, and breathe an inward sigh of relief when he's called away by someone who looks like they could be his brother or boss or possibly both.

I go to find my mom in the crowd, hoping for permission to retire early from the party and find Ares, but she's busy speaking to someone else. Someone familiar, but not from a red carpet or TV show. Blood roars in my ears.

It's him.

The scar on his cheek. The gelled hair.

Long Ge is here.

"Oh, this is my daughter, Chanel," my mom says, beckoning me closer. This should be my cue to say "Shushu hao" in my sweetest voice and smile, but all I can do is stare at the man in horror, my heart thudding so fast I feel sick.

The man turns slowly toward me. "Chanel, is it? Pleasure to meet you."

There's no malice in his expression, yet my gut won't stop churning. In my head, I see the paparazzi photos of my mom tucked into a drawer, the unsent love letters, the proof of his obsession. I want to recoil. Scream at him to get away. "Nice to meet you," I manage.

"This is my friend Long Ge," my mom introduces. "Or, well—I should call you Long Zong now."

He waves his hand, looking exceptionally pleased. "Oh, please, don't embarrass me. Just Long Ge is fine."

"You're being far too humble," my mom insists. "Long Zong here is the CEO of *multiple* highly successful corporations, including this exciting new media advertising agency he was just telling me about."

"Yes, well, as I was saying, you would be the perfect fit," Long Ge says, and the bad feeling in my stomach solidifies. "We've recently signed a few models, but just between us, none of them have quite the reach and influence you do."

My mom laughs. "Okay, now you're the one embarrassing me."

"I'm being serious. And you know we'd work well together—"

"Mom," I can't help interrupting. "Mom, I need to talk to you about . . ." I try to think of a good excuse, but my thoughts are all jumbled, falling apart on the spot. "My wardrobe. I think I lost one of my dresses. The really pretty pink one I bought last weekend."

Without moving a single facial muscle that could cause a premature wrinkle, my mom shoots me a look that screams *Can't you see I'm talking to someone important?*

I act like I don't see it. "If you could just help me for a second—"

"*Later*, Chanel," she says through gritted teeth. "Sorry about that," she adds to Long Ge, her voice pleasant. "As we were saying . . ."

"I'll have my assistant send you the details of the contract tonight, if you're interested," Long Ge tells her.

"That would be fabulous—"

"Mom," I try again, the panic closing in around me like a physical force, as if the air has turned solid. "Seriously, I really need to talk—"

She ignores me. "I'll have my team look over it."

"If you have any questions, we could always discuss it in greater depth over dinner," Long Ge says, extending a hand, and all I can see is him in the vision, the flames licking the sky.

My mom reaches out to shake it, but I grab her arm. Pull her back.

"Oh my god, Mom, please," I whisper. "Stop talking to him. You don't know what he wants."

She whips toward me, her eyes wide with incredulity. "What is going on with you?" she hisses under her breath. "You're acting very rude, Chanel. He's an old classmate of mine, and he's been extremely sympathetic and supportive after hearing the news—"

"He's dangerous," I blurt out. "He . . . he's *obsessed* with you."

My words are met with a terrible silence.

In the background, conversations are still flowing, more wine poured into fancy glasses, the appetizers being passed from tray to tray: crystal bowls of sweetened red bean congee and platters of iced fruits—peeled longans from Guangxi, sliced dragon fruit from Hainan, glistening purple grapes from Australia.

But the silence seems to spread and congeal, until the whole room feels suspended in motion, amplifying the loud, ragged beat of my heart. Long Ge's expression appears frozen in a mask of polite confusion, but something dark shifts in his eyes as he appraises me. A look so chilling that I actually stumble back a step, my fingers trembling so hard I drop the phone in my hand.

It falls with a loud clatter to the hardwood floor, and before I can move, Long Ge bends down calmly to pick it up.

"Here you go," he says, his voice still perfectly amiable. But as he starts handing my phone over, he glances at the lock screen, the photo of Ares glowing over it. It's the photo I'd taken of him at the tattoo parlor, zoomed in to his collarbones and the arm he has propped up on one knee, the ring glinting on his thumb. For a second, recognition flickers over Long Ge's face.

I think back to the dragon symbol carved into the office door at the fight club. Is Long Ge the reason why Ares has been fighting there the whole time? And just how well does Long Ge know Ares?

"What are you talking about?" my mom demands. "You've never even met Long Zong before."

"No," I say. Shake my head, frustration choking off the very air in my lungs. I don't have enough time to explain, can't find the right words to. "I mean . . . please, you have to trust me—"

"I think your daughter has confused me with someone else," Long Ge says gently. "We certainly have not met before. I understand, I have one of those faces, you know. Happens all the time." He lets out a generous laugh, and my mom joins in, though the sound is strained.

I stare between them. Suddenly I can see this moment playing out like I'm a bystander: Long Ge, the successful, dignified businessman, a trusted old classmate, with his pressed suit and expensive watch and cheerful, patient manner. And me, the spoiled daughter, volatile, impulsive, impossible to reason with. Two adults in a world of their own, while I'm just a kid throwing a tantrum. I can't convince my mom to steer clear of him, not without evidence, and I can't provide any evidence without telling her about the vision—and why would she believe me?

It feels like the ground is turning to quicksand beneath my feet. Desperate, I twist around before I can sink completely to the bottom. My heels click against the marble, my hair flowing behind me, my breathing tight and shallow and too loud in my ears. I walk so fast I almost crash into one of the waitresses, who tries to offer me congee.

Behind me, I hear my mom's voice over the crowd, sweet and apologetic: "I'm *so* sorry about her. I have no idea what that was—"

"No, I get it. Teenagers—they can be very emotional, can't they?"

"I don't remember us being quite so dramatic when we were younger."

"Ah, who knows what the new generation is thinking, hmm? Though you're still very young. If I hadn't known you all those years ago, I would've confused you for a teenager."

"Please, you flatter me."

Their laughter chases me all the way out the door.

22

ARES

As Ares inches forward in the bakery line, he mentally lists out all the reasons why he should not fall for Chanel Cao.

One: She can be incredibly vain. Although he supposes that any girl who looked like her and had hundreds of dedicated fan accounts *would* be at least a little vain. And can he really blame her for often staring at her own reflection, when even he finds it hard to stop staring at her sometimes? But never mind that.

Two: She takes over an hour to get ready before heading out anywhere. Kind of tied in to point one, but he could see this seriously impacting their schedule if they were ever to start dating, not that he's imagined dating her or anything like that.

"Next in line, please."

As the customer in front of him finishes scanning the WeChat pay code on his phone, he takes another half step forward, eyeing the glass displays around him. The pastries have been carefully laid out on shelves and lit up so you can see the shine of sugar, neat white plaques printed beneath them like they're priceless works of art in a museum.

He doesn't usually stop by Holiland, but he's seen the photos trending across the internet: the futuristic setup, the soft swirls of fresh-baked bread tucked in paper bags, the pastel pink walls and pastel pink trays and pastel pink uniforms. The bakery is even brighter in real life, and though he's personally indifferent to this kind of aesthetic, he can imagine Chanel loving it here.

But back to his list.

Three: She's too good at dodging questions. He has to press to get an answer, and even then, he can never tell if she's saying something because she means it, or because she knows it's what he wants to hear.

Four: She's also too good at kissing. So good it feels like he's losing his mind whenever her lips brush his. That could be a dangerous weapon, if she ever decided to use it against him.

Five: She loses things easily. In the time he's known her, he's already witnessed her misplace her phone, forget her keys, forget her purse *containing* her keys, search around for a claw clip that was in her hair minutes before and somehow vanished into thin air, and drop two different rings and a ruby earring that could probably cover someone's rent for six months. He finds himself fighting the constant, irritating urge to remind her to check that she has everything, or to simply carry her purse for her.

Six: She seems determined to remain unknowable.

Yet he's addicted to the process of trying to know her anyway, to decoding her words, remembering her little habits—or maybe he's simply addicted to her. Even if they must exist in separate galaxies, every detail he picks up on feels like taking one small step closer to her planet, and the closer he is, the more beautiful she looks. He likes knowing the way she draws her hair back over her shoulder to spray her signature scent—Chanel No. 5, which she's been using religiously ever since she received a bottle of it for her fourteenth birthday—or that she secretly hates when people call her by her Chinese name, or that she only becomes irritable when she's feeling guilty, which is usually connected to how much she ate for lunch, even though she's never eating enough.

"Next."

He can feel the bakery worker's curious gaze on him, taking in his new tattoo—still raw red around the edges—and piercings and dark jeans, entirely at odds with all the surrounding pink. Or maybe it's more wariness than curiosity; every time he walks into a store, people act like they expect him to try and rob the place. "I'll just have that," he says, pointing at the lychee cream cake behind the counter.

The girl relaxes slightly and spins around to slide the glass panel open. "Is it for your girlfriend?"

He makes a noncommittal sound, though he can't stop thinking about it. Getting to call Chanel Cao his girlfriend. *His.* He hates how much he likes the idea of it.

"Thanks," he says. His mind manages to assemble three more reasons—*never cleans out her camera roll, can't pass a stray dog in the street without trying to feed it or adopt it, perfume is so strong that you keep smelling it hours after she's gone*—before he pays for the cake, holding the pastel box carefully in both hands.

His phone buzzes as he heads out the door, and he tries to balance the cake while he picks up. "Hello?"

"Are you free right now?" It's Chanel's voice, but she doesn't quite sound like herself. She sounds scared. Shaken.

"What's wrong?" he asks immediately. "Are you hurt? Did something happen to you?"

"I . . . I'm fine."

She's such a liar. "Where are you? I'll find you right now," he tells her.

A pause, and he hears the faint rush of water in the background before she replies, "I'm at the lake."

"Okay. Wait there."

The most important reason he should not fall for Chanel Cao: She's the only other person who's seen the vision, the root of all his hopes for the future, but he's increasingly starting to suspect that she doesn't want the vision to happen. Which should, by all accounts, make her his enemy.

Yet he runs to her anyway.

23

CHANEL

I don't expect Ares to find me so fast.

But within ten minutes of hanging up, he's here, panting, eyes wild and worried. He crosses the grass in three long strides. The air between us tightens into nothing, our breaths intermingling like ghosts in the darkness. "Are you okay?"

"I saw him," I say. This was the decision I'd reached as I left the party; I know it's risky, telling Ares about it, but I can't bear not knowing. I'll offer up the information I have in return for the information he has. It'll even the playing field between us, and then—and then it'll simply be a matter of who can be smarter, crueler, faster. "The man in the vision. Long Ge."

Ares stares at me. "How do you know who he is?"

"You tell me first," I say. "How much do you already know about him?"

He hesitates, and I can see him making the same silent calculations. How much to say, how much to withhold, how much we can give each other.

Sometimes I feel closer to Ares Yin than I've ever felt with anyone in my whole life—closer than I thought two people could possibly be. Times when he's as intimate and essential as the air in my lungs, the very blood in my veins.

Then there are times, like now, when he's as distant and cold as the moon. Even when he's right in front of me, there's this impenetrable look in his eyes, an entire universe between us, filled with every question I'm too scared to ask. I want to shake him, force him to really *look* at me, tell me what he's thinking.

Or better yet, I want to crawl inside his brain and rifle through it like a thief in a mansion, ripping through the closets and turning over the drawers, desperate to find something of value. And it's startling how I know the exact half-stifled sound he makes when we're kissing and he loses control, how I've memorized the contours of his chest, all the softest and hardest places on his body, but I couldn't begin to guess what he'll do next.

"The fight club I was in . . . ," Ares says haltingly. "He's the one who founded it. He commands a lot of respect and power there. But from what I've gathered, it's not just the fight club that he owns. He moves between circles, gets up to a bunch of shady stuff."

"Right," I say, a little dizzy, trying to piece everything together. Reminds me of when I'd sit through entire lectures at school, not understanding a single word the teachers had said, until the night before the exam, when Alice would patiently explain the fundamental concepts to me, and things would only start making sense in hindsight. Like why Ares had been tracking Long Ge down at the nightclub. I'd initially feared they might be accomplices, but it doesn't sound like Ares has even spoken to the man before. "Right, okay."

"Where did you see him?" Ares asks. Then, more urgently: "Did he hurt you?"

I shake my head. "No, but . . . he was at my mom's party tonight."

Surprise flashes over his face. "At her party? Why?"

"They've been talking. He reached out to her after hearing about the divorce, but they used to be high school classmates. Friends. I think . . ." I swallow. My throat feels constricted, like I can't inhale fully. "No, I *know*. He's obsessed with my mom. At the party just now . . . he was trying to convince my mom to sign with this new media agency of his or whatever, but I feel like that's all just a ruse to get closer to her." I watch Ares's face intently as I speak, searching for the version of him I'd seen in the lake, the one holding the lighter as my house burned with my mom inside it.

But he only looks confused, if not concerned, his dark brows furrowed. "Did you warn your mom about him?"

Like he actually cares about my mom's safety. And maybe he really does in the present moment. So what will happen between now and then to change that? "I tried to warn my mom," I say. "But I can't get through to her. She won't take me seriously."

"Did Long Ge do anything else? Say anything?"

"I left the party early, so I'm not sure. I didn't think he'd do anything terrible while there were so many people around. Not for tonight, at least."

"No, you're right. He's more careful than that," Ares says. "Or else he wouldn't have made it this far." He releases a low breath. "Look, whatever, we can figure that shit out later—I'm just glad you're safe."

I glance up at him, and it's only then that I register the pastel pink box in his hands.

"What is that?"

His fingers shift over it, like he has half a mind to hide the whole box behind his back and pretend it doesn't exist. He licks his lips but doesn't speak. If I didn't know better, I'd think he was nervous.

"Well?" I prompt, when the silence stretches on long enough that I wonder if his plan is actually just to wait for me to get distracted and forget my own question.

"It's . . . a birthday cake," he says at last, as if he's confessing a grave sin.

"A birthday cake?" I repeat. "Whose birthday is it?"

"Nobody's."

"So are we just celebrating random days now? I don't have anything against the idea, by the way—I'm as much a fan of nonevents as I am of events."

"No. Or . . . yes, yours. It's for you," he tells me, setting the box down on one of the tables the old Beijing uncles like to use for their chess games, the surface marked with lines for weiqi pieces. He tugs the ribbon free, then pushes the pink flaps of the cardboard to the side, revealing the cake within.

My eyes widen.

All of a sudden I'm back in Paris, staring longingly at the

birthday cake on display before me. It could be the exact same cake, transported through time and space. Everything about it is how I remember: the shiny lychees glistening like gems atop the thick white cream, the delicate strawberry-pink swirls, the chocolate icing spelling out my full name, all the details illuminated by the soft orange glow of the lamppost.

But instead of near-strangers crowding around me in a foreign room, singing "Happy Birthday" like a hired chorus, the rapid-fire clicks of cameras sounding in the background, there's only the whisper of the wind through the grass, and Ares. Ares, who's watching me intently, waiting for my reaction.

"You got this for me," I say slowly. "Why?"

I can see him weighing his response. "That story you told me, about your thirteenth birthday party. I couldn't stop thinking about it." The pulse of his throat as he swallows. "You."

And there it is again, louder than ever, the awful truth slamming up against my better judgment: *But I love him.*

I love him and it's killing me.

For now, though, we have cake. I rip into the packet of disposable spoons and he prepares the flimsy paper plates and I cut the cake into eight wobbly slices just for the two of us. I lick the frosting off the knife and I taste the sweetness of the icing instead of guilt and regret. The breeze rises, sending the edges of the plates fluttering madly like butterfly wings and blowing my hair across my face. It's everywhere, sticking to my lip gloss and my lashes.

Then Ares reaches over and carefully bunches my hair in his fingers, brushing the stray wisps away from my cheeks and holding it back for me at the nape of my neck. "Is that better?"

"Much better," I say. "Thank you." I don't even know if I'm referring to the cake or the makeshift ponytail or him coming here to meet me tonight or just him, the existence of him, despite the consequences of him. The words feel useless, insignificant anyway, when really what I want to say is, *It's never been like this with anyone before* and *It's not fair of you to keep offering me tenderness when I know it'll be taken away.*

He looks over at my plate. "Do you like the lychees?"

When I nod, he picks all the lychees off his slice and adds them to mine. And I recall the stories my mom would tell me of the Four Beauties of ancient China. Her favorite has always been the legend of Xishi, the concubine spy sent off to an enemy kingdom to destroy it, this grand, twisting, epic tale of court intrigue and betrayal that ends with Xishi sailing across Taihu with her one true love.

But the one I remembered most vividly was Yang Guifei, the emperor's beloved consort. She'd adored lychees, but they were only grown in the south. The emperor was so obsessed with her, so determined to please her, that he had his couriers ride out on their fastest horses for thousands of miles to bring the fresh fruit back to the palace. A journey across a whole kingdom, just for a taste.

I'd thought that kind of fierce devotion was only the stuff of myth, exaggerated with each retelling over the centuries, a fantasy fed to hopeless romantics. And yet . . .

I pop one of the lychees into my mouth, relishing the cool,

sweet burst of it when I bite down. I can't explain how nice it is, not having to scrape off the buttercream or ration my bites.

Something warm unfurls in my chest, so potent it almost hurts, like brushing your fingers along the edge of a wound. There's the moonlight splashing across the grass, and the stars glistening like sugar above his head, and the scent of spring's first flowers sweetening the cool, dark air.

"Did you hear? The lunar eclipse is happening in four days," Ares says, staring up at the moon.

I stiffen. The blood moon. Prom. The vision. The night where everything is destined to change. I can't afford to wait any longer, and now seems like the best possible time. Between the cake, and the way he'd rushed over to find me tonight . . . despite myself, I feel an excruciating surge of hope. Even if he hasn't brought it up himself, it no longer seems so impossible that he could care about me, care enough to agree to go to prom with me.

"Ares," I begin. *Just say it. Just ask him. Doesn't matter that you've never had to ask a guy out before; now's not the time to worry about embarrassment or prom etiquette.* All the chess pieces have been set on the board already—Ares, his brother, Long Ge— and the next few moves are critical. I'll beg Ares if I have to. Anything to keep my mom safe and alive.

"Yeah?" His tone is so soft, so gentle, it gives me the courage to keep going.

I set my fork down and take a deep breath. "Will you . . . will you go to prom with me?" My own voice shocks me with its softness. Not a weapon at all. No more tricks, no games, but a hand outstretched, praying for peace, my sleeves rolled up to reveal bare wrists, the veins leading up to my heart. *Please.*

Please, please, please.

Please say yes.

Please don't hurt me.

His eyes widen a fraction in surprise. "Chanel," he says, still softly, but the softness feels like a slow death, a sweet poison. Like he almost pities me for what he's about to say next, which makes everything so much worse. "I want to. Believe me, I really, really want to."

"Then why can't you?" I whisper, hating how my lips tremble over the words, how the pain is pressing in. How stupid I feel.

"There's something I have to do that night," he says, shaking his head slowly. "Something more valuable to me than my own life. I promise, if it weren't for that—I'd go to prom with you. I'd go in a heartbeat."

"That simply means you don't want to go to prom with me enough," I say, but we both know what I actually mean, what I can't bring myself to say out loud. *You don't want me enough.* The truce between us cracks, and the sudden change sends a wave of cold washing over my stomach. How quickly we can go from sitting side by side, sharing cake and speaking of childhood memories, to standing like soldiers on enemy lines, staring each other down. How quickly intimacy can vanish.

My mom was right to warn me against love. All love really does is give someone the power to hurt you.

"It's not that simple," he tells me, his jaw taut, his eyes inscrutably dark.

"It *is* that simple."

"There are too many things out of my control. I can't . . . I'll explain everything to you later—"

"So you're rejecting me?" I cut in. "You're not going to prom with me? That's your final answer?"

A moment of silence trickles between us like moonlight.

And in it, I can hear the ending notes of a melody, an old memory of the first time I had my ears pierced, the woman speaking to me seconds before she stepped forward with the needle, gentle but matter-of-fact. *This is going to hurt.*

I know it's going to hurt, but I still can't help hoping that he'll prove me wrong. That maybe I can change his mind. That's what I've been doing this entire time: not trying to change the future, but trying to change *him*. Making the same mistake thousands upon thousands of girls have made in the past, thinking everything would be different if only I could make him like me more.

I should've known how this would go. Should've known it was doomed from the start.

"Chanel," he says quietly, "I would give you almost anything you asked for. I'd wait in line outside the bakery every morning to buy you the lychee cake you like, whether it's your birthday or not. I'd fly to the other end of the world with you if you simply wanted a change of weather. I'd gladly be your chauffeur, your bodyguard, your confidant, your private chef, your personal photographer, your tour guide in any city. I'd plant an entire field of your favorite pink lilies and pluck the brightest ones to deliver to your door. I could build a tower in the middle of the ocean just to give you a better view of the sunset. I could claw the stars from the sky for you. I could give you the moon. Anything," he whispers, "but this."

I should've known how this would go, but the actual blow still knocks the breath out of my lungs. I've failed. After everything I've done, all my scheming, all the ways I tried to contort myself into something he wanted, all that I offered, I still haven't escaped the age-old curse: *He just doesn't love you enough.*

I clench my teeth and let my hand drop, the heat of his skin gone completely. Now there's only the cold and the ink-black waters and the distance between us.

Strange, how a few inches can feel like infinity, the turn of an era.

I wait until my voice hardens enough for me to speak. "Okay." This time, it comes out exactly how I want it to. Curt, sharp, removed. "Then I should probably go."

Something ripples across his face, fleeting as a sparrow's shadow over the surface of a lake, there and then gone. But he doesn't ask me to stay.

24

ARES

Ares wishes someone would just punch him already.

He can feel the compulsion crawling along his skin like an itch, the desire to be hurt, to be hurt so badly he can stop thinking. Forget the wounded, betrayed look on Chanel's face at the lake tonight, how she'd walked away without glancing back at him. She's always been so composed, every word and action calculated, laughing as if nothing in the world could ever affect her. But he'd seen her composure slip. Heard the shakiness in her voice.

Will you go to prom with me?

You're rejecting me?

Why can't you?

The bell rings, the crowds of the fight club come alive with bloodlust, stamping their feet, and Ares pushes his way forward into the ring, relieved that it's finally happening.

The tension in the air is palpable as he takes his place before a man his father's age. In his peripheral vision, he can make out the faces of his spectators from the shadows. Suspicion. Distrust. Outright disdain. After Chanel had showed up the other night, he'd sworn to them that he hadn't known she would be coming, that she was merely a classmate who must've tailed him out of curiosity, that it would never happen again. Despite his insistence, he'd worried that because he'd let her run away, the Cave wouldn't let him back in. But then Sangui had informed him of the final match happening tonight, with the same instructions as usual.

Make sure you win.

If he wins this round, he'll be the final victor. He'll get to meet Long Ge at last, get to save his brother. *That's* the part he has to focus on now, not the shine of tears in Chanel's eyes when he'd turned her down—

His opponent rushes him, fists swinging.

The first punch lands just as Ares had hoped it would. An astounding burst of pain to his temple, so violent his vision flashes white. He staggers back, panting, metallic taste of blood in his mouth. Rights himself.

The man is surprisingly fast and nimble on his feet for someone so much older. Ares had heard that he was released from prison not long ago. Sentenced for murder. He believes it. The man looks like he's spent the past decade pacing by himself, imprisoned in his own mind, the life leaking out of him like watercolor until all that's left is the feral, bloodshot red of his eyes, the sickly yellowish tint of his skin and teeth.

Ares tries to take charge by feinting left—and it works, at first. He gets in three rapid jabs to the man's stomach before his hands claw into Ares's shoulders, forcing him back again. In most matches, there's usually some kind of unspoken etiquette about avoiding the face, but he strikes Ares hard across the cheek, an obliterating, searing sensation, the sheer pressure and force of it more shocking than the pain itself. Ares feels his head swim, his legs swaying beneath him.

He can no longer tell if the dampness on his neck is from sweat or his own blood.

"The kid's definitely losing," someone remarks behind him.

Another voice agrees. "Yeah, just look at him."

If he looks anything like he feels, then Ares can understand why they'd think so. He's struggling to stay standing, to keep breathing in and out. His body seems sluggish, like a foreign object controlled only by a remote with a bad connection, every command registered a beat too slow. Then, a new source of pain.

Sharp, too sharp. Wrong and unfamiliar, cutting open his side, right under his rib cage.

Disoriented, Ares glances down just in time to see the silver flash of a pocketknife as it retracts from his wound, shining red.

Even seeing it, he feels numb with disbelief, a refusal to accept that this is something that has happened to him, to his body, that he must now deal with the consequences of it. A pocketknife, in the middle of a boxing match. But outside weapons aren't allowed.

He waits for someone to stop the fight. They must have noticed the knife, or at least the cut. The blood is spreading fast through his shirt, and he reaches uselessly for it, his hand pressing down over his torn flesh.

But the crowd only watches.

The floor flips upside down, and he feels the cool cement on his cheek. Has he fallen? He's lost his sense of direction; everything's blurry. When he squints up at the lights, he sees his opponent approaching, the knife gleaming in his hand, his shadow falling over him. It shouldn't be allowed, surely, by now, someone will speak up—

They're letting it happen, he realizes dimly, his heartbeat pounding in his ears. This is his punishment for the other night, for letting Chanel escape. He'd violated the second rule: He'd fought the men outside the ring. They don't trust him anymore, and they're certainly not going to do anything to help him.

He could die here.

Like this. Alone, bleeding, curled up against himself like an injured animal.

And as soon as he becomes aware of this, he thinks, unwillingly, of Chanel Cao again. If he dies, the last time he ever saw her would be at the lake tonight. The last words he'd ever spoken to her would be to disappoint her—

He struggles to rise, fingers scrabbling at the cement. His body feels like it's made of lead, something he has to carry rather than something he owns. He lifts his head inch by agonizing inch, eyes watering from the effort. He's barely managed to shift his knee forward when the man kicks his stomach so hard he gasps, his muscles seizing.

Bright, blunt pain.

He falls back down as the crowds roar in delight. The noise encases him like a cage, amplifying every shout of glee, every barked laugh. It seems almost impossible, like this level of cruelty defies the governing laws of the universe.

A boot grinds down over his arm, pinning him there. He wants to scream, to run, to fight back, but he can't find the strength to even open his eyes properly to look at the man who's going to kill him. Fuck, someone's actually going to *kill* him—

"Wait." Sangui's voice rings through the noise with enough urgency that everyone goes quiet. "Stop right now."

Is he taking pity on me? Ares thinks in disbelief. *Does he actually care enough to save me?*

Then, as if from a great distance, he hears Sangui say, "Long Ge wants to see him."

25

CHANEL

The worst thing about heartbreak is how spectacularly predictable it is.

You know exactly what's coming. You know, and yet you're powerless to stop it, a bystander in your own disaster, frozen to the spot as the train tears off its tracks, as the avalanche crushes everything in its path, as the meteor falls and sets the city ablaze. Every piece of advice I've ever given to my friends comes back around to point and laugh in my face. "If he's not willing to do this for you," I recall a younger and wiser version of myself saying, my heart carefully tucked away, "he isn't worth it. Don't cry over him. Don't bother texting him. There's no point getting upset."

As if it's that easy, that logical.

I do cry over him.

It feels like I'm grieving, but the person is dead to me by his own volition, and somehow that's worse. When I drag myself out of bed the next morning, the tears spill faster than I can reapply my mascara.

I give up after the fourth try, wiping angrily at the black clumps on my lower lashes until they're smudged across my cheeks, my eyes rimmed red, my lips chapped and trembling. I look like every girl who's ever secretly envisioned a life with a guy she has no future with. I've become a walking, sobbing cliché, a perfect case study about the risks of falling in love.

Yet, for all its predictability, heartbreak is also so isolating. So contradictory. I'm simultaneously aware that everyone has gone through something like this and stubbornly convinced that nobody on earth has ever suffered this way before. I'm not interested in talking about anything except him, but I also don't want to tell anybody about him. Don't want to share him, even after everything.

I grant myself exactly one day to mope in private. That already feels overly self-indulgent, considering that the lunar eclipse is in three days.

Then I get to business. I make a booking for my mom's favorite resort in Sanya, the one with the goat enclosure and the underwater restaurant. I choose the flight that leaves on the night of the vision, calculating it so that she'll need to head off to the airport before it gets dark.

I start collecting my belongings. Putting childhood photos and precious gifts in boxes, to be stored somewhere else until I can be sure the house is safe.

I log into my mom's email account while she's showering and track her latest correspondence with Long Ge. He's already sent her the documents and the agency pitch deck, but she hasn't signed anything just yet.

And if I catch myself wondering about Ares from time to time—

Well, I tried it, I think to myself, with a mental slap on the wrist. I'd been frank and disgustingly earnest, offered up a small piece of my heart—and look what happened. Exactly what I knew would happen. Now there's no getting that piece of my heart back ever, no refund or replacement for damaged goods, and I can be certain that I'm never putting myself through it again.

Back to games and tricks and lying through my teeth.

26

ARES

The receptionist doesn't even try to welcome him when he limps into the office.

Fair enough. He knows he doesn't belong here. He's too young, his hair is too long, his skin too tattooed and bruised. Meanwhile, the receptionist looks like a walking résumé, with her no-nonsense bun and Yale-issued tote bag and the shiny company badge pinned to the front of her wrinkle-free button-down shirt.

"Could I please see Long Ge?" he asks.

She makes a sound that he's pretty sure is a scoff, though she's professional enough to keep it quiet. "Do you have an appointment with him?"

"Yes, I do, actually," he says.

She regards him with open skepticism. He doesn't blame her. He can barely believe he's here. All his searching, all the fighting, just for a chance to track Long Ge down—only to be invited over by the man himself.

"He's in a meeting right now, but I'll let him know you've arrived." The receptionist nods to the seats by the water cooler. "Feel free to wait there."

He does, though the seats are horribly uncomfortable, shaped in a way that sends a judder of pain through the roughly stitched cut in his side. Not like he'd be able to get comfortable anyway.

Despite being owned by the same person, everything about this place is the opposite of the Cave—neat, orderly, sterile. Safe. His eyes pass over the complimentary tea bags offered at the entrance, the two pots of mandarin trees with shiny red packets hanging from the branches for good fortune. One of the office walls is made entirely of glass, so that when the sun sweeps in through the windows, it floods the entire level, burnishing all the glass panes and glossy posters promoting this year's annual gala dinner.

It's exactly what he expected after scrolling through images on the company website at three in the morning to verify if the company truly did belong to Long Ge. He hadn't stopped until he'd come across Long Ge's photo in the About Us section.

He waits a whole hour before the man appears. A faint rustling accompanies his movements as he walks through the headquarters—people standing up behind their desks, stopping halfway in the corridor, setting down their papers.

"Morning, sir."

"Would you like some tea, sir?"

"Sir, we just need you to sign. . . ."

Long Ge stops before Ares. He looks like a harmless, ordinary middle-aged man, except for that scar on his cheek, and the sharp, inquisitive look in his eyes, behind the thick glasses. "Oh, good. You're here." He extends a hand. "I'm Long Ge. Nice to meet you in person."

Ares stands up, feeling wrong-footed, somehow. Cautiously, he takes the man's hand and shakes it once. It's all too civil and normal, these polite greetings and handshakes. But what can he do? Lunge across the space, scream at him, "Give me my brother back!" while around them white-collar workers fill out tax forms and make phone calls about preparations for the gala? "Yes, hi, I know," he says, trying to match the man's businesslike tone.

Long Ge smiles. "Follow me."

He leads Ares into his office, an impressive space that leaves no room to question Long Ge's position in the company. The city unfolds beyond the floor-to-ceiling windows, the skyscrapers peeking out over the autumn-brushed trees. Ares can see the CCTV tower from here, the seemingly gravity-defying glass structure shaped like a giant pair of pants, all the cars racing each other around the ring roads. Beijing moves at such a restless, breathless pace, forever marching doggedly on and on into the future; you either try to keep up with it, or you get left behind.

"I've heard a few interesting things about you," Long Ge says, sitting back in the white swivel chair. He gestures for Ares to do the same across the desk. Ares notices his own chair is much shorter. Either the person who'd sat here before him has uncommonly short legs, or it's a power thing.

"You have?" Ares says.

"Caused a bit of a commotion at the Cave the other week,

didn't you? But a good fighter, Sangui tells me. Many of my men were betting on you to go all the way."

Disoriented, Ares finds himself unable to muster a response. Like his brain has forgotten the conventions of the English language, grammar abandoned, logic gone. "I . . . It wasn't—"

"But that's not even the most interesting part about you," Long Ge says. He leans back, still smiling wide, his eyes twinkling. "Why don't you tell me more about your friend Chanel Cao?"

His chest seizes. A sick sensation, spreading fast through him. "Chanel Cao?"

"You're very close, aren't you?" Long Ge says.

He doesn't know where Long Ge is going with this, but he thinks back to Chanel's expression last night by the lake, those large, frightened eyes in her lovely face. Frightened, because of Long Ge.

"No, not very," he tells Long Ge, feeling a desperate, almost dangerous urge to protect her, the same feeling that had over-taken him when he saw her cornered at the Cave. "She's just a classmate."

"Don't lie to me," Long Ge says pleasantly, picking up a ballpoint pen on his desk, pressing it twice with a quick, light clicking noise, then setting it down again. "Would 'just a class-mate' accompany you to get that new tattoo? You were acting like quite the couple, Zaizai told me. And I saw a photo of you on Chanel's phone with my very own eyes."

The tattoo parlor. Ares's breathing grows shallow. He hadn't understood why the scene had even featured in the vision, but now it makes sense. The tattoo artist must have recognized

Chanel and told Long Ge. Eyes and ears all over the city. Always watching, listening.

"She's also the girl you were risking your life to defend at the Cave, weren't you?" Long Ge says, with the leisure of a kidnapper circling his hostage. Nowhere for Ares to run, they both know it. Pinned down by fear, his ties to Chanel, ties to his brother. Might as well have his hands bound to this chair. "I should've made the connection sooner. Fancy playing the part of the hero, hmm?"

Ares stays silent.

Yet Long Ge keeps talking, unbothered by the task of carrying the conversation alone. "Though I can see how a girl like that would inspire heroic feelings in anyone. Very beautiful, isn't she? I met her just yesterday, and she looks so much like her mother it's shocking. Almost identical to her mother at her age. Her *behavior*, though—now, that was very disappointing. Kept interfering with my business for some reason. Seems to be under the impression I'm going to harm her mother, the silly girl."

A chill creeps down Ares's spine. "What do you want?"

"It's very simple. Coco Cao hasn't signed my contract yet," Long Ge says. "I have reason to believe that her hesitation stems from Chanel. But since you and Chanel are so obviously in love with each other, why don't you put in a good word for me? Assure her I have her mother's best interests at heart? I don't care how you go about it—propose to her, if you must. I just want the contract finalized."

"He's obsessed with my mother," Chanel had said.

Ares starts to protest, but Long Ge lifts a finger to silence him.

"Bring the contract," he says, "and I'll have your brother come pick it up. How's that sound? It's been a while since you last saw him, hasn't it? It'll be a nice family reunion."

Ares freezes in his chair, trapped by some force infinitely greater than he is.

It all comes back to power, or the lack of it. It's his fault his brother is gone in the first place, but also his fault that his brother is still missing. It wouldn't be like this if he were stronger, braver, wiser, richer, smarter, faster, *better.*

He swallows, silently hating Long Ge, hating all the men who flounder around and waste away their fortunes on luxury watches and boring mansions and private jets and overpriced booze. If he could command their resources, he would bring his brother back home in an instant. Power, he's realized, is the closest thing to magic in real life. It can open up entire worlds, create options that simply wouldn't exist otherwise. If he were more powerful, he wouldn't have to choose between two futures. Wouldn't have to bleed for clues. Wouldn't have to fight against Chanel when all he really wants is to drop the weapons and draw her to his chest.

Wouldn't have to make an impossible decision now.

"I'll send you the time and address," Long Ge says cheerily. "And forgive me for not seeing you out—I do have a rather full schedule today."

27

CHANEL

When the dreaded day arrives, my only remaining obstacle is Ares.

I wait until the middle of history class to execute my plan. While everyone else is studying, I frown down at my collar, patting the empty space there. Then I speak up, my voice ringing clearly through the classroom. "Hey, has anyone seen my necklace?"

The response is instant. Everyone except Ares lifts their head from their worksheets, and even Mr. Murphy pushes away the bowl of Caesar salad he's been loudly munching on for the past ten minutes.

"What does it look like?" Bobby asks.

"It's kind of shaped like a heart. Red rubies, with this huge diamond in the middle." I shake my head, feigning confusion. "I was literally wearing it when I walked into the room half an hour ago, I swear. I don't know how it isn't here anymore. . . ."

"Did it fall off just now, maybe?" Rainie asks.

"Maybe," I say. "But I've looked around my desk, and it's not here. It's not on the floor either." I heave a dramatic sigh, then add in a deliberately unconvincing voice. "No, that's fine. Sorry, guys, go back to what you were doing. I'll try to find it myself."

"We can help you search for it," one of the guys at the back volunteers. Jason. He'd asked me out three times last year, even though we'd never had a proper conversation, and had once written a poem about my eyes, which he'd started reading out loud to me before I stopped him for the sake of his own dignity. "It must be somewhere in this room."

"Really?" I shoot him my brightest, most grateful smile. "That's *so* nice of you to offer."

He almost leaps out of his seat. "Don't worry. We'll find it," he says, like he's making a solemn vow.

There's a flurry of activity as people start checking around them, flipping their textbooks over and pushing aside their laptops and scanning the gray carpets and chairs. I pretend to join in, routinely shuffling some papers and remembering to look concerned. But I keep my attention pinned on Ares's pencil case, waiting for someone to notice the silver glint of the chain dangling out the half-open zipper.

Jason's the one who finds it. "Hey, isn't that—" He pulls the chain out, holding up the evidence.

The classroom falls silent.

"Dude, did you steal Chanel's necklace?" Jason demands.

As murmurs circle the room, Ares's eyes flash to mine, betrayal and accusation burning in them, and I know he knows. *This is what you get,* I imagine myself saying to him, my voice as cold and hard as my heart. Since he's refusing to go to prom with me, there's no point in trying to act like a cute prom couple anymore. I just have to make sure he can't go *anywhere* tonight.

"What the hell?" someone else says.

"I didn't take it," Ares protests, but I can tell that nobody believes him. They probably assume we had a lovers' spat or a falling-out.

"Ares." Mr. Murphy rises from his desk, his voice serious. "Theft is strictly prohibited on school grounds—well, *anywhere*."

Ares glowers at the teacher, which isn't helping his case. "I'm telling you, I *didn't take it*. Why would I steal something like that?"

"I'm afraid I'm going to have to ask you to stay behind for detention after school," Mr. Murphy says gravely. "Please return the necklace to Chanel right now."

I try to keep my face passive as he walks over, but my heart thuds with each step he takes in my direction. We haven't been face-to-face like this since the night by the lake, and it's only when he comes closer that I notice the new bruises on his face. His split lip. The way he's holding himself gingerly to one side, like there's something sharp digging into his left rib cage.

I frown, helpless to control the concern that rises up inside me; a knee-jerk reaction, like shaking your hand when you've been burned. I almost open my mouth to ask if he's okay, if he's been fighting at the Cave again, to demand to know why he isn't protecting himself. Then I remember I no longer have the right to ask him these things, if I ever did. That I shouldn't care in the first place. And he doesn't give me a chance to speak to him anyway. He doesn't even look at me properly when he drops the necklace on my desk, his movements quick, as if he's eager to discard it. Then he's already turning around, hands in his pockets, his back to me.

Pain sears through my chest, threading together every strand of the past and future shared between us, from the moment I first saw him walking down the dark alley to the vision of flames engulfing my only home.

But this is necessary. I just have to do this, and everything will be okay. Ares will be kept after school for detention. The house will be empty, and my mom will be safe, and there will be no fire tonight.

But when I get home, my mom is still standing around in the middle of the living room, her suitcase lying wide open, her clothes strewn everywhere.

"What are you still doing here?" I ask, my words coming out too fast, too panicked.

My mom frowns up at me. "Should I not be here? This is where I live."

"Sorry," I say, fighting to regain control of my expression. "I just mean . . . isn't your flight leaving in, like, an hour?"

"That's plenty of time," she says, tossing in silk dresses and travel-sized packets of makeup wipes without any sense of urgency. "It's not like I have to wait in line. Oh, I probably should bring my other jacket," she adds under her breath, rummaging around in her suitcase and pulling out a blazer.

Which is really just great. It's not even that she hasn't finished packing for her trip. She is now actively *unpacking*. I can feel a scream building inside me, but I clench my teeth, take a deep, steadying breath, and dart a glance outside the window.

It's not too late; the sky is a deep blue, the moon not visible yet. As long as I can get my mom out the door before darkness falls . . .

"Which jacket are you looking for?" I ask as calmly as I can, even as a low, buzzing sound fills my head, like a violent swarm of bees. I can barely even hear myself speaking, just the desperate thud of my heartbeat.

"The leather one with the gold clasp—"

"I'll fetch it for you," I say, rushing toward the bedroom before she's finished her sentence.

When I return, she's staring at herself in the mirror, but she looks exhausted. Defeated. She touches a finger to the faintest crow's-feet around her eyes, stretching the skin there like she can magically erase any lines. Sighs.

My heart aches for her.

There was a time—even if it feels like an era ago now, a past life—when my mom was happy. When she did her makeup because she enjoyed showing off her beauty and not to cover the dark circles under her eyes. When she'd float through the house humming, with a bouquet of lilies in her arms.

I remember a random November evening, coming home from school and smelling the briny scent of boiled crabs and my dad's famous sugar-and-vinegar sauce before I even crossed the threshold. Listening to the clatter of chopsticks against plates, cracked shells, my mom planning out her next trip to Paris with my father. Both of them smiling when they saw me step inside.

We had all been happy here, and it's hard not to imagine those moments of happiness stored inside this very house, in the curtains my mom had chosen and the dining room where we shared countless dinners and the massive walk-in closet where I'd wobble around in my mom's heels as a kid while my dad watched, laughing. If the house burns, where does that happiness go? Where else am I meant to find proof that we'd been a real family once?

"Here," I say quietly, passing my mom the jacket. "You look beautiful, by the way."

She manages a small smile. "Thank you, darling."

"Really. You're beautiful."

"I know," she says, but without her usual conviction, and presses a quick kiss to my forehead. "Call me if you need anything, okay?"

"I will," I assure her, and then finally, *finally,* she's leaving. Once the door closes, I slump back against the wood, allowing the relief to wash over me for approximately three seconds before I rush into my bedroom to change. I still have one last stop to make tonight.

28

ARES

"Why did you steal it?" Mr. Murphy asks Ares for the tenth time, leaning forward in his armchair, his expression furrowed in that way Ares has seen on the faces of so many teachers before: worried, disapproving, deeply unhappy to be here.

That makes two of us, Ares thinks to himself, and contemplates punching an exit route through the classroom wall.

A clock ticks above the whiteboard. With every second, he can feel the vision slipping further and further away from him. What is Chanel up to? Was this whole necklace scheme her way of getting back at him for the prom rejection? He wouldn't put it past her. Has to almost admire her for her nerve—if he weren't trapped here, the only person in detention, watching the sun stoop lower behind the trees while Mr. Murphy tries to introduce to him the concept of moral integrity.

". . . can't be about the money," Mr. Murphy says. "You are evidently in a very fortunate financial position, Ares. Few people have donated as much to the school as your mother."

He frowns. "My mother? No, that can't be right."

"I assure you it is," Mr. Murphy tells him. "She donated a significant sum only last semester."

He considers reasoning—*But dead people can't make donations*—except he never brings up his mother, and certainly won't now. There must have been a mix-up.

"Is it for the thrill of it? The adrenaline rush?" Mr. Murphy goes on. "Is that what you're chasing? I know, with all the media youths are consuming nowadays, you might have been led to believe that stealing is cool. But I can tell you, Ares, that it is very much *un*cool to steal from your classmates."

"I didn't steal it," Ares says flatly.

Mr. Murphy sighs. "I would like to believe you. I really, really would—"

"Believe me, then."

"But you cannot expect me to think that the necklace unchained itself from Chanel's neck, sprouted a pair of legs, and wandered into your pencil case on its own, did it?" Mr. Murphy asks. "So what's the *real* reason here? I won't judge."

It could just be the quiet of the room, but the clock's ticking seems to grow louder. Ares clenches, then unclenches his jaw. "Will you release me from detention if I give you a reason?"

"No," Mr. Murphy says simply. "Either way, you should take some time to think over your actions today."

He doesn't have any time left. Maybe he can just make a run for it. There's no way Mr. Murphy would have the speed, stamina, or willpower to actually chase after him. . . .

The classroom door slides open, and Ms. Hoang steps inside, her teacher's badge swinging over her blouse.

"Oh, is my shift over already?" Mr. Murphy asks, looking visibly relieved.

"You're free to go," Ms. Hoang tells him. "I'm on detention duty for the evening." She turns to Ares with some surprise. "And what did you do to land yourself here, young man?"

"He stole a necklace," Mr. Murphy says, but moral integrity doesn't seem to hold very strong against the relief of clocking off, because he's already on his way out.

"I didn't," Ares mutters. "They *think* I stole a necklace."

"Ah." Ms. Hoang nods, like this could be a real possibility. She waves politely to Mr. Murphy. "Have a nice night, Jon. Hope you get some quality time with the kids." When the door shuts after him, she turns back to Ares. "You're saying you were falsely accused?" Still with the same receptive expression, sympathetic even.

And Ares feels a faint flutter of hope. Thanks to his help with the peer tutoring sessions and his consistently impressive math grades, Ms. Hoang is much nicer to him than any of the other teachers. He'd daresay that she even likes him. "Yeah," he says. "Exactly."

She nods slowly. "Hmm."

Sensing an opening, Ares asks in his politest voice, a voice that doesn't even sound like his, "Do you think I could go get my math workbooks from my locker? There's nothing else for me to do in detention, so, you know, I might as well prepare for the next math test."

Ms. Hoang considers him for a moment. "That sounds like a sensible idea," she says at last.

"Thank you," he says, with genuine gratitude. He stands, the chair screeching behind him, and heads out into the bluish light of the corridor, but he doesn't stop at his locker. He keeps walking, his strides lengthening, phone in his hand as he calls the earliest available DiDi to take him home. He just has to hurry, and everything will be okay. He will meet Long Ge, and his brother will be safe, and there will be a fire tonight.

Chanel's here.

Even in the darkness, even from a distance, he knows it's her. He could recognize her just by the shape of her silhouette. The very sound of her breathing. She's as inevitable as the future, as familiar as his own past, and for reasons he can't possibly fathom, she's waiting below his apartment on the night everything changes.

He's still struggling to process the fact that she's here when she whips around at his footsteps, marches right up to him, eyes blazing, and grabs him by the throat.

"Chanel? What are you—"

She crushes her lips to his, the smooth, floral notes of her perfume enveloping him. He can't think. Can't do anything except kiss her back. He forgets the meeting, the deadline, everyone and everything except Chanel.

Her fingers snake around the top two buttons of his shirt and she's pushing him toward the front entrance, somehow keeping her balance while leaning her full weight against his body, her mouth on his the entire time. She tastes like cherries, and his mind dances toward some old poem about forbidden fruit before everything goes dangerously fuzzy again, because her hand is braced around the nape of his neck.

"Let's go up," she whispers into his ear.

He's barely aware of himself fumbling for the key card in his pocket, the automatic *beep* of the entrance as it unlocks, and he shoves his shoulder against the heavy glass, unwilling to lift his hands from her waist for even a second. A small voice in the back of his head reminds him that he's meant to be mad at her for framing him and for something else, other things, he forgets now, but her touch is like a sedative. All the anger leaks out of him as she tugs him toward the lift.

The second the doors slide closed around them, she's backing him into the wall, kissing him hard like she's never kissed him before. Without restraint, without any care for who might see them, the security cameras blinking down at them from the top right corner. More half-solid thoughts about how this is a terrible idea appear, then vanish in Ares's head, erased by the sensation of her quick, uneven breaths against his neck. He knows the elevator is moving upward, but he feels like he's falling, down and down and down, stomach flipping, the air rushing around him. The whole world seems to blur into the background until there's only her.

She's standing so close that he can see the dark flecks of mascara smudged just underneath her waterline, the tiny mole above her full lips, the shiny powder dotted on the very tip of her nose.

She's beautiful.

She's so beautiful it's unfair, there should be legal warnings that come with this kind of thing, the same labels you find on gunpowder and deadly poisons, because who could possibly stand a chance against it? She shifts even farther forward, her leg pressing into the space between his. Then she lifts her knee by just a few calculated inches, and all the blood in his body rushes to the point of contact. A hoarse, almost pained sound escapes his lips, and he can only hope the security cameras don't have audio systems built in.

Then they're on his level, stumbling through the corridor, into his apartment, and he's struck by this sense of unreality as she discards her jacket at the entrance, revealing a white lace dress perfectly fitted to her body. Selected for the occasion, he suspects, as a soldier would select their best sword before riding off into battle.

"Do you want me?" Chanel asks, taking his hand and lifting it to the delicate strap of her dress, her gaze intent on his.

He freezes in place, his heart throbbing behind his ribs. He almost laughs. What kind of question is that? There is no universe where he doesn't want her.

"If you want me," she whispers, "you can have me like this. You can have me in any way you want. Just stay here tonight."

Her fingers curl into his hair, the gesture as intimate as it is possessive, and he thinks, woozily, that if this is what it feels like to be possessed by her, then by all means, go ahead.

No, another voice rattles in the back of his mind. *That's why she's doing this.* Even when she's kissing him, she's being calculating, determined to gain the upper hand. She must have an ulterior motive. Maybe this is another form of revenge, like the setup with the necklace—

But she's trembling.

He wouldn't have been able to detect it if they weren't so close, if he couldn't feel her fingers quivering at his throat, couldn't hear the hitch in her breathing.

Something's wrong.

"Wait," he says, pulling back.

Chanel stops. Stares up at him, confusion flickering through her eyes. "What? Don't you like it?"

"It's not that. Tell me what's wrong," he says.

She shakes her head. Even manages to laugh. "Nothing's wrong."

She's such a good liar that he has no doubt she'd fool anyone else, but he knows her better than that. "You're clearly upset," he says. "Did somebody hurt you? Or is this—is it about prom, still? About me not going with you? Because I really do want to, Chanel, I just—"

"Why do you care?" she cuts in, and finally, he catches a glimpse of real emotion underneath her act. It's odd, because Chanel Cao can be so worldly, so mature, navigating every social interaction with ease, carrying herself with more grace and confidence than most adults he's met before. But right now she only looks like a girl who's scared, who doesn't know what to do.

"I care about you," he says. Swallows. "I thought that was obvious."

She falters, her eyes searching his face like she's running his words through an invisible lie detector. Then the shrill sound of a ringtone breaks into the space between them.

She steps back, pulls her phone out, frowning. "Hello? Mom? What—"

He can't hear what her mother is saying, but Chanel's face pales.

"*No,*" she whispers.

29

CHANEL

I can feel Ares watching me as I grip the phone, all my carefully laid plans falling apart within seconds.

"I'm heading back now," my mom says. "I doubt the driver's gone that far—"

"*No*," I say again, resisting the urge to scream. This isn't happening. This can't be happening. "Mom, you can't just—you're going to miss your flight—"

"But I need my sunglasses, Chanel," she says matter-of-factly. I can hear the buzz of activity in the background, suitcase wheels rolling against polished concrete, the announcements calling for boarding, repeating the names of passengers who need to come to the gate. "I can't go to Sanya without those sunglasses."

"Right. But . . . couldn't you just buy another pair once you get there?" I suggest, my stomach churning. "Sanya has that huge duty-free shop—"

"You know I can't just get any *regular pair*," she says, like I'm being absurd. "I need my customized VCL sunglasses. They're the only ones that properly complement my face shape."

"No, but . . . Mom, I . . . please—" I press a hand to my temple and blink hard, like I can somehow blink this reality away, hit restart the way you do on a malfunctioning computer. It's too much. I don't have enough control, you simply can't control other people. I've always known this, but it's hitting me now, the full, paralyzing weight of it. There are only so many strings you can pull, there's only so much you can manipulate. But every single person has an individual life of their own, their own history and plans for the future and mistakes and their own way of seeing the world and carrying their pain. Like my mom right now, like my father, like Ares, who's still staring at me while I try not to hyperventilate. Everything is spiraling out of my control, and there isn't enough time to do anything. "Can you please stay at the airport?" I ask my mom. "I'll get your sunglasses for you—it's faster that way."

"Really?" She sounds skeptical. "They're in the bottom drawer of my walk-in closet—the smaller one. I don't know if you'll be able to find them—"

"I will, trust me," I say quickly. "Just . . . just stay there. I'll bring them."

It's only when I hang up that I hear how strained my breathing is, like I'm choking on air.

"What's wrong? What happened?" Ares asks at once, his hand stretched out toward me as if he wants to take away whatever is hurting me. There's no lust in his eyes, only concern. That's what makes me pause, an idea dawning on me, new and utterly terrifying. I can't control him, I know that, as hard as it is to accept. If I run back to my house right now, there's nothing else I can do to stop him, unless—

Unless I tell him where the house is. That's my last card, the only thing I haven't tried: total, terrible, damning vulnerability. It would be a massive gamble; the consequences wouldn't be just devastating but deadly if I'm wrong. I'd be giving him exactly what he needs to make the fire happen.

But maybe that's the risk I have to take. Maybe that's always the risk with falling in love. You can't just decide for yourself whether or not someone will hurt you, you can't move them around like a chess piece, keeping them a safe, calculated distance away at all times, and you can't expect them to love you if you don't let them.

So I let him.

I take a deep breath, look him straight in the eye, and I tell him. "I was lying before, about the vision. I do recognize the house."

Shock ripples over his face. "What are you saying? How . . . how do you know?"

"Because," I say slowly, and as I do, I imagine all the countless possibilities, all the moments shared between us, all the versions of our lives that might exist, leading up to now, to the two of us here, "the house is mine."

The moon is slowly starting to rise by the time the driver drops me and Ares off at my house. I give Ares a quick nod before I rush inside alone, the door slamming shut behind me, and practically run to the closet, fumbling through all the drawers, not caring how much of a mess I'll have to clean up later, if there even is a later.

At last my fingers close around the leather case. Thank god. I brandish it high in the air, as if I've just procured the elixir of life.

got them, I text my mom.

I take one final look around my home: at my parents' bedroom, where I'd hover on nights when I had a stomachache, whining until my mom murmured sleepily for me to come inside; the birthday gifts collected over the years, crystal roses to blossom in perpetuity and yellow wine from the last century; the photos displayed on the mantel, snapshots of my childhood, hiding from the sun at the beach, picking baskets of strawberries.

Then I turn around to leave, to hurry back to Ares, who promised he'd be waiting outside the house for me. He had looked so sincere when he said it, like he couldn't even imagine himself setting my house on fire, that I'd almost felt safe coming back here tonight.

But when I pull the door, it won't budge.

No, no, no—

My heartbeat kicks against my chest. I hear a low buzzing in my ears, panic lashing through me. I yank again, harder, with clammy palms, but the door's stuck. It shouldn't be. It was working just fine this morning—

I wriggle the lock with all my strength, but it doesn't do anything. The buzzing has dialed up to a shriek inside my head, the realization pounding against my skull. *Someone's locked me in here.*

"Fuck," I whisper.

30

ARES

Ares has envisioned this scene a thousand times over, in a thousand different ways. But nothing could have prepared him for the reality of it, for the moment he steps out of the DiDi and takes two steps down the street and stops. It's a rich neighborhood, the illuminated villas sprawled out in a way that reminds him of the American suburbs he's seen in movies. He's never been here before, and barely has time to wonder why Long Ge would choose this place in particular when another car door slams shut in the distance, and the boy appears as if from a dream.

His brother.

Ares feels the ground wobble beneath him. He'd glimpsed Luke's face in the vision, but the difference is more pronounced than ever in real life. He's no longer a child. Most of the softness has dissolved from his face, his hair has been cropped short, and he must've grown six inches since they last saw each other. He's almost as tall as Ares now, though it's hard to judge exactly from here. Something's changed about his eyes too. They're darker, difficult to read; before, Ares would only need to take one glance at his brother to know what he was thinking.

Then he says, "Ge?"

Not Gege anymore, just Ge. His voice is deeper, but it's not a stranger's voice either.

"Luke," Ares says. He should've prepared a speech, there's so much he wants to ask his brother, starting and ending with *Sorry, I'm so sorry, I fucked up*, but he finds himself at a complete loss for words. "Luke—I—"

"Not so fast," Long Ge calls out pleasantly, coming to stand beside Luke. His hand sets itself on Luke's shoulder, and Luke flinches. There's a lit cigarette dangling from his other fingers, and he blows out a puff of smoke, whitening the night air, before he says, "Give me the contract first."

Ares retrieves the crumpled contract from his pocket. "I have it here."

"Signed?" Long Ge presses.

Forged. But once Ares gives him the contract, he'll take his brother and they'll escape together.

"As promised," Ares says, fighting to keep his voice calm. He's so close now. He approaches Long Ge slowly, the way you'd approach a beast in a cage. He hands the contract over. Breathes in.

Then he grabs hold of his brother's hand, and there's one terrifying, heart-stopping second where he half expects his brother to shake him off, to turn his back on him, to blame him for what happened, those stupid, thoughtless words he's regretted every night since. *Can you just leave me alone for once?* A moment where he wonders if he'd been presumptuous to think his brother even *wants* to go back with him.

But then Luke squeezes his hand, and he wants to sink to the ground with relief.

"Let's go," he urges, and they're sprinting down the street, and Long Ge yells something after them, and he makes the mistake of glancing back. Long Ge's dropped the contract—must have figured out it was fake—and is chasing them, and he's so much faster than Ares expected, and he realizes, with a crush of despair, that this won't work. "Leave without me," he tells his brother. "I'll meet you back at our old house."

Luke's eyes are wide with fear, and all of a sudden he looks closer to his thirteen-year-old self, the boy who ran away. "No, Ge—"

"*Listen to me,*" Ares says. "Now. There's no time."

He hears his brother's footsteps slapping against the concrete, fading away into the distance while Long Ge's footsteps draw closer and closer. He holds his ground, remembers everything he learned during those fights in the ring, and turns.

He slams his fist into Long Ge's face, and he's never enjoyed violence before, but there's something awfully satisfying about this. The darkness cloaks their movements as he shoves Long Ge down. He punches until his hands are numb, and he thinks he might be bleeding too, but that's normal for him these days. He can feel Long Ge struggling underneath him, and it really is just like any fight. Hold on for long enough and his opponent will stay down. He imagines the crowd chanting around them.

Five . . . four . . .

Three . . .

Two . . .

Long Ge is shaking. No, laughing. A wild, unnerving noise that sends a chill through Ares, almost a wheezing, as if the man has lost his mind completely. Or maybe he has. When Ares stares down at him, Long Ge stares right back, a bruise already swelling on his temple, fresh blood glistening on his teeth.

"You think it's that simple?" he asks, laughing louder, the sound reverberating through his body. "You can just trick me and run away with your brother?"

Ares feels suddenly very frightened, but of what, he doesn't know. He's still pinning the man in place, but it's as if their positions are reversed, and he's the one frozen, back pressed to the ground, unable to move or even breathe.

"I made my instructions very clear," Long Ge goes on, his black eyes gleaming. Ares can make out his own reflection in them, distorted, and he's struck by how young he looks, not that much older than Luke. "I wanted to play fair, be nice, give the boy a chance and so on. I have been extraordinarily generous, you know. Made it so, so easy for you. All you had to do was convince your little girlfriend to do this one thing, and you couldn't even manage that. Useless, compared to your little brother."

The words land like a slap. *Useless, compared to your little brother.* No doubt what his own father had thought, often, or maybe every time he looked at them together. His sweet, clever, beloved son, and—that other one. Useless. Something wrong with him. A mistake.

Ares's fingers are going numb and cold, too cold, but he doesn't release his grip on the man. "Well, it wouldn't have worked anyway," he says.

"What?"

"What did you imagine would happen?" Ares says, more to buy himself time than anything, assemble the thoughts in his head, which feels like an overheated computer, the fans whirring loudly but feebly. "If she had actually signed the contract? You believe she would have fallen in love with you? She works with you long days and nights, you rope her into your life, she's impressed by this empire you built, and the two of you live happily ever after?"

For the first time, something human flickers in Long Ge's expression. Then rage flashes. "You don't understand the situation," he snaps. "You don't understand her."

"And you do?"

"I love her more than anyone else in the world," Long Ge says vehemently. "I love her, I've loved her my whole life, I love her so much I would cut off my own arm if it made her happy. And if she just spent more time around me now, she'd realize that I'm the best person for her. I'm not that awkward, pathetic little boy who lost fights in the schoolyard. I taught myself to be charming, cultured. I have money now, ten properties, hundreds of men who'll do my very bidding. My companies are worth far more than the nightclubs that scumbag ex-husband of hers has opened up—"

Ares is still staring down at the man, and watching him, hearing the desperation in his voice as he describes this warped fantasy, he experiences a surge of something utterly unexpected: pity.

All this work. The Cave, the empire he's built for himself, the suit and hair. Just to impress a woman he knew decades ago, a woman who wouldn't even spend that much time with him unless a legally binding contract demanded she do so.

Long Ge must see the pity in his face too, because his features twist. "Don't look at me like that. Don't you dare—" He struggles again under Ares, breathing hard. "She'll see," he says. "She's starting to see already, now that the divorce news is out—"

"That was *you*?" Ares demands. "You leaked the news. You did that to her." To Chanel too. He remembers, painfully, how she had arrived at school the morning the news broke, how hard she'd tried to act nonchalant, like it didn't affect her, like nothing could.

But Long Ge doesn't show any sign of shame. "The news was going to leak eventually. I just needed to move things along, to make her understand. When she has nobody else left, nobody else to love her, comfort her, hold her, protect her, she'll realize she has only me, that it's been me all along. I just need to clear away the obstacles."

Again, the terror, juddering through Ares. Clear away the obstacles. What does he mean, what could he—

Long Ge reaches into his pocket and pulls out a lighter, an open flame dancing from the end, and Ares's vision flashes white. *No.* He lunges for it, yanks the lighter out of Long Ge's grip, holding it so tight in his own hand that his nails dig into the flesh of his palm, but Long Ge doesn't even try to resist. He's started laughing again, bloodied spittle flying from his lips.

"This lighter's just for my cigarette," he says. "But don't worry, you'll see what a real fire looks like soon enough."

A spark catches his eye. Ares glances wildly to his left, just in time to spot a masked figure slip out through the front yard of a villa. One of Long Ge's men, stationed there in secret all along.

"I'm sorry about your girlfriend," Long Ge says, baring his teeth in a horrible smile. "But again, we could have gone about this the peaceful way. You chose not to listen."

And Ares watches it happen. Watches the fire catch.

The sky is burning.

Smoke wafts up over the roof, spreading fast through the glowing orange haze.

Someone screams from inside the house.

Chanel.

31

CHANEL

"Help. Please—"

The heat presses against my back, sticks to my throat, my eyeballs, coating my skin in sweat and soot. It's everywhere. The taste of ash in my mouth. I cough—on the smoke, on my own terror, the voice in my head yelling at me to *get out, get out, get out.* But how?

I'm trapped.

The fire has spread all around the living room, flames engulfing the couches and the coffee table, blocking the way to the windows, the last possible exit. I can't step back without being burned, but I can't get out with the front door still locked.

This shouldn't be happening. It shouldn't be like this, but then—the scene is so familiar. I'd seen my mother screaming for help, or thought that's what I saw. Her face. Or my own, I realize with a jolt, remembering every single time someone confused the two of us. *Blessed with her mother's genes, god, the resemblance is striking, you look just like each other—*

We look just like each other.

A hysterical laugh chokes out of me. The vision is the same, but it means something different now. I hadn't recognized myself in the lake. I'd never even considered that it could be me trapped inside the fire, because I didn't think I'd ever put myself in such a dangerous position in the first place. I didn't think I would tell Ares where the house was, and now—

Where is he?

Did he start the fire after all, after everything I told him, after he promised me he wouldn't? I had taken the risk—but had I bet wrong? Gambled everything I had for nothing?

Useless, fragmented thoughts race through my head, trying to make sense of it. Piece on a chessboard, or the player standing behind it. God rolling some dice. Fate. Destiny. Invisible hands of the universe. Immovable forces and timelines, splitting apart, reconciling, splitting once more. Moon and sun, chasing each other across the sky. A butterfly flutters its wings, and somewhere else a house erupts in flames. The beginning and middle and end, and the end is here.

I just never thought that it would be like this. That after all the blood spilled, the boys I've kissed, I would feel like a little girl again. Helpless. Abandoned. Shaking and slamming against doors that won't open, trapped inside my own house while I watch it burn down.

As the smoke fills my throat and my vision darkens, I see flickers of my own life, its extraordinary beauty and its cruelty, the highlights and the excruciating moments I've buried in the back of my mind.

Rationed bites of birthday cake, buttercream frosting scraped off with a fork. The flash of camera lights outside a French restaurant in Shanghai. Wiping off mascara specks from my eyelids with a cotton swab. My parents smiling from across the dinner table as I unwrapped the new Tiffany necklace they bought me for Christmas, the blue satin ribbons unspooling in my fingers. Crying on a bathroom floor, the cold of the tiles against my thighs. Laughing together with Alice in our old dorm, cross-legged on the bed while the sunlight puddled through the windows. Ares, trembling under my touch, his eyes dark and unfathomable; kissing him like every second mattered, and it did, like it was the apocalypse, and maybe it is.

And even though I'm gasping for air, the heat pressing in and the room swaying and every strained breath bringing in new, bright gashes of pain, I still keep my hand on the doorknob, my knuckles white. I still want so badly to change the future when it's already here.

I dream of him before I die.

It's an incredible dream, more vivid than anything I've ever experienced before. He's running over to me like I always wanted, the angles of his face burning bronze against the flames, and I think, half delirious, *God, I'm really going to miss that face.* Even when he isn't smiling, even when he's looking the other way. How his eyes always seem to change in the light, so I can never entirely pinpoint what shade they are, bitter black or coffee brown or brilliant molten gold; the smooth, firm line of his jaw; the shape of his mouth, which is exactly as soft as it looks.

I'm pretty sure I'd made a comment about that once, when I was kissing him. "Nobody's complimented my lips before," he'd said, breaking away to laugh breathlessly into my shoulder, and the gesture somehow felt more intimate than when he had his fingers in my mouth. I loved him like that, unspooled and vulnerable and happy, or the closest thing to it. "Good," I'd told him. "I don't want other girls complimenting your lips. I don't want anyone else to know what you feel like." Or maybe I had only said it inside my head, afraid he'd hear the jealousy clawing up my throat.

The memories are getting jumbled now. Everything's fuzzy, except the clarity of his arms around me. He's holding me tight to his chest like I'm his whole world, so careful not to drop me, and I remember the games I'd play as a kid, when the floor was lava and you had to leap from sofa to sofa to avoid it. I was never good at getting from one end of the room to the other—I kept slipping or missing my jumps. But maybe the trick is that you need someone to carry you. Someone who'll wade through the lava for you, like he is now.

"Chanel," he whispers, his voice raw from the smoke. His shoulders are shaking, and it's only when something cold splashes onto my cheek from above that I realize he's crying. "Chanel, please—"

It's okay, I try to say, but the words won't come out. The fire dances in my peripheral vision, charring the wood and melting the walls of my childhood. Something crashes from another room. The tinkling of porcelain. It feels like the universe is shrinking and shrinking until there's only the two of us left here, and maybe that wouldn't be such a bad thing. Maybe I could simply stay in this dream forever with him.

A window shatters to our right, and I glimpse the sky through the cracked glass, the crimson glow of the blood moon. It seems to hang lower in the horizon than usual, so low that it feels like I could reach up and take it for myself, if only I could move my hands. . . .

Then the darkness washes over me, and even the moon disappears.

32

ARES

Ares thought he knew fear.

He had felt it the morning he found his little brother's bed empty, all those years ago. When he'd first stumbled across the vision in the lake, convinced that he was hallucinating. When the knife had cut through his side, lying on the floor of the Cave, tasting the blood in his mouth. But nothing can compare to the fear thrumming through him as he rushes down the hospital corridor, almost barreling straight into the nurse.

"She hasn't woken up yet," the nurse tells him with a sympathetic kind of grimace.

"Can I . . . can I visit her?" he asks. His voice is so hoarse it barely sounds like his own. He doesn't know if it's from the screaming or the smoke.

The nurse's eyes pass over him. "You should really go get your own wounds treated first—"

"I'm fine," he says quickly. "I'm used to it. I just . . . please. Can I see her?"

The nurse hesitates, maybe senses the desperation in him, this wild, animal feeling, maybe can tell that he's losing his sanity, because she nods, pushes the door open for him.

Chanel lies on the hospital bed, almost motionless except for her slow breathing. He hates how small she looks, how fragile, hates seeing the tubes in her skin, the raw, puckered burn marks that extend along the entire length of her left collarbone. She would hate seeing herself like this too.

"Chanel," he whispers, crouching down by her side.

He would give up thirty years of his own life for her to sit up and talk to him. Tell him again about her childhood hikes up Lingshan Mountain, where the air tasted like pine and dew and there were butterflies everywhere, and how this one white butterfly landed on her shoulder and wouldn't leave her. About the first and last time she went camping, far enough away from the city to escape the light pollution and count every single star in the sky, but they headed home early because she couldn't stand not showering for longer than a day. About late afternoons spent strolling the lanes of Solana, watching the sun skim over the river, and the surprise birthday parties she's thrown for her friends, with themed outfits and hired videographers and free disposable cameras for everyone to use. About crowded airports and lonely limousines, looming skyscrapers and responsibilities, summer trips to New York and Seoul and Venice.

About anything.

33

CHANEL

My senses come to me slowly, in fragments. The cool touch of the pillow. The distant beeping of a machine, shuffling footsteps. An ache, deep in my chest.

I rub my eyes open, and rise gingerly from the bed to take in my surroundings. It takes me a moment to realize I'm in a hospital room, and not an indoor garden.

"Oh my god," I murmur, picking up the fat bouquet of fresh-plucked roses laid right beside my pillow.

Every surface in the private room is flooded with flowers, their rich fragrance almost entirely covering the smell of antiseptic. Lilacs and daffodils bloom aggressively over my bedside table, some of them bearing signed cards, others tied with satin ribbons. The only colors missing from this vibrant display of well-wishes are yellow and white. If not for this small detail, the absence of mourning colors, I would've thought that I'd died.

Ares is asleep on the floor beside me, his head resting against the edge of my mattress. The ache in my chest sharpens. I don't know how long he's been there.

"Hey," I say softly.

He wakes with a start, his eyes focusing on me, the intensity of his features almost too bright to look at. "Chanel?" He makes a movement as if to hug me, then thinks better of it. "I . . . I'll go call the nurse. Does anything hurt? How do you feel? Do you need water? Fruit?"

"I want . . . lip gloss," I say.

I don't expect him to have any, but he produces a tube of lip gloss from his pocket. It's the same cherry one I always use. "Here," he says immediately.

"You remember how to apply it for me, right?"

He nods. I thought he was gentle last time, but now he's so careful with his movements that I'm tempted to laugh at him. Then, staring down at the IV strip on the back of my hand, he says, very quiet, "I didn't realize what Long Ge was planning, with the fire. I was so scared. By the time I found you, I thought it was too late."

Long Ge. So it hadn't been Ares who'd started the fire; it had been Ares who had rescued me from the burning house. I hadn't bet wrong, after all. "You came for me," I say aloud, just to confirm it, to prove it wasn't a dream.

"Of course I did," he says.

The TV is turned on behind him, the news playing at a just-audible volume, more background noise than anything. But familiar images flash over the screen: my childhood house in its former glory, contrasted against a smoldering pile of ruins, the walls of the nearby buildings stained black, the dead lawn littered with shattered glass.

My throat tightens.

Then the scene changes to Long Ge in handcuffs, being dragged away by the police. He looks like he's lost his mind, or maybe his soul; his eyes are wild, his teeth bared as he shouts something inaudible.

"He's in prison now," Ares tells me quietly. "He'll be there for some time; he did a bunch of illegal shit on top of making minors work for him and burning houses down. They've freed all of them now, the minors."

"Okay. Okay, thank god," I say.

His expression darkens. "But he deserves worse than prison." He's staring down at my collarbones, and only when I follow his gaze do I see the burn mark peeking out from under the gauze.

I inhale. "Oh." It's about the size of my palm, too high to be covered up unless I wear turtlenecks for the rest of my life.

"I asked the doctors about it," he says. "It'll get better, but . . . it'll leave a scar."

"Okay," I repeat in a daze, my head buzzing. A scar. A permanent mark. My perfect image, irrevocably changed. I should be freaking out about it, speed-dialing the top surgeons in China right this second, and yet . . . maybe it's the fact that I almost actually died, but it doesn't feel like life-and-death, the way it would have a month ago. "Well," I say weakly. "At least prom is already over. I don't have to worry about how it'll look in prom photos."

"For what it's worth, you won," he says.

"What?"

"Prom. I saw the results. Even though you weren't there, you had the most votes. You were crowned prom queen—as you deserve," he adds, his voice soft. "But I'm really sorry you had to miss it. I know how much it meant to you."

It does. Or it did. But prom feels like such a small thing now, so silly and frivolous and insignificant. Even the news of my win doesn't give me the rush of validation I'd always imagined. It's just something that happened, a past life, the concerns of a girl who hadn't almost been burned alive.

"They also voted for me for prom king," Ares says.

I bite back a small smile. "Congratulations? I mean, not that it matters to you."

"Anything that matters to you matters to me," he tells me simply, and he's about to say something else when the door bursts open.

"Chanel?" My mom rushes in, still wearing the same clothes I last saw her in, which is so rare that it's all I can focus on for a moment. My mom refuses to even wear the same pajamas two nights in a row.

Ares stands up and steps back from me with what seems like a superhuman level of self-restraint, letting my mom take his place by my hospital bed. Then he excuses himself quietly from the room, glancing over his shoulder at me with every step on his way out.

"Thank *god* you're okay," my mom says, her face ashen. "I still can't believe it—"

"I'm sorry, Mom," I whisper. Because even underneath the

overwhelming relief that she's alive, that I was the one caught in the fire instead of her, there's the guilt gnawing at my insides. I should've been more strategic, more careful. I should've prevented the fire from happening at all.

"What are you talking about?"

"The house," I say, too weak to lift my arms all the way, so I nod toward the TV screen instead. "Everything's ruined."

"It's just a house. You're safe and I'm safe."

"But it was our home," I say, my voice breaking. It's not just the house I'm grieving. It's my childhood, the last happy memories I had of my family together, burning into rubble. Now my dad's gone, and the house is gone, and I guess my childhood really is over. I was never going to save it in time.

Even if it hadn't burned . . . there's simply no way to return to what it was before.

"I'm really, really sorry," I tell her.

"Stop *apologizing*. How is any of it your fault?" my mom demands. "If anything, I should've known . . . you tried to warn me about Long Ge," she says, her complexion paling further. "Ever since they told me what happened at the house, I've been thinking about it. At the party, you tried to warn me. And I didn't listen."

"To be fair, he was your old friend," I say softly.

"Barely," my mom says, shaking her head. "We weren't even that close in high school. He wasn't close with anybody—he was picked on a lot by the other kids. Mostly they tried to humiliate him, but sometimes they got violent with him too. They'd challenge him to fights he could never win, and they never played fair. That's how he got the scar on his cheek. One of the older boys had brought a knife to the fight and . . ." She trails off, wincing at the memory. "I felt sorry for him, especially after that fight, so I would try to be nicer to him. Invite him to join me and my friends for lunch if he was alone. Smile at him when I saw him in the corridors. I suppose I was the only person he could have considered a friend at school, but I never thought much about it. I certainly wouldn't have thought it'd end up like this."

"That's just . . . that's so sad," I whisper.

"Which part?"

"All of it. Everyone."

"It is," she says, folding her hands on her lap. She touches the empty space on her ring finger, a phantom feeling maybe, an old habit that hasn't died yet. "When he reached out after the divorce, it surprised me, but I—I didn't suspect anything, when I should have." Her fingers curl. "Instead I just let myself enjoy his affection and attention and all the shiny business opportunities he was offering me—"

"You needed someone. I get it," I say.

"But you needed someone too. You needed me," my mom says, and I feel my throat burn with the truth of it. Because even when I'd conditioned myself to need nobody, I *did* need her.

"Mom, I—" My voice cracks over the word, a sob rising inside me.

"Shh. It's okay, come here, baobao," my mom says, drawing me into a tight hug. I breathe in the familiar floral notes of her perfume. Chanel No. 5, the same as my own. I'd always loved the smell on her, had begged her for my first bottle on my fourteenth birthday. "Ba ni xia zhao le ba?" *You were scared, weren't you?*

This whole time, I've been trying to keep it together, to act like a grown-up who knows exactly what to do, to be there for my mom. But now, the last of the fight in my body shatters. Of course I was scared, terrified out of my mind, terrified still, and I'm clutching her, sobbing, nose running, while she strokes my hair.

"Don't worry about the house. We can always build another home," my mom says softly.

I sniff. "It won't be the same, though."

"It won't be," she agrees. Doesn't try to convince me it'll be better, but somehow, that's what calms me down. Her acceptance of it. I can't bring myself to do the same, not yet, but in time—who knows?

And for now, I bury my face against the soft fabric of her shirt, and I cry and I cry and I no longer bother pretending, and it's weirdly cathartic, to just *feel*, even if the feeling isn't pleasant.

"I'm here," my mom murmurs. "I'm here."

So I guess not everything is ruined. Say there was a version of the future where the house had burned, but my mother had also been trapped inside. Or Ares hadn't come to save me. Say that had been the original vision all along. What I did couldn't have been utterly futile, then. I couldn't stop the future in its tracks, but I could change it, even if only by a little. That matters. It all matters.

★ ★ ★

"How are you feeling?" Ares asks for the seventh time the next morning.

"Not too different from when you asked just a few seconds ago," I tease him.

"Just checking," he says.

I shake my head. "You know, I don't think I'm used to you like this. I didn't know you could be this nice."

"I'm not this nice to anyone else."

"I know you're not," I say, smiling as I stretch. "It's just kind of a culture shock. Maybe you should throw in a few insults, help ease me into it."

He shoots me an incredulous look from across the room, where he's peeling an apple for me with a pocketknife, his fingers fast and steady, the strips of skin falling away like crimson ribbons into the plastic bag spread underneath it. Now that his little brother is resting at home, Ares has basically been living inside the hospital. And despite my half-hearted insistence that I don't need him around to take care of me, I'm grateful he's here, grateful for the time that we have alone together, at last. "Are you asking me to insult you?"

"Is it hard to?"

"Very," he says. "I can't come up with anything at all."

I scoff. "That can't be right. There's so much material to work with."

"I'd disagree."

"Maybe you don't know me that well, then," I say, and I'm still aiming to sound light, joking, but it's a real worry of mine. I've been thinking about it ever since I woke up and saw Ares there, still waiting in my room. It feels like a beginning, but I want to start things right. I want to be honest with him in a way that I've never been honest with anyone else before. Want him to know me, actually *know* me, not the image I've perfected for other's eyes.

"What is there that I don't know, still?" Ares asks, sounding genuinely curious.

"Oh, I could go on."

The knife pauses in his hand. "I'm listening."

So much I could say. So many faults and flaws, accumulated over time, hidden from view. Like how sometimes I make plans I'm genuinely excited about in the beginning, then cancel them the night of, not because I hate other people, but because I hate the way I look. But then if I stay indoors too long, I get restless and start feeling like I'm wasting my life away. My mood in the morning is far too dependent on how well my makeup turns out and whether I woke up feeling slim. I know how to make an entrance, but I never know how to leave. I'm too fixated on being skinny, and I'm aware that it's bad for my health and my sanity but I just can't seem to eat intuitively anymore; I ruined that intuition fifteen years and five personal trainers ago. I always look up the menu before dining at a restaurant so I can calculate how much I'll be able to eat and start rationing for it two meals ahead of time. It's stupid, but I can't change it, like most of my bad habits. I think there's something wrong with me, and not in a fixable or relatable way.

Or how I'm secretly a little jealous of all of my friends for tiny, silly things—for the shape of their nose, or their laugh, or their ability to solve a math equation or talk politics at the dinner table or how they're able to maintain their weight without watching every single morsel of food they put into their mouth—even though I would cross oceans for them, strangle any man who ever tried to hurt them.

Or how there are days where I feel like I have everything—an outrageous amount of money in my bank account, the most coveted designer collections in my closet, a long list of numbers saved to my phone—and other days where it feels like I'll never have enough of anything. I crave attention so desperately, even if it's in the form of envy. I occasionally loathe myself, but I always, always want the best for myself.

Yet when the best things do fall in my lap, I find myself questioning if I really deserve it. I suspect that everyone pretends to enjoy hanging out with me far more than they actually do. I laugh loudest when I'm saddest, and I'm vain enough to believe that plenty of people are interested in me—but give it time, and they'll inevitably find out that I'm not really very interesting at all.

How, when I was eight, a boy in my class pointed out that my lips are too thin and now that's the first place I zoom in on whenever I look at a photo of myself. Had considered getting fillers, and would have probably gone ahead with it if I didn't have trust issues, leading me to worry the doctors would somehow mess up the procedure and make me look worse.

I begin to tell him as much, all of it, but I break off somewhere between the eighth and ninth major flaw. Honestly, I'd expected him to run out of the room within a minute, but he's still sitting there, gazing over at me, his expression tender, patient, filled with such irresistible affection that I have to wonder if he'd heard a single word that came out of my mouth just now.

"If you're trying to scare me off, it's not working very well," he says.

"I'm not. I just . . . I want to be honest. Because you might think you like me right now, but once you get to know me—"

Before I can go on, he's dropping the knife and crossing the space toward me, and his long, slender fingers are tangled in my hair. His other hand curves around my back.

His lips soft on mine. Warm.

The world tilts.

He kisses me with a hard-repressed hunger, edged by something I can't quite discern, something almost dangerous. His whole body is trembling with it, his hands deliberately, carefully light over my skin, as though aware of all the parts of me that are still wounded, still hurting. I feel drunk, in a dream, sick with desire. What really hurts now is the too-quick beat of my pulse, the strain of my heart against my chest.

Hot, feverish skin; the smell of his cologne and the blankets falling; the distant, out-of-body shock that this is happening, no games or tricks, we're just doing this because we want to and we can.

At last, at last, at last.

"Chanel," he murmurs, his mouth against mine. He tastes like cold, sweet moonlight, everything that's beautiful and terrible in the world. He pulls away for a second, breathing hard.

Then he presses his lips to the hollow of my throat. I stay still and let him, lightheaded, one hand curled tight around his shirt.

"I *want* to know you," he says. "I want to know everything about you, and none of it could ever, ever scare me off."

"Is that a threat?"

"A promise," he says, and I think that I could actually do this. Try it, at least, why not. For once, I want to be the girl who gives love a chance.

"I'm holding you to your promise," I tell him. "If you break it, I'm going to ruin your life, you realize?"

I can feel his lips on my neck, feel how they curve into a smile. "I wouldn't expect anything less from you."

34

ARES

During his first three days back home, Luke doesn't say anything to Ares and their father.

Or, barely. He remains quiet when Ares shows him the way to his old bedroom, where everything has been preserved, a time capsule of Luke's old science posters and car models and the faded teddy bear with the plaid shirt and missing eye. The only time he speaks is to ask Ares whether he has a spare toothbrush.

Ares isn't sure what he'd thought would happen. Tears? A brotherly embrace? Staying up late and sharing a drink? He considers offering Luke a beer—technically illegal, but he was younger than his brother when *he'd* started drinking—or an apple juice, but maybe Luke would find that too childish now. In the end he plays it safe by getting Luke a glass of warm water, which he accepts wordlessly.

There may not have been tears, but there was far more talking in Ares's imagined version of events. Sentimentality. Instead he feels mostly a lingering sense of awkwardness, like when you find yourself sitting next to the only other person your age at an adult gathering, and the silent expectation is for you to become friends by the end of the night. But what to say first? How to cover all that ground and distance, the regret, the loss, the relief? And what if his brother still blames him?

"Give it some time," Chanel tells him on the phone after her checkup appointment. Luke is sleeping, his snores soft through the walls, but Ares keeps his voice down just in case, the doors closed. The thin red bar in the corner of his screen warns him he only has thirteen percent of battery left, so he finds himself sitting cross-legged on the floor while his phone charges, playing absently with the wire. "He must be in shock."

He can hear the gargle of hospital noises in the background. Doctors coming around to check patients' vitals. Beeping of monitors. "Yeah, you're right, I don't know. It's stupid, but I just thought things would be . . . different."

"Well, you've both been through a lot," she says gently. "If he doesn't feel like talking about it yet, maybe you can do something together."

"Do something?" he repeats.

"Like an activity. Something fun that you both used to enjoy. It might help him open up to you, or at least remind him of how things used to be."

He thinks about this for a moment. "Hey, you know, you give pretty good advice."

She laughs, low and lilting, and he feels a warm jolt of pleasure. "You just realized?"

So on Thursday, he takes Luke down to the arcade. From

memory, the place was packed on the weekends, you had to wait in line for every game, but tonight they're one of the few people here. A family, the father collecting tokens while the mother holds their drinks. Three teenagers younger than he is. A couple on a first date, probably, judging from how often the girl keeps checking her lipstick using her phone's front camera mirror, how the guy's carrying himself with a forced kind of confidence, trying to teach her how to play pool.

"Want to play Street Fighter?" he asks Luke.

Luke gives a quick nod, and it feels easier like this, performing the series of motions the game naturally requires of them without much thought: piling their bags and jackets on the machine behind them, holding the tokens out to Luke, slotting them into the machine, hands finding the buttons, picking their fighters. Luke goes for the same character he always used to, the one with flame-red hair and long claws.

Then the game starts, and he slams his hand down, urging his fighter onward. Memories float up from the Cave, flashes of broken bone and blood drying on walls. What a relief, to be away from all of that now, to fight without getting his knuckles dirty in the safety of the arcade, his brother beside him.

He lets Luke win the starting round, and for the first time, his brother smiles. The same dimples, even in the sharper face. Looks more like a child this way, different, but not changed completely.

"Again?" he offers.

"Okay," Luke says.

They play five more rounds, and he makes sure to win two of

them, so Luke won't suspect he's going easy on him. Then they wander over to the adjoining food court, where he buys them a bucket of fried chicken wings dusted with cheese powder. Together they sit by the window, and Luke wipes his hands, picks up one of the wings but doesn't eat it yet. Just blinks at Ares. Swallows. At last he asks, "Are you . . . mad at me?"

"What? No," Ares says, so surprised he can't even think of anything else. "No. Why would I be?"

"I should've come back," Luke says quietly, staring down at the table. "Or I should never have left. But at the time, running away seemed like the best thing to do, and on the first night . . . I was hungry and cold and I bumped into this group of boys who were, like, maybe a year older. They seemed really cool and we got to talking and I told them I didn't have anywhere to go, which was a stupid thing to say, but it *felt* true. Then they asked me if I wanted to join them for dinner, and I did, and . . . that's when they brought me to Long Ge."

Ares listens with horror, gut churning, everything he'd wondered about in the past three years unfolding before him.

"Long Ge said that if I wanted to be really independent, live on my own and not burden anyone, I needed a job. And he could get me one at his company. He offered me a contract, and it seemed legit, like, this serious adult was giving me this opportunity, and I was just glad he was going to give me money. I had no sense of what was a lot and what wasn't; I mean, I realized after, but then it was too late. Long Ge, and the men around him—I was so scared of them. I didn't want to do anything to upset them, and they said that if I tried to leave, they'd not only chase me down, but they'd make you and Dad suffer as well. . . . I had no idea how to get out of it. I—I know I should've been smarter about it."

"We could've helped you," Ares says. "You were just a child—that's exactly why men like Long Ge target people like you. Because you don't know any better. Of course you don't."

"Well, you did help me, didn't you? In the end," Luke says, and nibbles at the end of the chicken wing. Brushes the cheese powder from the corner of his mouth. "I just didn't want anyone to see me like that. With the wrong group, a failure."

"You're not a failure," Ares says firmly. "You didn't fail anything. I was the one who . . . I should never have said it. None of it would've happened if I hadn't said it."

"It's okay," Luke mumbles. "I had a lot of time to think about it, you know. While I was gone. And if I'd been you, if our dad had treated me that way . . . not that he didn't care about you. I'm sure he did, even more than he realizes."

"He doesn't care at all," Ares says. Not with resentment or accusation. Just one of those hard facts about life. You wished it wasn't the case, but, well, what could you do?

Luke shakes his head. "That's not true. Or else why would he have asked you to come to Beijing? After all those years growing up in America with your grandparents?"

"To babysit you," Ares says. "To cook for you, to protect you. Better inside help than outside help. Even though every time he looked at me, I know—I know it just reminded him of my mother."

"You really think that?"

"What else is there to think?"

Luke hesitates. Peels part of the chicken skin off with oily fingers. "There was a video I found of him with your mom."

Ares's throat tightens painfully. His mom. Someone too abstract and unknowable for him to really think about for long, like trying to imagine what exists beyond the universe—your brain hits a dead end. And yet he thinks about her all the time still, on some subconscious level, every time he sees a mother and son strolling in a park or grabbing dinner or heading home from school together. "What video?"

"From before you were born. They looked very happy together, and she was saying—I think he was meant to show it to you. Or that was the plan, before she . . ." Silently, lightly, he sidesteps the fact of her death like a ditch in the road. "She was talking about the life you would have together. The three of you. She wanted to move to Beijing and spend the first year at home, cooking for you, and he was pretending to be jealous, saying she only cooked for him like, twice a year or something, and she was laughing. . . . Like I said, they were happy. He really loved her, you could tell. And I think—not to find excuses for him, or anything like that—maybe it felt . . ." His forehead scrunches as he reaches for the right word. "It made him too sad, to try and have that life in Beijing without her, but he still wanted to look after you, or have you close. I'm not sure. That's just what I think."

The donations. Significant donations, Mr. Murphy had said, from his mother. He had been deeply skeptical at the time, thought it was a mistake, but—maybe. Maybe his father had intended it. Let his mother be seen as a good mother, generous, supportive, even when she wasn't around. Or maybe that was the only language he knew: money. *I can't speak to my own son, but here's a couple million, make sure he's doing okay at school, won't you?*

Sitting there in the corner, amid the chatter of arcade games, a happy robotic voice urging people to play again, Ares feels a deep wrenching in him, an emotion so intense he wishes to weep. But it isn't awful, this feeling. A catharsis. Resolution, or redemption, even. For his old self, for his father.

He breathes out. "Right. I see," he says.

They both eat in silence, until there is a pile of small bones stacked up on the napkins. "These aren't as good as the chicken wings you make," Luke says, licking the cheese powder off his fingers.

"Yeah?"

"I missed your cooking," Luke admits. "Long Ge fed us, but . . . just enough so we didn't starve. Sometimes I'd literally lie awake at night with my stomach rumbling and try to remember how the food tasted at home."

"Tell me what you're craving," Ares says. "I'll make it for you."

This earns him a tentative smile. "I will." Luke pauses, seems to think of something, his face turning serious again. "By the way, is that girl okay? I've been meaning to ask."

Ares knows instantly who he means. "Yes. Yeah, she's okay. She's out of the hospital now. Just has a couple more checkup appointments, but the doctors say she's healing fine."

"Who is she, anyway?" Luke asks.

"Chanel Cao," he says, with a stirring of pride. How many people have said her name today alone, but how many can claim to know her the way he does?

Maybe his thoughts are more transparent than he realizes, because Luke regards him in a new way. "And are you two . . . together?"

"Not yet," he says. "Not officially. I'm planning on asking at a better time. I want to do it right." He's never discussed girls with Luke before, he realizes. Not that there was ever much to discuss. Only fleeting moments of fondness, shallow desire, mutual flattery, strangers who more or less remained as much. None of them really count, not anymore.

"How did you meet?"

Ares feels himself smiling. Can't seem to help it. "You want to hear the full story?"

Luke nods, eager.

"Okay, well, I guess it began with the moon. . . ."

35

CHANEL

The moon hangs high tonight, a perfect silver pendant in the sky.

I find Ares standing underneath it, waiting by the lake banks where I'd first followed him. I stay still, allowing myself the luxury of simply admiring him from a distance. He's always looked so beautiful in the moonlight. Almost surreal, like something out of a dream.

Then I step forward—silently, or so I think, hoping to catch him by surprise, but he turns around at once, his dark eyes finding mine.

"Have you been waiting long?" I ask.

"No, not at all," he says, his lips sliding into a smile. "I know you usually need two hours to get ready."

"Well, being hot takes time," I say. I shrug off my fur jacket as I cross the grass toward him, revealing the tight crimson dress I'd picked out just for him, the one that's softer than silk and fits like a second skin around my body. A warm, pleasant breeze fans my hair back from my bare shoulders. It's finally starting to feel like summer, and even the air is sweeter, balmy with the fragrance of begonias and yesterday's rain. Children are staying out later, chasing each other around the park, licking hawthorn ice pops and scooping traditional Beijing yogurt out of little glass jars. The yeyes and nainais are back to playing their chess matches and dancing in the courtyards, swaying together to ballads from the nineties, slightly off-rhythm but laughing.

Everything feels fresh and full of promise, like new beginnings.

"I like the dress," Ares says, his fingers skimming over the fabric around my waist.

I gaze up at him. "Of course you do."

"This too," he says, tugging at the black velvet bow in my hair. "And this," he says, hands drifting down to my jaw, tilting my chin gently up toward him. The cuts in his knuckles have almost healed, I notice, the dark red scars fading into a pinkish color. No new bruises, no blood.

"I think you like everything about me," I murmur against his lips.

"You think so?"

"I'm actually certain of it," I amend, and pull away, teasing, before he can kiss me.

"You do make it very, very difficult not to like everything about you," he agrees.

I'm biting back a ridiculous grin as I cast my eyes on the lake. The pale moonlight ripples over the surface, and out of habit, my stomach tenses, dreading what future might form from the murky shapes, but the water doesn't change. The house fire, the smoke, the destruction—all of it is gone now, as if the vision had never existed in the first place. You can only see the liquid reflections of the lamps, and the two of us, standing side by side, the red of my dress the closest thing to flames.

"Isn't it so strange?" I murmur, and I don't have to say more than that. He knows exactly what I'm thinking.

"Very," he says. "Sometimes I think I made it all up inside my head. If it weren't for you . . . I would've thought I'd lost my grip on reality ages ago."

"Do you reckon anyone else will see a vision like we did? If maybe—maybe there are more lakes out there similar to this one? Or if maybe it isn't about the lake at all. Maybe it's the moonlight."

"Maybe it's all of it. The exact combination—the place, the timing. You and me," he says, with a readiness that makes it clear he's been wondering about it too, drawing up his own theories that can never be tested. He pauses. Looks over at me, his gaze catching on the burn scar underneath my collarbone, his face tightening like it's been seared into his own flesh. "Chanel . . . I'm still really, really sorry."

"Sorry? What's there to be sorry about?"

"I just . . ." He swallows. Shakes his head. "You shouldn't have had to go through that. Every time I remember it . . . how close you were to—"

"But you saved me," I remind him. "And besides, it's all in the past now, isn't it?"

The past. I can barely believe it, even when I say the words out loud. The worst has happened, and somehow we survived it, and we're both here.

"How's your brother these days, by the way?" I ask Ares, deliberately changing the subject before he can sink too deep into his own guilt. I don't know if anything I say can ever convince him to forgive himself, even if I've remained adamant that there's nothing to forgive.

"Luke is . . . adjusting," Ares says. "I've enrolled him at Airington, and he should be ready to start classes next semester. It's just that he hasn't been to school in so long. . . . He hasn't said anything about it, but I think he's a little nervous."

"Luke's so smart, I bet he's going to be at the top of his class in no time," I say. "I can already see him fitting in; he can be Airington's next genius, after Henry Li graduates."

"Those are pretty big shoes to fill," he says.

"I mean, nobody can replace *Henry Li*. But trust me, being smart will get him far. And if anyone *does* give him a hard time, I'll step in."

His expression softens, the line of his mouth loosening. "Yeah?"

"Yeah. Though I doubt I'd need to, when everyone's already terrified of you."

"You're not terrified of me," he points out.

"That's because you're my boyfriend," I say. This has the exact effect I wanted. His eyes turn to molten amber, some bright emotion flickering across his features, and the curve of his smile is almost shy, even though he's had three weeks to get used to this.

Part of me had thought that maybe he wouldn't ask me outright. He was, after all, already doing everything a boyfriend would, and more. While I was still stuck in the hospital, he visited every day with fresh flowers and fruit baskets. He was the one who thought to bring me my favorite brand of face masks, who bought a scented lychee plush toy to keep me company at night, though I barely needed it, because he'd stay with me all the way until I fell asleep. Then, once the bandages came off and I was finally given permission to go anywhere I wanted, he went everywhere with me; he took me shopping again, carried my bags in the hand that wasn't holding mine, dutifully followed me through dozens of stores, waited for me to try on dress after dress without the slightest hint of impatience. And when one of the retail assistants started unabashedly flirting with him, he'd turned to me, grabbed my waist, and kissed me until my jaw unclenched and the jealousy in my stomach dissolved. I could feel him smiling when I pulled away.

"What was that for?" I'd asked.

"To make it clear that I'm yours," he murmured into my ear. "And because I wanted to. Are those good enough reasons?"

"Maybe," I allowed, fighting to keep my facial muscles in check so he couldn't see how hopelessly, absurdly happy those few simple sentences made me.

He started planning out our dates too. Long midday walks around Chaoyang Park, finding a patch of grass to fall back on when we were tired, him using his arm to shield the sun from my eyes. A nighttime visit to the local aquarium, his silhouette edged by the blue glow of the water, pointing out all the different fish he knew, laughing when I admitted that I only knew two, and that was from *Finding Nemo*. Baking at his place, his hands around mine to steady them as I squeezed blueberry batter into heart-shaped pans. Building forts in my new living room, pushing the chairs back to make space for the hot flush of pleasure in my chest, lying together on the cushions imported from France and gazing at the glow-in-the-dark star stickers he'd ordered for me.

It was his idea to try a new restaurant every couple days. "What are you craving?" he would ask, and I would tell him whatever came to mind: Korean barbecue tonight, or Sichuan food, or something as specific as scallion beef pancakes. And every time, he would return an hour later with at least three different restaurant options to choose from and a detailed overview of each, noting which ones had good lighting for photos and which ones offered the best seating. He would let me pick whatever I wanted from the menu, and he would always offer me a bite of his dish first, and if I decided I actually liked his meal over what I'd chosen, he would just smile and slide it over to me.

When we did go out to eat, I could still hear my mom's voice in my head. *Are you really going to finish all that? Control yourself, Chanel.* There were still those flashes of guilt where I felt the compulsion to make a list of all the foods I ate like someone at a confessional, sorting them into good and bad and inventing new, arbitrary rules to torture myself over what was on my plate. But it was getting easier to ignore the voices and the rules, easier to sink my teeth into the food and actually enjoy it, to say yes to dessert because I felt like it and maybe it *could* be that simple. Life could be that good.

Then, three weeks ago, we watched a new action blockbuster together at the theater in Solana.

A movie date. Our very first one—something that felt extraordinary because of how ordinary it was, the kind of couple activity I used to dream about when the idea of being together with Ares seemed impossible.

The movie itself was awful. Despite the rave reviews, all the promotion that had been slapped onto billboards and bus station posters and social media ads, I could barely bring myself to watch it. Influencers had been filming themselves walking out of theaters crying; the only times my eyes teared up was from yawning.

And yet I had no desire to leave. I was happy to lie on those leather seats for hours, watching the actors stumble through recycled jokes and buses explode on-screen with Ares next to me, his arm around my shoulders, leaning over to grab a handful of caramel popcorn or whisper in my ear about how horrible the acting was.

After, we went back to his apartment, debating the whole way whether the glowing reviews were fake or if there was some kind of bigger conspiracy involved, and as soon as the door clicked shut behind us, I was pulling him to me. I still held the half-filled popcorn bucket in one hand, didn't have time to think about setting it down, didn't care. He tasted like caramel and butter when he kissed me, his lips just as soft, and I stood on my tiptoes, wanting even more.

"Wait, Chanel," he said between breaths. "There's something I . . . need to ask you."

"What? Don't tell me you're proposing." I was joking, but his face flushed as he drew back a few inches to look at me properly.

"I know we've been doing this for a while, and it's never been a question, whether I belong to you," he began, more formal than I'd ever heard him. "But I did want to make sure, in case you felt differently—do I get to call you my girlfriend?"

I stared at him, the champagne-bubble thrill of the moment— the burnt sugar on my tongue, his hands on my waist—melting into a deeper, more potent pleasure, almost an ache. The emotion rose in my throat, and I ducked my head, laughing, barely able to form words.

"What's so funny?" he asked.

"No, it's not funny," I said, wondering how I could possibly explain it to him. This was what the poems and the ballads and the paintings were for, I thought. This precise feeling. "I'm just really, really happy."

But maybe I didn't need to explain, because the look that crossed his face—I suspected he knew. He took the popcorn bucket from me and placed it on the counter behind him, eliminating any remaining obstacle between us, any distance, any doubts I'd ever had. I could feel the hitch in his breath when he wrapped his arms around me and murmured, "Is that a *yes*?"

"Yes," I said. *Yes, yes, yes*, my heart echoed, a thousand times over. "I feel like I should warn you, though. Being my boyfriend isn't an easy job. I like to buy pretty things—"

"I'll buy you anything you want," he said instantly.

I bit back a smile. "I can take forever to pick out my outfits, especially if we're going to a big event—"

"I don't mind waiting for you. However long it takes."

"And there are *a lot* of big events I need to go to," I continued, my words half muffled by the cotton of his shirt.

"I can hold your purse and your coat on the way there, and I can hold your heels for you on the way back."

"People might gossip about you, if you're with me. I mean, they're definitely going to find out, one way or another."

"That's a good thing," he said, without missing a beat. "That way they'll all know you're taken."

"I can be temperamental too."

"Helps keep things interesting."

"I'm extremely high-maintenance."

"It'd be an honor to maintain you."

"And I might need you to help take photos of me."

"I would hope so. It gives me an excuse to look at you."

With a small, contented sigh, I did something I'd never done with anyone else before: I sank completely into his arms, letting him carry the full weight of me. "You really have an answer for everything, don't you?"

"It's a basic requirement for being Chanel Cao's boyfriend."

And he's met every other requirement since, things I didn't even know to ask for, like bringing a scrunchie for me when I forget my own so I can eat without fussing over my hair, or walking me the five steps from the car to my house when it's dark, or filling up a thermos of hot water for me to sip when the weather's cold. I've never been so glad to be wrong about how love works.

"I'm taking Luke out to get pizza next weekend," Ares is

saying, pulling me back to the present. "Do you . . . want to maybe come meet him?"

I lift my head. "Wow. Are you officially introducing me to your family now?"

"Can I?"

"What do you think?" I say, laughing. "*Obviously.* I was hoping you'd ask. I'll put it on my calendar."

Next weekend. Next month, and the one after that. A whole future to look forward to, more things to get excited about than to dread.

For a few moments, everything is quiet. Quiet enough to hear the lake water sloshing against the stone banks, the whisper of wind through the willows, my own heartbeat when he touches me. Just the underside of my wrist with his pinkie finger, as if to reassure himself that I'm real, that I exist.

"I bought something, by the way," he says.

"That's good. You should start spending more money on yourself," I say seriously.

"Something for *you*," he clarifies.

I blink. "What, another nonbirthday birthday gift?"

"Something like that. Here." He retrieves a small velvet pouch from his jacket pocket, and gestures for me to hold up my hand. A silver necklace spills out onto my outstretched palm. I stare down at it, speechless, my heart straining to contain all that I feel. The pendant is a crescent moon, with a single diamond dangling like a star from the end. It's beautiful. It might be the most beautiful gift I've ever received in my entire life.

Softly Ares says, "I hope you know I really mean it. I would be willing to give you everything. Even the moon."

"You already have," I tell him. I push my hair over one shoulder, exposing the back of my neck to him, the most vulnerable part of my body. "Can you help me?" I ask, even though I could clasp and unclasp a necklace with my hands tied. Yet it's nice to be helped anyway, to let myself want him even when I don't always need him.

The silver is cool against my skin as he moves behind me to adjust the chain, but his fingers are warm, careful, wonderfully gentle. When he's done, the necklace falls over the burn mark on my collarbone, just above my heart.

"Thank you." I whirl back around to wrap my arms around him again, and I have to marvel at how safe I feel, how much it makes sense, even though it's the last thing I'd expected. If I'd seen a vision of this future two months ago, I would've sworn I was hallucinating. It should be impossible to feel this much, really, to be this open and tender and happy and *known*, but so is seeing visions in a midnight lake's reflection. So is giving someone the moon.

"Anything, for you," Ares says, pulling me closer to him.

And the moon glows above us, its light just as beautiful as the present, just as bright.

EPILOGUE

When the flowers arrive, I assume they're from the founder of a perfume company.

Probably a thank-you for collaborating with them in my last post. The bouquet is far bigger than these kinds of gifts usually are, spilling over my arms when I pick them up. Pink lilies, my favorite flower. I give a faint nod of approval. The marketing intern must have done their research.

But then I spot the cream box underneath it, and the little handwritten note tied with a gold ribbon. No corporate branding, no perfunctory "We look forward to working together again in the future!" Just a messy cursive:

I'll see you in a bit. —A

My lips split into a grin. I hold the flowers closer to my chest, inhaling their scent, before placing them in the empty crystal vase on the dining table. When Ares had come over to my new house the other night, I'd made a passing remark that we hadn't finished fully decorating everything yet; the walls weren't so bare anymore, but I wanted more greenery, something to liven up the space. I hadn't realized he was listening so closely.

Then there's the box itself. I push the white wrapping paper aside, and my fingers find the softness of scarlet silk. A familiar shade. For a few moments, I can only stare in disbelief, my heart swelling inside my chest. It's the dress I tried on that time I dragged Ares to the shopping mall with me. Everything about it is the exact same, except the straps—the broad straps I'd complained about are gone, replaced by elegant spaghetti straps.

He'd remembered.

I don't even have time to process everything, the flowers, the spontaneous gift, the thought that must have gone into it—the brand *never* does alterations for their dresses, so how did he convince them to make this?—when my phone rings. The perfect sight of his name flashing over my screen. My grin widens as I lift the phone to my ear.

"I think someone has a crush on me," I inform him.

"Really?" His voice, low and amused, the hum of cars in the background. "Who?"

"I can't be sure, but, like, they just got me my favorite flowers *and* my dream dress."

"Wow. You know, that doesn't sound like a crush."

"No?"

"Sounds like they're in love with you or something."

I tip my head back and laugh. "You think?"

"Possibly. I'll be there in five," he adds. "Try the dress on."

"Wait. Right now? But I thought we were getting sushi tonight."

"Slight change of plans. I'm taking you somewhere fancier."

"But we just went somewhere fancy two days ago. We don't have to always—"

"Just try the dress on. For me? Please?"

"Okay, okay, fine. Only because you asked nicely," I say.

When he rings the doorbell five minutes later, I'm ready. More than ready. The dress fabric is so light and fitted so well to my body that it moves like water when I do, reaching for the door and smiling up at him, my stilettos clicking as I step back with a little twirl to let him admire me.

"Definitely," he says, his gaze so scorching that I can feel the full weight of it, like the press of the sun against your eyelids.

"Definitely what?"

He picks up my purse for me, then grabs my hand, lacing his fingers through mine. "I think the person who sent the flowers is definitely in love with you. Who wouldn't be?" The expression aglow on his face: helpless, irresistible affection. I can hear it in his voice too, when he murmurs, "I mean, just look at you."

He doesn't stop looking until we've headed downstairs, where a limo is waiting outside the iron gates. The chauffeur, dressed better than most businessmen, starts to open the car door, but Ares beats him to it, helping me into the back seat the way he had that night I was acting drunk.

"A limo?" I ask in wonder.

"Don't act like you've never seen one before."

"Ares," I say, with suspicion now, studying him. He's paired his jeans with a white button-down shirt and black tie, brand new, from the looks of it. Formal attire, for him. "What do you have planned for tonight?"

A conspiratorial smile plays on his lips, and I'd almost forgotten how good he is at keeping secrets. Can't force an extra word out of him if he doesn't want to tell you. "You'll see."

The drive is pure comfort, even with the traffic. The leather seats warm, Ares's hands warmer around my thigh, brushing bare skin through the high slit, and dusk falling beyond the windows. Vivid pinks and purples, the color saturated like an eyeshadow palette.

We arrive outside a building I recognize only from Airington's past prom photos, would have otherwise mistaken for a winery or a museum, with the high hedge wrapping around the driveway and the Pegasus statue poised at the entrance. Rivera Restaurant.

I turn to Ares, wide-eyed. "You made a reservation for us here? But the wait-list is literally, like, half a year."

"It's only half a year if you're not Chanel Cao," he says, guiding me inside. "What do you think? It's your kind of place, isn't it?"

It's *exactly* my kind of place. Aesthetic extravagance, high chandeliers and rich mahogany, silvery light glancing off marble, every corner designed for photos. Stunning views of the river, almost as deep a blue as the mountains in the distance. Heavy velvet drapes pushed back by eager waitresses, revealing a grand ballroom—

"Chanel!"

Alice rushes up to me, and I think to myself, laughing in

surprise as I hug her back, *Wow, what a coincidence, that she's here too*, but after a delayed beat remembering *where* we are, and wondering if Henry had also made a reservation and brought her here, when I see him behind her. Wearing a suit that would be considered casual for him, the same shade as Alice's dress. Then other familiar faces, Rainie and Mina and Bobby from school, and Haili, beaming, pink-cheeked, recovered from the heartbreak, arms wrapped around a guy I've never met before. New boyfriend, maybe. But it can't be a coincidence that they're *all* here, and then I realize—

"You . . . arranged all of this?" I ask Ares.

"He did," Alice answers for him. "He's been planning this out for weeks. God, you have no idea how hard it's been keeping it a secret from you."

Ares is watching my reaction, proud and a little shy. "I know how badly you wanted to go to prom, and this isn't the same, of course, but . . . I thought I'd at least try to give you something close to it."

"This isn't the same," I say, my throat thick, the feeling in my chest so immense I can barely speak. "This is . . . Ares, this is so much better." Because maybe I don't need to be loved by everyone, after all; I just want to be in the same room as everyone I love.

Looking around now, I can't fathom the amount of planning that must have gone into making this happen. Guests invited from different circles: childhood friends, Xiaohongshu mutuals, models and socialites, the two girls I met at Dave's thing last summer, the entrepreneur I really hit it off with at a Christmas party. Somehow, Ares had known exactly who I would want to see tonight—and he would have had to reach out to them. I imagine him, usually so closed off, unwilling and unlikely to even call the doctor if he was in pain, messaging my friends one by one: *hey, this is Chanel's boyfriend, I'm planning a surprise for her. can you make it? would this time work? oh, amazing. dress fancy, you know her.* Then ordering the flowers, the dress, the limo, not just making a reservation for two but renting the whole venue. The hot canapés brought out on trays are all my favorites too, and the music playing softly in the background could be taken straight from my playlist.

To think I'd once been afraid of him.

I'm pulled into the crowd, round after round of hugs and air kisses, floating atop the compliments, "You look gorgeous, like a princess, that dress was made for you, an icon, a star," and Ares stays back, letting me have my moment, walking up to my side only when someone asks after him.

"Hey, man." One of the guys from my history class offers Ares a tentative fist bump, like he's half scared Ares will punch him for real. "Um, totally cool if you're no longer interested or whatever, but just wanted to pass along the message from my cousin to hit him up if you ever need those bots again—he'll get you a discount."

Ares darts a glance at me, then nods. "Yeah, sure. Appreciate it, bro."

"Bots?" I say, confused. "Why did you need bots?"

"Just. Personal reasons," Ares tells me, but in my head I can hear Henry's voice telling me slowly, confused, "Someone's drowned out the top result already. . . . Must be bots. Organic engagement doesn't work this way. . . ."

I meet Ares's eyes. Ask the question without asking it. *That was you?*

His smile is an admission.

The crowd surges around us again, and only after the food and the thank you so much for comings are evenly distributed do we settle into the dark leather couches by the bar. Cherry cocktails red as my lipstick, served with little umbrellas. The air sweet with perfume, flashing jewelry, pearly whites. Youth and our awareness of it, intoxicating even before we've finished the first round of drinks, the splendor of a night like this, shrieking laughter and endless conversation and freshly filled glasses raised to me. Rainie is telling an anecdote about someone beatboxing on the train during the school's annual Experiencing China trip, and Ares is sitting on the other couch across from me, one elbow rested against his knee, swirling his whiskey around and around. Sipping it without haste. He's smiling, half listening, when his gaze finds mine, as if he'd known I was looking. And I go on talking to the girl next to me about my travel plans for the summer, and he's reacting at all the right beats to Rainie's story, but he tilts his head at me, checking if I'm okay, if I'm enjoying myself, whether I need anything. A private language shared between us, unnoticed by everyone else in the room. Team of our own, and how nice that is, to belong in the same camp finally. Another head tilt, his eyebrows lifting. Invitation to get up, which I do, excusing myself as the others push their purses back and shuffle over on the couch.

He joins me at the bar, asks over the music, "Are you having fun?"

There's something so endearing about the question, an innocence to it. "I am," I reply. "Time of my life."

The quirk of his lips, pleased with my response, with himself for earning my approval. "Really?"

"Really, truly," I say. My fingers find the back of his neck and he leans into my touch, tender, tipsy. *Definitely.* Definitely in love, god help me. Our foreheads so close I can feel him breathing, and his hands in my hair, open about his desire, and why not? Hardly a secret that we're together.

The receptive warmth of his mouth when I kiss him, slow and soft, the sound he releases deep in his throat. I kiss him there too, then return to his lips. Taste of whiskey. Rough fabric of his jeans, my pinkie curling into the loop of his belt, pulling him to me. Perfect, pure sensation. Actually can't remember a time better than this, ever. I should tell him that, maybe later tonight, or tomorrow, there's no rush anymore, plenty of chances in the future. So many things I want to tell him, can't believe I get to.

"Okay, so like, I love everything about this place," I say, breaking away for a moment, "but you know what I've been craving all day?"

"What?" he asks at once.

"Your egg-and-tomato noodles."

He laughs, the sound all the more lovely because of how rare it is, reserved just for me. "We're at a Michelin-starred restaurant where they serve twelve-course meals, and you want to eat my egg-and-tomato noodles?" he says incredulously.

"Please?"

"You're not joking?"

"I would never joke about those noodles," I say. "They're *that* good."

He brushes a thumb over my jaw, his laughter still alive in his eyes. "Okay," he says. "I'll make them for you as soon as we get home tonight."

Home. Such a beautiful word. Home, and him; one and the same, in a way. A new life or, rather, a new way of living it, built from the ashes.

ACKNOWLEDGMENTS

Writing this book felt like coming home, and I'm beyond grateful for all the people in my life who made my return possible.

Thank you endlessly to my agent, Kathleen Rushall—there's nothing more inspiring than getting to work alongside someone so brilliant, so thoughtful, and so dedicated. How wonderful and surreal it is to now have seven books together, none of which would exist without you. Thank you also to the incredible, passionate team at Andrea Brown Literary Agency.

Thank you to Sara Schonfeld for seeing my vision, even when it was still blurry at the edges, and for helping me fill it in on the page. Thank you to everyone at HarperCollins for your efforts and expertise.

Thank you to Carolina Rodríguez Fuenmayor for yet another absolutely stunning cover, and for capturing the heart of this book with your beautiful art.

Many thanks to the wonderful Taryn Fagerness at Taryn Fagerness Agency for bringing my books to readers around the world.

Thank you to Grace for bringing so much joy and light into my life and for always cheering me on. I'm so grateful we met.

Thank you to my parents for building such a beautiful life for me when I was a child, and for supporting me as I strive to build a life for myself now.

Thank you to Alyssa, of course, for your patience and encouragement and enthusiasm, for your sharp eye and even sharper sense of humor. There's nobody else I'd rather share my stories with.

And thank you, a thousand, million times over, to my readers. I've always believed that the greatest form of love is to feel seen, and by reading my books, you have given me exactly that. I still can't believe how lucky I am.